MURDER
OUT OF
CHARACTER

A PEACH COAST LIBRARY MYSTERY,
BOOK 2

OLIVIA MATTHEWS

DEDICATION

To My Dream Team:
My sister, Bernadette, for giving me the dream.
My husband, Michael, for supporting the dream.
My brother, Richard, for believing in the dream.
My brother, Gideon, for encouraging the dream.
And to Mom and Dad, always, with love.

CHAPTER 1

"I'M AS NERVOUS AS A long-tail cat in a room fulla rockin' chairs." Adrian Hobbs, the lanky twenty-six-year-old library assistant at my right, shifted from foot to foot.

Would these Southernisms ever get old? I was a recent transplant to Peach Coast, a small town in Georgia—I'd relocated five months ago from my native New York—but I couldn't imagine that ever happening.

Adrian had good reason to be anxious. Our library was hosting its first Summer Solicitation Drive Cocktail to launch our fundraising season. I didn't want any of the seventy-six attendees who'd joined us this Thursday evening to sense his discomfort, though. Everything had to appear perfect…even if it wasn't.

Masking my own nerves with a confident smile, I turned to him. Adrian loomed nine inches above my five-foot-three-inch height; seven, if you adjusted for my navy Oxford pumps. Placing a hand on his arm, I felt the tension knotting his muscles. Perhaps I should offer him another praline.

"Try to enjoy yourself, Adrian." I let my arm drop,

but held his over-bright blue eyes. He may have had enough sugar. "After all your hard work, you deserve to. Besides, you're making the rest of us uneasy."

"Marvey's right. You're gonna cause a panic." Floyd Petty, our rapidly-nearing-retirement reference librarian, settled his features into a deeper scowl. He tugged again at his gray and black striped tie. Would he tear it off this time? He lowered his hand and I breathed again.

Vivian Liu jerked a look toward Floyd beside her. Her raven bob slashed above her narrow shoulders. As Adrian's supervisor, the circulation manager was protective of him. "His anxiety's understandable. This is his first fundraising event."

Viv and I were wearing almost identical black cocktail dresses. I was doing my best to avoid standing next to her.

Floyd snorted. "It's a first for all of us, except Marvey and Corrinne. You don't see me jumping out of my skin."

Actually, I did, but I didn't think it would be prudent to point that out.

Corrinne Carpenter, our head librarian and boss, stood apart from us, seemingly unaware of the anxiety behind her. She focused on the podium where Cecelia Jean Holt, our new chair of the Peach Coast Library Board of Directors, was wrapping up her greeting and underscoring the importance of our summer fundraising campaign.

Corrinne embodied serenity. I admired that about her. But after working with her for five months, I could identify small signs that gave away her tension: the clouds darkening her grass-green eyes and the tightness around her wide pink lips. This event was critical to establishing an annual calendar of donor solicitations.

We were hosting it after hours in our upper activities room. The library was a renovated bus depot. When it had opened in 1951, it had arranged travel along the coast and around town for residents and tourists. Ticketing, departures, and arrivals had occurred on the main floor, which was now the heart of the library. A cafeteria for passengers and employees had operated up here. The floor hadn't been used in the five years before my arrival, but it hadn't taken much effort to reopen and decorate it. And it was free, something our budget appreciated.

Our long-term goal was to expand the library's offerings and services into this space. But for tonight, the room was comfortably crowded with devoted patrons and donors.

The festive decorations—balloons, streamers, and table centerpieces—were on loan from staff and volunteers. The eclectic mix of styles and colors looked deliberate and emphasized the evening's fun and relaxed tone. Classic jazz from Floyd's surprisingly diverse compact disc collection provided the background entertainment.

Cecelia ended her remarks, then made a beeline from the podium to our group.

I pitched my voice over the applause as she joined us. "You were perfect."

The expression on the older woman's smooth sienna features was pure relief. Her eyes gleamed with triumph. "Thank you again for writing it. You provided a lot of critical information on the value of a strong library system that I wouldn't have thought to include. I love the library, but I can't always put my finger on all the reasons why."

I offered Cecelia a plastic flute of nonalcoholic strawberry margarita. We hadn't had time to apply for a temporary liquor license. No one seemed to mind. "I've worked for libraries even before graduating with a degree in library science. That information's second nature to me, especially the summer slide statistics."

The slide was an estimated forty-seven percent drop in students' academic skills. It occurred during summer breaks when kids were less likely to be reading.

"Is that the reason the library's issued a Summer Reading Challenge for students?" Spencer Holt joined our conversation. His tall, lean frame was impressive in a smoke gray business suit and red tie. But then the man looked good in everything, even a backwards University of Georgia Bulldog baseball cap and crimson apron that read, *I Cook, Therefore, I Am.*

Spence was Cecelia's only child and one of my new best friends. The Holts was the richest family in Peach Coast and one of the wealthiest in Camden County. In addition to a bed and breakfast, a hotel, and a community bank, they owned *The Peach Coast Crier*, the town's daily newspaper. Spence was its editor and publisher. The paper had written a substantial article on the reading challenge, which had help boost our efforts to register students for the program.

The Holts were generous with their philanthropy. They were Peach Coast's version of Gotham City's Wayne Foundation. Spence was like a Southern Bruce Wayne/Batman. The impression went beyond his appearance, money, and prestige, though. He and his mother were local celebrities. He didn't like it when

I reminded him of that, and who could blame him? I wouldn't want that kind of attention, either.

"Summer slide's one of the reasons for the challenge." I blinked away a mental image of Spence in a cape.

"Our budget restrictions forced us to take six programming hours away from students this summer." Corrinne crossed her arms over the jacket of her cream linen skirt suit. She was tall and fashion-model slim. "None of us are happy about that."

Viv shook her head. "No, we're not."

Floyd's scowl returned. "That's right."

Adrian nodded while eating another praline. His eyes glowed like high beams. Perhaps it had been a bad idea to stand so close to the refreshments. The pecan confections, an old-fashioned Southern tradition, *were* hard to resist.

Cecelia considered us as she sipped her margarita. "I hope these fundraising programs are successful. I don't want to have reduced hours again next summer, either."

Because of its pencil-thin budget, last weekend— Memorial Weekend—the library had transitioned to its summer schedule. Weekly hours had been cut from sixty-nine to sixty-three. I couldn't be the only one who feared that if our finances didn't improve, the next cost-saving measure could be staff layoffs.

I was suddenly cold in the warm room. I'd left my home in Brooklyn less than six months ago, bought a house, and resettled my rescue tabby. What would I do if the library let me go? I drew a deep breath, catching the scents of pastries and sauces, and crammed those fears back into their box.

"I understand your concern." Spence angled his

squared chin to indicate the guests circulating nearby. His close-cropped natural emphasized his spare sienna features. "On a positive note, the shortened hours allowed the library to hold this fundraiser onsite."

"You have a talent for turning lemons into lemonade." Feeling marginally better, I shared a smile with him before turning to my colleagues. "We should mingle." I considered Floyd, who once again tugged at his tie. "Will you be okay speaking with our guests?"

"Sure." He grunted before burrowing into the crowd of very important, very loyal donors.

"I won't let him out of my sight." Corrinne's firm hand on my back felt like a lifeline.

She and Cecelia went after Floyd. It would take both of them to minimize the damage he could do in social settings. I still had chilling flashbacks of his participation in our first small business seminar. We'd had to convince the presenter to continue the series and encourage Floyd to take those evenings off.

"Can I tag along with you?" Adrian's request of Viv was muffled by another praline.

"Sure—but no more treats. You've had enough sugar for the evening." Viv's voice was thick with amusement.

Spence looked at me, sweeping his right arm before him. "Lead the way."

I hesitated. It would be wonderful to have Spence's help navigating the room. He had a way of breaking the ice. And I enjoyed being with him. Still... "Are you sure you don't mind keeping me company? You're not here to work the room. You're here as our guest."

He gave me his Bruce Wayne smile, confident and charismatic. "Even guests need to work the room. We might as well do it together."

"In that case, thank you."

I set a course for Anna May Weekley. The red-haired café owner shared a tabletop at the opposite corner of the room with her younger sister, Lisa May DuVeaux.

"Pardon me, Anna May." I stopped beside her and offered Lisa May an apologetic smile. "Thank you again for donating the refreshments. Your generosity is a big reason this event is going so well."

My sentiment earned me the Anna May Weekley Seal of Approval. Her peaches-and-cream features glowed and her periwinkle eyes twinkled. "I'm glad to do it for a good cause. Besides, Nolan said I can deduct it from my taxes as a charitable donation."

Nolan Duggan was a certified public accountant and Lisa May's boss. He also was one of Spence's best friends.

Anna May shifted her attention to Spence. "Your mama did a fine job with her remarks."

Spence inclined his head. "Thank you, Ms. Anna May. I'll pass your kind words on to her."

"People do seem to be enjoying themselves, don't they?" Lisa May's blue dress complemented her shoulder-length reddish gold curls. Her gaze drifted back to a spot behind Anna May. Her expression was smug.

Anna May looked over her shoulder. "Don't you see enough of Nolan during the workday? Why are you spying on him after hours?"

"Because it's past time for Nolan to settle down and get married. I'd say it's also past time for Jolene to do the same." Lisa May's eyes, so like her sister's, gleamed with determination as they remained fixed on a nearby tabletop.

Nolan stood there with my other best friend, Jolene

Gomez, owner of To Be Read, an independent bookstore and one of my favorite places in my adopted hometown. Jo and I had become best friends bonding over our love of literature, her bookstore, the library, and chocolate.

Lisa May portioned a speculative look between Spence and me. "You're friends with Jolene and Nolan. Have either of them said anything to you about their... relationship?"

Anna May gaped at her. "Lisa May DuVeaux, that's none of your business."

Lisa May sniffed. "I'm just looking out for the health and well-being of my employer."

Ann May snorted. "That dog won't hunt."

I adjusted my impression of Lisa May to include her newly discovered role as Peach Coast Matchmaker. "Jo hasn't said anything to me, but I've noticed Nolan spending more time with her at the bookstore."

Ignoring her sister, Lisa May turned to Spence. "You're Nolan's best friend. Has he confided in you?"

"He's very private." Spence sipped his drink as though warding off additional questioning.

That was just the kind of response the Caped Crusader would give. Understandable. If Bruce Wayne expected his friends to protect his secrets, he'd have to do the same for them.

"Jo has a rival for his affections, though." Lisa May inclined her head toward one of the refreshment tables lining the perimeter.

Like the other stations, it was burdened with hot and cold hors d'oeuvres, punchbowls of lemonade, iced tea, and Anna May's prize-winning pastries. Groups of people orbited the treats laughing and chatting.

The young woman in question stood slightly apart

from the crowd. She was with a man who was working hard to appear fun and interesting. I didn't think he was succeeding. The woman kept glancing toward Jo and Nolan as she picked at the frosted pecan brownie she'd balanced on a clear plastic plate. Her expression was wistful.

She looked to be in her mid-thirties. Three-inch black stilettos boosted her average height. The silhouette of her knee-length cocktail dress hugged her slim figure. The crimson material made her pale skin appear almost luminescent. She'd gathered her light brown hair at the crown of her head, revealing a long, elegant neck.

I could understand her seeming infatuation with Nolan. He was kind, intelligent, interesting and handsome. Much like another Peach Coast resident I knew. I slid a look toward Spence. But if Jo was attracted to Nolan, I wanted to know more about her potential rival. "Who is she?"

Lisa May looked away from the refreshment table. "That's Gertrude Trueman."

"Most people call her Trudie." Anna May gave her sister a pointed look.

"Trudie Trueman?" I'd probably go with Gertrude as well.

Lisa May continued her report. "She's recently returned to town and inherited her family's construction company, Camden County Construction Contractors."

I blinked. "The Trueman family's fond of alliteration."

Lisa May either didn't hear my comment or chose to ignore it. "She doesn't seem interested in waiting in line for the eligible bachelors. Nolan's the accountant for her family's company. She uses every conceivable feeble excuse to see him—*without* an appointment."

"Nolan built a successful accounting firm. I'm sure he can handle Trudie." Anna May waved her praline between Spence and me. "So can Spence, so you don't have to worry either."

CHAPTER 2

M Y CHEEKS FILLED WITH HEAT. "We're not—"

"Why didn't Ms. Cecelia read your name with the Class of 2006 gift announcement?" Anna May asked, narrowing her eyes at Spence. The Class of 2006's gift had given the library fundraiser a significant pre-launch boost as well as publicity for the Summer Solicitation Drive.

"I didn't graduate in 2006, ma'am," Spence corrected her. "I'm Class of 2008. This year, we're making a gift to the medical center."

"That's wonderful." Lisa May gave him an approving look. "Our community has a lot of worthy organizations in need of help."

"Yes, we do." I stepped back. "We're going to mingle some more. Thank you so much for coming. I look forward to seeing you at the library."

"Why are young couples always so worried about work?" Lisa May shimmied her shoulders. "You need to sneak away for some quality time, just the two of you."

The idea of quality time alone with Spencer Holt made my pulse skip. I understood why he was considered one of the most eligible bachelors in Peach Coast. Still...

"We're not—"

"It won't do any good," Spence said, placing a hand onto the small of my back and leading me away.

I fell into step beside him. His peppermint-and-sandalwood scent was distracting. "Aren't you concerned people have the wrong impression of our relationship?"

"Not even a little." Spence's Barry White voice rumbled with amusement. "You're providing me with cover from well-meaning people who've been playing matchmaker with me for years."

I didn't think that was as funny as he seemed to. He was using me for cover? How did I feel about that?

Nudging the question aside for now, I brought us to a stop at Jo and Nolan's table. "I'm so glad you came," I told Jo.

"Are you kidding?" Her waist-length raven hair was free of its ponytail holder. The thick mass oscillated behind her as she looked from me to Spence and back. "You had me at, 'Anna May's pastries.' Besides my bookstore has benefited from all the work you've done to increase the community's interest in reading."

"Before you started promoting the library, I didn't think I had much time for reading." Nolan dragged his gaze from Jo to smile at me. "I was always busy with work...but now I *make* time."

His words filled my heart. It was as though he'd presented me with a box of chocolates. "I'm so glad. And thank you for agreeing to do a presentation on taxes for small business owners. People are already registering for it."

"I should've thought about doing something like this

sooner." Nolan smoothed the white tie he'd worn with his navy shirt and suit. "It's a good way to attract new clients."

Jo reached over to press the back of Nolan's hand on the table beside her. The gesture drew my attention to the University of Florida Gator logo inked onto the inside of her small right wrist. The orange, blue, green, and white tattoo peeked beneath the sleeve of her citrus orange skirt suit. "You're in your office from dusk to dawn as it is."

How did she know that?

I sent Spence a curious look. He shrugged and turned away. Yep. Peach Coast's Caped Crusader knew more than he was willing to share.

I considered Nolan and Jo. Their eyes kept coming back to each other. There was definitely something there. "Speaking of bringing in business, Nolan, you've been working with Camden County Construction. Is Trudie Trueman a new client?"

He dragged his eyes away from Jo. "I'd been the company's accountant for quite a few years before her daddy passed. God rest his soul. He wasn't the same after his wife died."

Nolan didn't appear interested in discussing Trudie, but he was fascinated by Jo. Relieved, I decided she didn't have any competition for his affections.

Spence shook his head at me. "Do you have everything you need?"

I knew he was referring to my prying. "Yes, I do. Thank you."

A casual glance over my shoulder revealed that Trudie Trueman had moved on. I recognized several of the guests who now circulated the refreshment stations, including Delores Polly, the organist at St. Michael's Church; Philomena Fossey, proprietor of Shoreline Souvenirs near the pier; and Reba McRaney, owner of Hair on the Coast beauty salon and a member of the Peach Coast Town Council.

"Marvey, do you have any thoughts on Hank Figg's death?" Nolan's question was so sincere for a moment I wondered why I didn't. Then I remembered: I'm not law enforcement.

"I asked her the same thing this morning." Jo hid a smile behind her iced tea, or as the locals called it, "sweet tea." I didn't think I could get used to hearing it called that.

Ever since I'd helped solve Fiona Lyle-Hayes's murder, people had been asking me to weigh in on mysterious deaths and disappearances they'd read about all over Georgia and across the country. Fiona's death had been Peach Coast's first homicide in two and a half years. I'd only gotten involved because the sheriff's deputies considered Jo their prime suspect. Why? Because Fiona had been killed in Jo's bookstore. I know; their reasoning was flimsy at best.

My amateur sleuthing had been a one-time, never-to-be-repeated event. That's why instead of indulging the morbid fascination of some Peach Coast residents, I distracted them with information about upcoming library events. Why waste an opportunity to raise the library's profile in the community?

I gave Nolan an apologetic smile. "I don't have any more information than what I read in the *Crier*."

"And the story covered everything we have from the deputies on the scene." Spence's voice was somber and his midnight eyes were shadowed with grief.

A heavy silence settled over our group. It felt as though we were all thinking about one of Peach Coast's favorite sons. After welcoming our guests earlier, Corrinne had asked for a moment of silence to acknowledge Hank's death before returning to our programming. The vibe in the room had been somber and thoughtful then, too; a testament to how much the community missed him.

Hank had been found dead in his home two evenings ago. Deputies Jedidiah Whatley and Errol Cole hadn't found signs of a break-in or foul play. They'd estimated Hank had been dead at least seventy-two hours before they'd been called to the scene, but they were waiting on the coroner to confirm that and the cause of death.

Jed and Errol were the deputies who'd been assigned to investigate Fiona's murder. My amateur sleuthing had gotten our relationship off to a rocky start, but I was working to repair it. I suspected I needed to work harder.

"Besides, it's not clear Hank was murdered." I looked from Spence to Nolan. "It could've been an unfortunate accident or a health condition."

Hank had been the beloved head coach of the boys' basketball team at Mother Mathilda Taylor Beasley High School, which had brought him full circle. Back in the day, the Peach Coast native had been team captain and a standout player at the school. He'd also been president of his graduating class.

I only knew him through my professional capacity, but I still felt his loss. He was so enthusiastic about the library and its mission. In the article about his death, the *Crier* had included remembrances from family, friends, and neighbors. Their words had painted a picture of a well-liked, respected, and admired member of the community. It was unthinkable that someone would kill him.

"The paper said Hank's body had been discovered by a friend who didn't want to be identified." I scanned the room. The lounge was crowded with library lovers, many of whom had been acquainted with the coach. "I wonder why the person wants to remain anonymous."

Jo's hair swept the middle of her back as she did a visual search of the room. "Hank had been dating June Bishop. I stopped by her flower shop yesterday to give her my condolences. She said she was going to be here."

The owner of Petals Palooza was also a member of the Class of 2006. Had the thought of attending the event and having her graduating class's gift acknowledged without Hank been too painful for her? I should've done more to reach out to her and express my condolences.

As I looked away, I caught another glimpse of Philomena Fossey. This time she was chatting with a guest at a high-top table. Did he look familiar? Yes, I recognized him from his photo in the *Crier*. He was the new assistant coach of the high school boys' basketball team. Perhaps his name would come to me later.

I turned back to the table. "Maybe June's not up to socializing yet."

"I could understand that." Jo's sigh held more than a hint of empathy.

"His players loved him." Nolan studied his beverage flute. "He was always coaching them to take responsibility for their actions on and off the court. It meant a lot to them that he did the same by taking responsibility for their losses as well as sharing credit for their wins. Not all coaches do that."

"His memorial is next Thursday." Spence's voice was low.

A hand came to rest on my shoulder. Startled, I looked behind me to see Reba McRaney. Her fair complexion was flushed and her hazel brown eyes sparkled.

"Marvey, this is such a wonderful event!" Her gaze bounced to Spence before returning to me. "You did a wonderful job putting it all together."

Her enthusiasm helped ease the sadness that had taken hold of me. "Thank you, Councilwoman McRaney, but this event was a team effort by our library staff and volunteers."

She waved the hand she'd removed from my shoulder while balancing a pecan custard in the other. "Call me Reba. This is a party. And that little black dress looks *great* on you." Her gaze once again swung toward Spence.

"Thank you." I kept my smile in place although her constant glances toward Spence were making me uncomfortable.

"But you'd look even better if you'd try something different with this." She wiggled her electric blue-tipped fingers in the direction of my dark brown shoulder-length tresses, styled in a simple flip. "You should come into the salon and let me give you a makeover."

It took all my self-control to keep from touching my hair. My gaze drifted up to Reba's blond streaked mane. The dramatic mass of complicated twists and curls probably needed a cup of hairspray and a hundred pins to keep it in place. The sculpture was striking and added at least three inches to her statuesque height. It reminded me of the mannequin heads in her display window that I was sure tracked me each time I walked past the salon. Creepy.

I sent an appeal toward Jo. She met my silent message with a deer-in-the-headlights stare. Not helpful.

Without backup, I turned back to Reba. "I'm really more of a wash-and-go type."

"But you'd look..." Her attention shifted to somewhere behind my shoulder. Reba's eyes narrowed and her lips thinned.

Alarmed, I turned to see what had upset her. Byron Flowers was talking with Corrinne. A reluctant smile curved my lips. It was well-known that Reba wasn't a fan of Peach Coast's mayor. I'd heard she'd run against him and lost in the last campaign. Had she challenged him because she didn't like him? Or did she not like him because she lost?

"Now there's one man who loves his hair." Reba harrumphed. "Maybe we'd get more county services if he paid as much attention to the town as he spent on his appearance—or on Corrinne Carpenter. That woman's obviously not interested in him."

Reba was right. My boss stood with her arms crossed and her body leaning away from the mayor. The stance screamed *I don't want to speak with you.* Either Byron couldn't hear that or he didn't care.

"Should we rescue her?" Jo's voice was uncertain.

"Corrinne doesn't strike me as the kind of person who needs rescuing." Spence sounded amused.

He had a point, but I was desperate to know the history between the mayor and my boss.

I caught his eyes. "We should mingle some more." I

smiled at the others around the table. "Thank you again for coming. I hope to see you at the library again soon."

I turned and was face to face with Sheriff's Deputy Errol Cole. "Thank you so much for coming, Deputy Cole. I hope you're enjoying yourself."

The young law enforcement officer swallowed a praline before responding. "You can call me Errol, Ms. Marvey. I'm not on duty tonight. Evenin', Mr. Spence." He inclined his head. "And, yes, ma'am. I'm having a very fine time. Good eats."

I flashed a grin at our newest library donor. "Thank you for supporting the library."

"Oh, yes, ma'am." His boyish grin displayed even white teeth. His light tan brought out his thick blond hair and bright green eyes. "Haven't read so much since college, but at least I'm enjoying myself this time around."

Our progress across the room was slow. Several guests stopped Mr. Popularity to greet him. Always the gentleman, Spence introduced me to the ones I hadn't yet met. I smiled at Viv and Adrian as we crossed paths through the crowd.

As I stopped with Spence for formal introductions to members of the town's school board, I caught the hissing of angry whispers. It came from close behind me, barely audible above the classic jazz from Floyd's CD. With as nonchalant a move as I could manage, I looked over my shoulder.

Philomena was venting her grievance to Nelle Kenton. The souvenir shop owner was a little taller than my five-foot-three and burdened with a wealth of honey-blond curls. She'd fisted her hands at her sides. Her curvaceous figure tilted toward Nelle, who stood a few inches above her. Nelle was the chief financial officer with Malcovich Savings and Loan, our lead donor for this summer fundraising drive.

My heart almost stopped. *Oh, boy.* We couldn't have a brawl breakout in the middle of our cocktail kickoff. After excusing myself from Spence and the school board members, I turned to Philomena and Nelle.

CHAPTER 3

"**L**ADIES, PERHAPS WE CAN TAKE this conversation into the hallway?" Then down the stairs and across the street.

Philomena's brown eyes shot daggers at me. How had I become the new source of her aggravation? "It's interesting that the bank doesn't have the financing to help small business owners, which are the life blood of the economy, but can throw all kinds of money at a library. Why is that?"

I wanted to correct her misperception that libraries didn't bring value to a community—hadn't she heard Cecelia's speech?—but my purpose was to defuse the tension, not exacerbate it.

"As I've explained, the bank's community budget is separate and apart from our business loans." Nelle's pale blue eyes were expressionless as they drilled into Philomena. Her tense features, framed by an asymmetrical chestnut bob, were impassive.

"And it's not personal, right?" Philomena's voice dripped with skepticism.

Nelle didn't blink. "Of course not. It's strictly business."

I could have chopped the tension with a butcher's knife. On top of that, I sensed the growing curiosity of the guests around us. "Ladies, we're attracting attention. Could we—"

Philomena spun on her heels and marched out of the activity room before I could finish. I smothered a sigh. I hadn't intended to run her off, but I wanted people to come away from the kickoff talking about the library, not a fight.

As we moved on from the school board members, an intimidating older woman broke off her conversation with Lucas Daniel, the assistant coach. A crimson, cap-shoulder power dress draped her tall, fit figure. Her features had settled into a cool, assessing expression.

After subjecting me to an intent examination from frosty dark eyes, she turned to Spence. Her eyes held him in place. Her voice sounded a command. "Mr. Spencer Holt. Here you go, running right past me. How long has it been?"

His face eased into a welcoming smile, undaunted by this force of nature. "I'd say it's been too long."

"And you'd be right." Her expression soured even more. "You could pick up the phone once in a while."

"The phone line runs both ways, Aunt Charlie."

Aunt Charlie? My jaw dropped. Now I saw the family resemblance. Tall. Fit. Warm sienna skin. Dark, intelligent eyes. I gave Spence a look, warning him I had a dozen questions. In response he lifted his shoulders in an almost imperceptible shrug.

Aunt Charlie's stone-faced expression melted into

an indulgent smile. She smacked him playfully on the shoulder. "All right, now. Gimme some sugar."

Spence kissed the older woman's cheek before settling his left hand on the small of my back. With gentle pressure, he propelled me forward. "Aunt Charlie, let me introduce you to Marvella Harris. She's the library's director of community engagement. Marvey, my aunt, Charlene Logan. She's my mother's little sister and president of Logan Investment Company."

Spence's family was packed with overachievers. I was impressed. "It's a pleasure to meet you, Ms. Logan. Thank you for your company's generous gift to our Summer Solicitation Drive."

Her dark eyes twinkled as they assessed me again. "I've heard a lot about you. Cecelia is impressed by all you've accomplished with the library, especially in such a short time."

I paused to catch my breath. "She's very supportive. That makes my work easier."

Charlene's eyes narrowed on the hand Spence used to cup my elbow before raising them again to mine. "I hadn't given much thought to the library until the paper started covering its events and presentations. I even got a library card. I haven't had one since elementary school."

A satisfied smile pulled at my lips. "I hope to see you at the library."

"It's hard to fit too many things into my busy calendar." Charlene spread her hands in as apologetic a gesture as possible from such a formidable woman.

"The book club meets once a month." Spence gave his aunt a sly smile. "Marvey serves Georgia Bourbon Pecan Pie and sweet tea after every gathering."

"Well, now. I might be able to fit in a few meetings." Charlene gave me a thoughtful expression. "Marvella, that's a beautiful pendant. May I ask where you bought it?"

I touched my glass pendant, which was suspended from a long antique silver chain. The image it held was a rough replica of the gray, white, and red original cover of the 2001 autobiography *Finding Fish: A Memoir* by Antwone Quenton Fisher. I'd struggled with the pencil rendering to duplicate the blurry photo of Mr. Fisher as a child.

"I didn't buy it," I said. "Making these book pendants is a hobby I've had since high school. It combines my love of drawing and celebrating books."

"Oh." Charlene's response came out on a long sigh. Was she disappointed? "It's lovely. You're quite talented."

"Thank you. I've gotten so many compliments on them, Spence suggested I give a workshop on making them to help raise money for the library." He'd understood I didn't want to turn a hobby I enjoyed into a second career.

Charlene's expression brightened. "I'd make time to attend that."

"Lisa and I had a great time." Anna May gave my shoulder a brief squeeze.

Her words made me smile. Her sentiment seemed unanimous among the evening's attendees. I waved at

a few school board members who called their compliments to me on their way out.

I turned back to the sisters. "I'm so glad. Thank you
again for coming. Your support means a lot."

Anna May adjusted the purse strap on her shoulder
as she moved toward the exit. "I'll send someone around
in the morning to collect the trays and serving utensils."

"Thank you, Anna May. Have a good night." I waved
the sisters off, then made my way back across the library's main floor toward the stairs to the activities
room. The cocktail kickoff was wrapping up. I left Corrinne and Cecelia to send off the rest of our guests while
I returned upstairs to help Viv, Floyd, and Adrian with
the cleanup.

Floyd had set aside the borrowed chairs and table
tops. The vendor who'd donated the furniture would
collect them tomorrow. Viv had cleared the food stations, carrying the dishes down to the break room for
Anna May's staff. Adrian was helping me return the
furniture we'd taken from the main library rooms back
where they belonged.

Once we were done, I did a final walkthrough of the
room, gathering up discarded event programs and invi-
tations to recycle. I wanted to do as much as we could
before leaving so we didn't overburden the night cleaning crew. Some of the programs had notes from the evening's presentations. "Book Swap Saturday." "Summer
Reading Challenge starts in June. Adults?" I smiled.
People had been paying attention. That was gratifying.
I liked the suggestion about an adult summer reading
challenge. I made a mental note to ask Corrinne's opinion of the idea.

I bent to rescue a stray sheet of paper peeking out

from beneath the cream tablecloth covering one of the dessert tables. It was a plain, blank sheet of stationery. I flipped it over.

Odd. Someone with small, tight handwriting had listed four names in dark blue ink. Hank Figg, the deceased high school basketball coach. Nelle Kenton, chief financial officer of Malcovich Savings and Loan. Brittany Wilson, who owned a bike shop, Coastal Cycles. I thought she also was a lawyer. But one name grabbed my attention and wouldn't let go: Spencer Holt.

Ice crawled up my spine. What was this list? Who'd created it? And why was Spence included with someone whose death was being investigated as a possible homicide?

Shaking off my discomfort, I added the page to my small collection of paper to recycle. There was probably a simple and silly explanation. No reason for me to worry. Right?

"Marvey, are you ready to leave?" Corrinne's voice carried from the main floor.

"Coming." Today was one of the few times I'd driven to work since I knew I'd be working late. I wasn't in Brooklyn anymore, but that didn't mean I wouldn't take precautions if I stayed out past dark.

I returned to my office to drop the papers into my recycle box before joining my team. As we walked out to the parking lot, I tried to ignore the hairs stirring on the back of my neck.

The next morning, my footfalls were almost silent

on the dirt path I'd discovered close to home. I'd left my house at five-fifteen for my Sunday jog. The trail was bursting with foliage that called this coastal Southern region home. I'd looked up a lot of them. Large, old sugar maples and sweetgum trees. Yucca plants, wax myrtle, and salt meadow cord grasses. The faint sound of birds greeting the day was in almost perfect sync with my steps. Each breath I drew brought the sharp scent of dew-laden grass and the musk of compost from the nearby swamp.

I came to the short, weathered wooden fence that blocked me from continuing to the swamp line that edged the town. Wiping the sweat from my eyes and upper lip, I turned to head home, which would complete my six-mile run.

A check of my black Apple iWatch showed the time was a quarter to six; right on schedule. I'd been running for thirty minutes. My navy wicking jersey clung to my torso. How much of the sweat was from exertion and how much was from the June weather? It wasn't yet six, but the temperature was already in the seventies.

My strides carried me out of the park and along the sleepy streets toward my house. I'd gotten lost the first couple of times I'd run this route. But I found my way when I'd made the effort to pay attention to my surroundings: the charming stone, brick, and wood houses; well-manicured yards; and the dancing wildflowers.

My house waited at the top of the block. I smiled at the little A-line cottage. It was so cute with its white wood façade and gray gable roof. Trees lined my sidewalk while black-eyed Susans shimmied in my front yard. The architect must have found their inspiration in a collection of fairytales.

I jogged up the four steps to my front porch, noted the time on my stopwatch, and collected my copy of the *Crier*.

My cat Phoenix greeted me as I let myself in and stood chatting as I deactivated my alarm. He didn't sound upset, so I made *I'm listening* sounds as I led him into the kitchen and poured myself a large glass of water. Along the way, I dropped my newspaper on my wooden dining table.

After I'd showered and changed, Phoenix and I returned downstairs to break our Sunday fast. My kitchen wasn't very big, but it was a bright, inviting space. Silver appliances picked up the gray pattern in the white tile. Three square windows invited sunlight to dance against the pale yellow walls.

"What are your plans for when your grandparents visit us in July?" I asked Phoenix, filling his water bowl and food dish. As I straightened, my attention paused on the original artwork decorating my refrigerator. My four-year-old nephew—soon to be five—had sent me a vibrant crayon rendering of the photograph of my home I'd sent to my family. The picture always made me smile. His talent was growing, but what he didn't yet have in skill was more than made up for in enthusiasm.

"I should focus more on the donor drive." I turned to prepare my own breakfast. "The fundraiser's happening now. I still have plenty of time to plan for Mom and Dad's visit. I'm just so excited. And it's the weekend. No one's thrilled about working on weekends."

I carried half of a pink grapefruit, a bowl of oatmeal, and chai orange tea instead of coffee into the dining room. Phoenix joined me so we could read the paper while I ate. But the first headline that captured my attention also destroyed my appetite.

Malcovich Savings and Loan CFO Found Dead.

Shock loosened my grip on the spoon and knocked the breath from my lungs. I was just getting to know Nelle. I liked and admired her. She was smart, enthusiastic, and driven. Her laughter was infectious, even when I didn't get the joke.

"Oh, Phoenix. I'm going to miss her."

He leaped onto the table as though curious to read what I was talking about.

With a heavy heart, I pushed aside my breakfast and read the news story. Deputies Jedidiah Whatley and Errol Cole were assigned to Nelle Kenton's case. Jed and Errol also were investigating Hank Figg's death. The article didn't state whether the deputies suspected a connection between the two tragedies, which made my questions feel more urgent. What if anything about the cases were similar? And what if anything about the deaths was suspicious?

My thoughts abruptly stopped as I remembered our kickoff three nights ago, the last time I'd spoken with Nelle. In my mind's eye, I saw again the sheet of note paper on which four names had been written: Hank Figg, Nelle Kenton, Brittany Wilson—and Spencer Holt. The same icy hand that had touched me when I'd found the list retraced my spine.

"Focus." I pushed away from the table and paced the length of my modest dining room. The oak flooring was warm beneath my bare feet. Sunlight streamed through the open cream venetian blinds over each of the room's three windows and from the rear French doors in the adjoining foyer.

"Could it be a coincidence that Hank's and Nelle's names were on that list and now they're dead? You know I don't believe in coincidences."

Phoenix stretched out on top of the *Crier*, which lay open on the table. He tracked my progress across the room, his vivid green eyes wide. Was he really listening? Or was he just humoring me? He did that sometimes.

"On the other hand, it's hard to believe someone would make a list of people they want to kill, take it to our fundraiser, then drop it on the floor." A chill raced down my spine. "Isn't it?"

Phoenix blinked at me. He wasn't taking a position, but at least he was willing to consider the question.

The soft voice in a far corner of my mind was growing louder and more impatient. "What if this isn't a fluke? Am I willing to take that risk with Spence's life?" That thought threatened to push me over into full-blown panic mode.

Take a breath.

Phoenix turned away. He jumped from the dining table and meandered to his favorite spot in front of the rear French doors.

"No, I won't take that risk." Breakfast would have to wait. "Phoenix, I need to speak with Spence about that list."

I stored my uneaten oatmeal and grapefruit in the refrigerator and chugged my now cool tea. Returning upstairs, I changed from my I'm-home-and-no-one's-going-to-see-me outfit to navy shorts and a pale yellow blouse that complemented my brown skin. Not that that mattered. *I'm going to see a friend*, I thought as I added long sterling silver earrings to my outfit.

I slipped on my sneakers and grabbed my purse.

The library was a short walk from my house, but due to the potential urgency of this situation, I thought it prudent to drive. The parking lot was empty. Granted, it was seven o'clock on a Sunday morning. Even during our normal schedule, the library wouldn't open for another six hours.

My sneakers muffled my footsteps as I strode across the marbled gray linoleum. I surveyed the surroundings with mixed feelings: pride for the promises and opportunities the institution offered, but sadness to see it in shadows because of insufficient funds.

I drew a breath and found comfort in the smell of millions of printed pages and the lemon polish that lingered on the aged quaint woodwork that framed the doorways and windows.

We'll get through this. The community supports us.

I didn't need to turn on lights to make my way across the customer service area to the offices. Natural light swept in through the large picture windows that framed the library's attractive landscaping.

The weathered, intricate oak circulation desk had served as the ticket counter when the building was a bus depot. I passed it and pushed through the dark wood swinging half doors to the managers' offices and small staff kitchen.

Thankfully, I hadn't yet emptied the box I used to collect my recyclable paper. It took a little digging, but within minutes, I'd recovered the anonymous list. My hands shook as I read it a third time: Hank Figg. Nelle Kenton. Brittany Wilson. *Spencer Holt.* My throat went dry. No, I couldn't ignore this. If anyone else died, I'd feel responsible for not speaking up. I shoved the paper into my purse and hurried back to my car.

Minutes later, I was ringing Spence's doorbell. A glance at my watch showed it was a few minutes past eight. Was he awake this early on a Sunday morning? Perhaps he was at church or getting ready for the Sunday service. Not everyone attended Saturday evening Mass the way I did.

As I debated trying the bell again or calling him on my phone, Spence's car pulled into his driveway. It came to a stop in front of his garage and he stepped out.

"Marvey? This is a surprise." He looked wide awake, if somewhat puzzled. In his crisp black chinos and steel gray short-sleeved polo shirt, he gave the impression that, like me, he'd been up for a while. He must have been coming home from the early Sunday service.

I retrieved the list from my purse and held it up. "We may have a problem.

CHAPTER 4

"YOU THINK THIS IS A hit list." Spence's voice was devoid of inflection, but I saw the skepticism in his narrowed midnight gaze.

That wasn't the term I used. In fact, I'd deliberately avoided calling it that.

"When you put it like that, it sounds crazy." I popped off one of the living room's three thick-cushioned copper and dark wood armchairs. "But how else do you explain two people on that list having recently died?"

"A tragic coincidence?" Spence tracked my restless movements from a matching chair that faced me. He sounded distracted as though he was trying to reason through this situation.

His living room communicated excitement and energy. Area rugs in vibrant crimson, gold, sapphire, and emerald splashed across the hardwood flooring. The room's centerpiece was a futuristic-looking two-tier metal-and-oak coffee table.

I paused in front of the electric fireplace. Its sleek, contemporary features included dark tobacco accents on a fresh white finish. Framed photographs across the metal mantel tracked his progression from his under-graduate years at Stanford, his graduate experiences at New York University, to his career as a journalist in Chicago. He also had pictures from his international travels to Canada, Mexico, the Caribbean, and Europe.

I turned back to Spence. "Neither of us believes in coincidence."

"But a discarded hit list? That's a stretch, especially one found after an event that more than seventy people attended." He continued to study the list. "What assassin writes the names of their targets, then leaves the list behind? Isn't that information supposed to be secret?"

Good point. I tossed him a disgruntled look. How could I protect him if he wouldn't even consider something was wrong? I took a calming breath. The room smelled of wood and peppermint. Like Spence. "Do you have another explanation for your name being on the same piece of paper as two people whose deaths are now 'under investigation' by the sheriff's department?" I made air quotes with my fingers for "under investigation."

Spence shrugged. "You found this note in the activity room after the event, right?"

"Right." I continued pacing, this time in front of the fake fireplace.

"It could be a list of attendees."

All right; I'll play along. "Seventy-six people came to the kickoff. Why were you, Hank, Nelle, and Brittany singled out?"

"It could be a list of high-profile residents."

"Why isn't the mayor on the list?"

"Maybe it's a partial list of library donors."

"Again, why only the four of you?" I rubbed my eyes.

This game of verbal tennis wasn't helping my anxiety. "Let's try looking at this another way. What do you have in common with the other people on that list?"

"We all live in Peach Coast." His words were dry.

I planted my hands on my hips and gritted my teeth. "Could you take this seriously? Please?"

"I *am*." Spence spread his arms. "And, honestly, growing up in Peach Coast is all I have in common with Hank, Nelle, and Brittany. We're friendly, but we've never been friends. We were in different graduating classes."

Nothing he said reassured me. If anything, I was more anxious now than when I'd first arrived. I hesitated before asking him the question we were both dancing around. "Spence, is it possible someone's trying to kill you?"

"For what?" His eyes were wide and clouded with confusion as though he couldn't believe we were having this conversation.

Neither could I.

I couldn't imagine anyone wanting to harm Spence in any way. He was thoughtful, kind, humble, and fun. The kind of person other people wanted to spend time with—not bump off. "I don't know."

"I don't, either."

I wanted answers, but only found more questions. "Have you fired anyone recently?"

Spence chuckled as though I'd told a hilarious joke. "No. I have a high turnover because most of my editors and reporters leave for bigger and better things after a few years."

Bigger and better things. Did he want those things as well?

I gave him a half smile. "It speaks well of your paper that your staff's in such high demand. My parents really like the reporting."

"Thank you." He dropped his eyes as though the compliment embarrassed him. His modesty was one of his many appealing traits.

"Have you broken up with anyone recently?" I was more interested in his response than I should've been.

"No." His expression was self-deprecating. "I've gone out a few times, but I haven't dated anyone seriously in a while."

I continued to grasp at straws. "Does anyone owe you money?"

"No." His response was quick and spare. If he had given someone money, he probably wouldn't consider it a loan.

Frustrated, I paced away from the fireplace and wandered to his front bay windows. These photos of Spence's family and friends were all set in Peach Coast. There were several posed and candid pictures of his parents with and without him. His father had been a handsome man. Spence's resemblance to him was striking. He'd also included photos of Nolan, Jo, and me.

I studied the photograph of the two of us taken after last month's Peach Coast Cobbler Crawl. We were covered in sweat. Shockingly, we'd taken first place. I hadn't been confident I'd be able to finish the event. We each had one hand around each other's waist. Our other hands held our medals aloft.

Through the window, I could admire his neighborhood. It was clean and quiet, and lush with trees, flowers and expansive yards. The scenery whispered wealth and elegance.

Planting my hands on my hips again, I spoke over my shoulder. "We need to take this list to the deputies."

"We could do that." Spence's voice sounded closer. "But they'll be more skeptical than I am."

That was an understatement. Factor in that I'd strained Jed's goodwill by investigating Fiona Lyle-Hayes's murder to prove Jo's innocence, and he'd probably be biased against anything I said or did. Ever.

I turned to find Spence an arm's length from me. "They still need to be aware of this list. It could be relevant to their investigations into Hank's and Nelle's deaths."

Spence rubbed the back of his neck. I sensed his frustration like a presence beside him. "We don't have any information beyond this list. Whatley won't take it seriously."

"That doesn't mean we shouldn't bring it to their attention."

He dropped his arm. "Why don't we take today to think it over? If you feel the same way in the morning, I'll speak to them with you."

I started to disagree. It was barely nine o'clock and he expected me to wait another twenty-four hours? This was another example of my New York background conflicting with Southern culture. They had a very different concept of "urgency."

Then I realized whether I go alone today or with Spence tomorrow, the deputies will most likely dismiss my concerns. However, my primary goal was to keep Spence safe. I'd shown him the list and shared my fears. That would have to be enough. For now.

"Promise me you'll be careful."

He squeezed my shoulder and held my eyes. "I promise."

A good book cures all ills. At the very least, it provides a comforting distraction. After returning from Spence's home, I changed back into my oversized teal T-shirt and faded black denim shorts. Both had seen better days. Phoenix and I curled up on my fluffy sky-blue sofa and fell into a newly released young adult fantasy. I loved young adult fantasy. Jo had read an advance review copy of the novel and recommended it to me. We planned to discuss the story once I'd finished it.

My cellphone rang, pulling me out of the paranormal universe and back into my living room. The sudden noise startled Phoenix. He launched himself from my lap and sent me a look of reproach.

"I didn't make my phone ring."

He waved his tail dismissively as he strode away.

The caller ID displayed my mother's number. "Hi! How are you?"

"We're fine. How're you?" My parents spoke in unison like low-tech stereo surround sound.

"I'm excited about your visit next month." Only six weeks and five days to go. *Yay!* I closed my book. "I'm already planning our activities."

Everything about New York moved quickly—except public transportation. During their visit, I wanted my parents to slow down and enjoy the moments as I was learning to do. Although, it wasn't in my nature to slow down too much.

We'd start the mornings with a run on the dirt trail near my home. Would they enjoy the idyllic surroundings, or would the trail's near-isolation cause them to be concerned for my safety? And how would they feel about On A Roll, To Be Read, the library, and my house? I really wanted them to like my adopted home. The trip was supposed to reassure them I was happy and safe. I didn't want them worrying about me for any reason, whether it was where I lived or what I was doing.

Urgh! I was making myself crazy, but I had to present the town in the best possible light. I didn't want my parents to be disappointed in my judgement.

At twenty-eight years old and living on my own, I didn't *need* Mom and Dad to approve of my decision to move to Peach Coast to advance my career, but I *wanted* it. They said they understood and supported my choice, but sometimes in their voices, I heard whispers of uncertainty.

The first couple of months had been hard. I'd missed my family so much, it had been like an ache. Sometimes it still was. Phoenix and I'd had a bumpy adjustment. My parents had known all about it, not just from our near-daily phone calls but also from their online subscription to the *Crier*. Yes, they'd subscribed to—and read—the town's paper to keep tabs on me. I know. That was next level.

Anyway, Phoenix and I were happier now. We'd fallen in love with the town and the characters who lived in it. I wanted my parents to see that.

"We're excited too." Mom didn't sound excited. Had something come up? Closing my eyes, I braced for disappointment. She continued. "Your father and I were thinking of coming early."

My eyes popped open. *What? Why—*

Oh. An image of the banner headline for this morning's *Crier* uploaded to my mind: *Malcovich Savings and Loan CFO Found Dead.*

"Mom, Dad, it's not necessary to move up your trip. I'm fine. Really. And as you read in the article, the deputies have everything under control."

Besides, if a serial killer was roaming Peach Coast, would I want my parents coming for a visit? No! The conflicting messages would be tricky, though: *Don't worry about my safety, Mom and Dad, but please stay home because I'm worried about yours.*

Dad snorted. "Are we supposed to be reassured with these deputies assigned to the case? Aren't they the ones who needed your help to solve the last murder?"

I flinched. Deputy Cole—and especially Deputy Whatley—wouldn't appreciate being described that way. *Note to self: When showing my parents around, skip the sheriff's department.*

"Your father's right, Marvey. You can't be dismissive of this danger. In less than a month, two people have died from unknown, possibly suspicious, circumstances. You have to take these events seriously." Mom sounded like me, talking with Spence this morning. He hadn't seemed to appreciate the danger of the situation, either. Maybe I should ask her to speak with him.

"I *am* taking them seriously, Mom. I promise. I knew the bank CFO. Nelle was warm and friendly." My eyes stung. I didn't want to think of her being gone. Beneath her professional demeanor, she had a playful sense of humor. I was going to miss her laughter. And she'd been a comic book fan. I loved comic books.

"I'm sorry, Marvey." Dad's low tone was gentle sympathy.

"Oh, I'm so sorry!" Mom's compassion was genuine, but short-lived. She quickly resumed her Mama Bear role. "That's even more reason for concern. If she was murdered, the killer attacked someone in your circle of acquaintances."

"I'm being careful. And remember, I have security systems on my house and my car." I'd gotten the home installation to appease my parents. It had come in handy last month during my amateur efforts to clear Jo's name. Apparently concerned by my inquiries, the killer had tried to break into my home in the middle of the night.

"The two suspicious deaths have already occurred in just the last two weeks." My father's apprehension carried across the nine-hundred-and-eight-point-four miles that separated us. "And it was a little more than a month ago that the author was killed at the bookstore. That's three murders in less than two months. We didn't know you were moving to such a dangerous town. You might as well have stayed in Brooklyn."

My lips curved into a reluctant smile. On which community's behalf was I more insulted, Brooklyn or Peach Coast? It was a toss-up. "That's an unfair comparison, Dad."

To be precise, it was actually three murders in five weeks, but I decided against correcting him. Besides, my name wasn't on the hit list. My eyes strayed toward the stairs leading to my bedroom where I'd stored the list inside my purse, ready to take to the sheriff's department Monday—with or without Spence.

"Perhaps your father and I will feel just as confident

of your safety once we see the town for ourselves." My mother had gone from insistence to persuasion.

I threw my head back and stared at the off-white ceiling. Of course I wanted my parents to visit as soon as possible, but we'd already made arrangements, and "as soon as possible" was next month. "I can't take time off from work now. You know we've just kicked off our summer fundraiser. And Corrinne approved my vacation request for July."

I sensed my parents' nonverbal fretting. Their minds were hard at work on a more convincing argument. But we couldn't dispute the facts, and the facts were this wasn't the best time for a visit.

"All right." Dad sounded resigned. "We'll wait until July, but you're friends with the newspaper's publisher, Spence Holt. Promise you'll keep us informed of whatever you learn about the investigation, whether it's in the paper or not."

I looked toward the staircase again. Should I tell them about the list? I rubbed away the wrinkle between my eyebrows. Now probably wasn't the right time. "I promise."

"Good." Mom seemed satisfied, at least for now. "And be careful."

"I will..." ...*do my best.*

CHAPTER 5

S EATED AT MY DINING TABLE early Monday morning, I folded open *The Peach Coast Crier*. "Are any of these news stories going to cause your grandparents to pack their bags and board a plane for Georgia?"

From his spot on the table on the other side of the newspaper, Phoenix scanned the page, then looked away.

"I don't think so, either." My shoulders relaxed and I re-read the headlines.

A local book conference was scheduled for the week my parents were visiting in July. *Excellent.* I made a note to ask if they wanted to attend. The Paw Babies & More rescue pet adoption was this Saturday, the same day as the library's book swap. People could swap books, then head around the corner to the pet shop to find a new furry family member. I might even have some books on pet care I'd be willing to part with. *Kismet.*

There was an update on the deputies' investigation into Hank Figg's death. According to Jed, the autopsy confirmed the high school basketball coach had been murdered. Beyond that, he wouldn't give any details, citing the ongoing investigation.

I shoved away from the table and stood. The sudden movement didn't dislodge the shards of ice filling my chest. I stared at the paper. Could this really be happening?

My mind screamed, *What kind of killer makes a list of their targets, then drops it in a crowded room like a half-written confession?*

All morning, I'd struggled to convince myself I was overreacting. I'd almost talked myself into believing there was nothing to the list. There had to be a simple explanation and if I tried, I'd uncover it. For a few minutes, I'd believed that. Now this news story had resurrected my fears. Every. Single. One. Hank Figg had been murdered. Would the autopsy reveal the same conclusion for Nelle Kenton? Was the same person behind both deaths?

And was that person also after Spence?

Bracing my hands on the dining table, I skimmed the rest of the article. The reporter had paraphrased Jed's claim that there was no connection between Hank's and Nelle's deaths at this time. That didn't mean they wouldn't find a connection later. I thought of the list in my purse. That connection would probably appear faster than they'd imagined.

Since the update had appeared in his newspaper, I assumed Spence had read it. Checking the time on my cell phone, I amended that thought. It wasn't quite seven o'clock. If he hadn't read the story yet, he soon would.

"Time for me to go, Phoenix." I packed my breakfast dishes into the dishwasher.

My tabby stretched, then leaped from the dining table. He trailed me as he did every workday morning as I collected my heavy chocolate handbag and American Library Association tote bag. The green message on the tan canvas tote stated, *Read, Renew, Repeat.*

I gathered Phoenix into my arms for our farewell ritual. I stroked his nose; he butted my head. Settling him back on the hardwood flooring, I sent a text to Spence before arming my home security system.

Taking list to deputies this afternoon. Could you meet me?

"Your usual, Marvey?" Anna May called out her customary greeting as I entered On A Roll on my way to work Monday. There was something so comfortable in our morning routine. It helped get my day off to a good start.

Her café and bakery was the town's unofficial gathering spot. It attracted residents from all stages of life: young, old, working, retired, single or committed. I'd known from the start On A Roll would be my gateway into the community, and the best place to help increase awareness of the library and its services. It was also a great way to start the day with good company and even better food.

"Yes, please, Anna May." I returned her smile as my low-heeled pumps tapped a path across the brown and gold tiled flooring to the order counter. Along the way, I exchanged greetings with other regulars, which was the majority of Anna May's customers.

The coffee shop was crowded, even this early in the morning. The circular pale wood laminate tables were all occupied. I breathed in the aromas of freshly baked rolls and sweet pastries, and had to remind myself I'd just eaten.

Time seemed to slow in the neighborhood café. It had taken me a while to accept Peach Coast was not on New York time. How would my parents react to this place?

At the register, I gave Anna May the exact amount for my order, which included a small café mocha with skim milk and extra espresso. "And a serving of your delicious peach cobbler to go, please."

Anna May's cherubic peaches-and-cream features glowed and her periwinkle eyes twinkled. This morning, her black T-shirt read, *Nothing Says 'I Love You' Like Coffee.* Truer words may never have been spoken.

I used to give the cobbler to Floyd but after four months, he complained his clothes were objecting to the indulgence. Since he hated shopping for clothes, he'd asked me not to bring the dessert to him, but I couldn't stop ordering them. The expression on Anna May's face the one and only time I'd rejected her cobbler wasn't something I wanted to see directed toward me ever again. No one would. I requested the cobbler separately just to reinforce her goodwill. My solution to the Cobbler Conundrum had been to put the pastry on an alphabetical rotation. Mondays they went to Adrian, Tuesdays to Corrinne, Wednesdays to Floyd, and Thursdays to Viv. Fridays, I treated myself. My colleagues had endorsed the remedy enthusiastically.

"Etta, Dabney, and I were talking about what a nice time we had at the fundraiser Thursday evening." Anna

May spoke over the cheerful refrain of the coffee bean grinder.

"I'm glad you enjoyed it." I looked over my shoulder to smile at Dabney McCoy and Etta Child, seated at their usual table near the counter. The retirees looked to be in their mid-to late seventies.

"I hadn't expected to have a good time around a bunch of people with their noses so high in the air they all could've drowned in a rainstorm." Dabney shoveled more peach cobbler into his mouth.

Etta gasped. "Dabney!"

"What?" The creases mapping his broad, pale forehead deepened as he paused with a spoonful of cobbler halfway to his mouth. "The food was good. Left as full as a tick."

"Anna May outdid herself." I exchanged a wry look with the café owner and caterer as she added espresso to the hot cocoa syrup before pouring the milk.

I enjoyed the cranky senior. Dabney wouldn't be Dabney if he wasn't complaining about something.

"Dabney's been spending more time at the library." Etta's wide blue eyes conveyed an unnecessary apology as she extended the olive branch. "Tell Marvey about that book you just borrowed."

Another nonreader converted? Her words were music to my ears.

Dabney swallowed his last cobbler crumb. His gray eyes strayed to Etta's bowl as he answered. "That's right. It's a book of supernatural stories."

It never ceased to surprise me what people gravitated toward for their reading pleasure. Dabney seemed too pragmatic for paranormal tales. "May I ask what drew you to that book?"

"Not what." Dabney shrugged. "Who. Viv Liu. After Etta dragged me into the library against my will, Viv chatted me up for a couple of minutes, then handed me that book. It's pretty good. I wish I'd enjoyed reading this much in my younger days."

High praise from Dabney. "It's never too late."

"Reading has opened a whole new world for him." Etta gestured toward Dabney with her empty spoon. "Now he actually has something interesting to talk about."

"I'm always interesting." Dabney gave a smiling Etta an indignant look. "But you should read it, Etta. The book has stories of headless people, ghosts, and spiders as big as houses."

Etta paled as she dropped her spoon. "Now why would I need to know about that?"

"You done with that cobbler?"

Etta scowled at him as he claimed the dish without waiting for her reply. Poor Etta. I'd been coming to the coffee shop every weekday morning since I moved to Peach Coast. During that time, I don't think I'd ever seen her finish a dessert.

I accepted my doctored café mocha and the cobbler to go from Anna May. "Will I see any of you at the library's book swap Saturday?"

"I don't have any books to swap." Dabney spoke around a mouthful of pastry, adding insult to Etta's injury.

"That's fine." I stepped closer to Etta and Dabney's table. "You can still come and peruse the books other people swap. If there are any titles that interest you, you can purchase them for a dollar each."

Etta's eyes widened with amazement. "How are you able to sell the books for so little?"

"Hey!" Dabney protested. "Don't spoil a good thing."

I smiled at Dabney before answering Etta. "It's part of our summer fundraiser. Proceeds from these sales will help support our programs. When I worked for the New York Public Library, our Big Book Sales were great revenue resources."

"Well, you know that Etta and I are always happy to do what we can to support the library." Dabney made the commitment with a straight face.

Peach Blossom Boulevard was a major thoroughfare in the quaint town. Six vehicles rolled down its broad asphalt street this Monday morning. For Peach Coast, this was rush-hour traffic. For New York, it would be heaven.

The short walk from On A Roll to the library was a breeze. The board redbrick sidewalks harbored few other early-morning pedestrians meandering to work. Stately sweetgum trees dressed the curbs. I had a sense of well-being as I passed homey businesses and charming shops preparing to greet their clientele. All the entrepreneurs knew each other and worked together to keep their business district thriving.

Across the boulevard, June Bishop owned Petals Palooza flower shop. She usually called out a cheeky morning greeting, and her boisterous laughter would bubble up and brighten my day. Our exchange was an enjoyable part of my morning routine. Today, she was setting out a few potted plants on the display tables in front of her store. She seemed solemn and preoccupied, which was contrary to her energetic, positive personality. Her grief over Hank's death was still fresh.

I crossed the boulevard to check on her. "Good morning, June." Even the bounty of roses and flowers arranged in her display window seemed muted.

"Oh, Marvey, I didn't see you there." She'd restrained her thick honey-blonde tresses with a bandanna as though she couldn't be bothered with her usual lively braid. Her floral dress hung on her slender frame.

"Is there anything I can do to help you?" My question seemed so inadequate.

"No, thank you. I'm fine." Her tawny brown eyes wavered, then drifted away. Her pale features were drawn. Was she having trouble sleeping? My heart hurt for her.

I suspected her answer wasn't honest, but I let it go. "We missed you at the kickoff Thursday evening."

June's smooth brow furrowed. "I'm so sorry. I know I said I was coming and all. I felt real bad to have backed out at the last minute. My driver was sick so I had to deliver the floral arrangements we'd created for a wedding Thursday night."

I hoped the task had helped distract June from her grief, if only for a little while. Although the coach had died sixteen days ago, the deputies hadn't released his body until Saturday, according to the *Crier*. Had that story restarted her grieving process? She'd cared a great deal about Hank.

"There's no need for you to apologize. I just wanted you to know we were thinking of you." I adjusted my purse and tote on my shoulder. "If you ever need to talk, I'm happy to listen. You can call me. Anytime."

June blinked rapidly. "Thank you, Marvey. You're a good friend. But the truth is Hank and I had broken up before he'd died." She brushed a tear from her cheek. "I could tell his heart was with someone else. And he's...he was...a good man. I just wanted for him to be happy."

I dug a packet of tissues from my purse and offered it to her. "What made you think he was interested in someone else?" A person would have to be crazy to break up with June. She was warm, funny, smart, and beautiful.

June whispered her thanks as she pulled a tissue free. "A woman knows these things."

I was tempted to ask who the other woman was, but I changed the topic. "It's a shame you missed the fuss we made over the Class of 2006. That was your graduating class, right? You weren't in the photo in the paper, either. I'm sorry."

June dried her eyes. "I graduated in 2006, but to be honest, I'm not sorry I missed the fuss or that I didn't make the paper. High school wasn't a good experience for me."

"Oh, I'm sorry—"

"Don't you worry about it, hon. You couldn't have known."

I stepped back, preparing to leave. "Promise me you'll call if you need to talk."

June's smile was a shadow of its usual cheery self. "I promise."

I returned to the other side of the street. In front of Paw Babies & More, Lonnie Norman, the pet shop's owner, offered me a half-hearted greeting.

"What's wrong, Lonnie?"

He released a gusty, irritated breath and ran a hand

over his thinning dark brown hair. "I'm about to fly off the handle."

My eyebrows reached for my hairline. I hadn't realized Peach Coast residents could get that frazzled. But on closer inspection, even Lonnie's uniform of beige pants and matching jacket with the shop's logo on his upper pocket had wrinkled under the tension. "Is there anything I could do to help?"

He looked at me in surprise, then managed to find a smile. "Thank you, but I don't think so. Not unless you know of a venue that's available for me to hold my annual pet adoption Saturday?"

I gaped at him. "You booked the community center months ago. What happened?"

In a blink of an eye, Lonnie's smile disappeared and his light brown eyes darkened behind his rimless glasses. "You 'n I are apparently the only ones who remember that." He set his fists on his stocky hips. "The scheduler overbooked the center. I argued with him for over an hour. Made me so mad, I wanted to cream his corn."

"Does he realize your event's Saturday?" A lightbulb flashed on in my head. "Your event's Saturday."

He adjusted his glasses and gave me a searching look. "That's right."

"Our book swap is Saturday." My pulse sped up as the possibilities raced across my mind. "Would you be able to hold your pet adoption in our parking lot?"

Lonnie's eyes stretched wide with hope, then narrowed with caution. "What about your customers? Won't you need the parking spaces?"

I waved both hands in front of me, warding off his objections. "We'll use orange cones to block the parking lot entrance, then place signs directing vehicles to the town's public lot across the street."

His frown cleared and his eyes sparkled. "Well, if you're sure..."

"I'm confident Corrinne'll support this idea." I thought of her rescue retriever mix. She'd named him Ballad because of his soulful brown eyes. She also claimed he loved singing along with the radio. So far, she was the only one who'd heard him do that. She blamed that on stage fright. "The library's just around the corner. You won't have far to go to set things up. And the weather's supposed to be beautiful. We should be fine to host the adoption and the swap outdoors. We can also cross-promote our events."

His grin brightened his features. "I'd like that. Yes, that would be fine indeed."

"Great." The excitement was contagious. "This afternoon, I'll bring you some of our book swap fliers and you can make up some fliers announcing the new adoption location so we can distribute them in the library."

"I can't thank you enough, Marvey." Lonnie's eyes shone with relief. "This will really help me out."

"My parents always told my older brother and me karma comes back, good and bad. If the library was in a similar situation, I'd hope people would help us."

"And they would." Lonnie awkwardly patted my shoulder. "You've only been in town a few months, but you've already built up a lot of good will."

"Thank you, Lonnie. That's very kind of you to say." My heart was full, but I didn't want to succumb to my emotions in the middle of Peach Blossom Boulevard where everyone could see me. "Anyway, I think the cross promotion will help us both."

Lonnie rubbed his hands together. "I reckon you're right. It could bring us both even more foot traffic."

Satisfied with our plans, I left Lonnie to create his fliers. The spring in my step carried me through the library's front doors right up to my desk. That's when my mind cleared and I recalled the mysterious list of names. Hopefully, the good will Lonnie referenced would be in attendance when Spence and I met with the sheriff's deputies.

CHAPTER 6

I'D GOTTEN INTO THE HABIT of arriving at work a little early. The extra minutes helped me ease into the day—especially if it was a Monday. I stowed my purse in the bottom desk drawer just in front of my economy-sized bag of chocolate-covered peanuts. While I waited for my computer to boot up, I strolled over to the employee breakroom. Nothing says *I'm a team player* like making the first pot of coffee.

"Good morning, Marvey." Corrinne's greeting carried over the sound of her practical pumps meeting the white and gray marbled linoleum as she advanced toward me. "And thank you for making the coffee."

"You're welcome." I glanced over as she stopped beside me.

Her eyes twinkled as we exchanged the smile that coffee lovers all over the world understood. Corrinne's fitted blush skirt suit complemented the warm undertones of her skin. The pearl necklace and matching earrings completed the image of polished professionalism.

"Is that a new pendant?" As she inclined her head toward me, her shoulder-length, honey blond bob swung forward, then immediately returned to place. Of course it would. Perfection.

"Yes, I made it this weekend." I filled my mug—my third of the morning; don't judge—before stepping aside to give Corrinne access to the coffee.

The image of Alexandre Dumas's triumphant *The Count of Monte Cristo* was encased in an oval glass pendant tray. The cover was the version with a weathered document superimposed over a crimson sky and framed by rusted chains. The vibrant colors went well with my Egyptian blue, short-sleeved blouse.

"It's lovely." Corrinne stirred her French vanilla creamer and four packets of sugar substitute into her oversized coffee mug. The head librarian had a wicked sweet tooth. I empathized. "Have you given any more thought to holding a pendant-making workshop?"

Like Corrinne, I thought the craft presentation was a great idea, and the proceeds would benefit the library. But several other projects had a higher priority.

"I want to get past this Summer Solicitation Drive and the launch of our Library Friends team first." I wrapped my hands around my warm porcelain mug. On the front, printed in white, bold block letters against its black surface was the message, *Keep Calm & Read a Good Book.*

Corrinne raised her left hand in surrender. "I understand, but I'm not the only one who's excited about it."

"She's right. I can't wait." Viv's voice drew my attention to the breakroom's entrance. She was leading Adrian and Floyd toward the coffee station.

Adrian tossed me a smile. "Thanks for the cobbler, Marvey."

"You're welcome." I moved away from the white tiled

counter to give our new arrivals space. Corrinne followed me.

It was interesting the way a hairstyle could change
a person's appearance. When I first met Adrian, his
shaggy brown hair had covered much of his face. Now it
was long enough to be brushed away from his thin features and secured into a ponytail that just reached his
shoulders. I liked it. But judging by the furtive glances
Floyd kept sending him, it might be a bigger adjustment
for some people.

"I don't know about the rest of y'all, but this weekend, I was worn slap out from the kickoff." Adrian
tugged at his ponytail as though trying to loosening the
band.

"It was probably the excitement that made you so
tired, Adrian." Corrinne settled onto a red vinyl break-
room chair, smoothing her linen skirt over her knees
and crossing her feet at the ankles. Not for the first
time, I wondered whether Corrinne had attended charm
school.

Adrian's eyes grew wider. "More like stress. A lot of
work went into just a couple of hours of fun. I'm never
lookin' at those fancy shindigs the same way again."

Viv was nodding her head in agreement. "That took
a lot of planning, preparation, and coordination. But it
was worth it. Even though the event was for donors, I
had a lot of fun too."

Her positive feedback made me smile with relief.
"That's the way it should be."

Floyd filled his plain white mug. He drank his coffee
black. The brew started to leak from the mug's hairline
fracture almost immediately. If I bought him a new one,
would he use it?

"It'll be weeks before we're able to tell whether it was successful, though." He grunted.

I was getting better at identifying the nuances of his nonverbal communication, but I couldn't tell if this was an agreeable sound or a dismissive one. Weighing it against his Bad Attitude Santa Claus persona—frosty blue eyes, salt-and-pepper buzz cut, and general negative disposition—I determined the sound was dismissive.

It was better not to correct Floyd regarding how long it could take to measure the fundraiser's success. Some donors didn't return pledge cards until a month after a solicitation drive ended. Knowing that could send my teammates over the edge.

"In terms of attendance, we can count the kickoff as a success." I gestured with my mug. "Nearly every invitee came."

Viv flashed a grin. "And a lot of attendees turned in their donor cards before the evening ended. I'm hoping Thursday's positive momentum will spill over to the book swap Saturday."

"Speaking of Saturday, Paw Babies and More is also holding its annual pet adoption." I informed the team of Lonnie's dire circumstances with the community center and my suggestion that he move the adoption to our parking lot.

"That's a brilliant solution." Corrinne pressed her palms together. Her eyes gleamed with enthusiasm for the synergy. "It emphasizes the library's commitment to the community and increases attendance for both events. Well done."

Viv and Floyd agreed. Adrian's eyes widened like a deer in headlights.

"But now there's pressure to keep that momentum going." His anxiety didn't seem to be dissipating.

I remembered my first big donor event. The food had been fabulous. The atmosphere had been festive. But like Adrian, anxiety had settled in my gut like a brick and hadn't gone away until we knew the fundraiser had been successful. What message would my younger self have found most comforting during that time?

Crossing to him, I placed a hand on his shoulder. "Adrian, you're doing a great job. Give yourself a break and celebrate every victory. We're still getting positive feedback on the kickoff and I know Saturday's book swap's going to be great."

Floyd's grunt made everyone smile. It was the sound of enthusiastic agreement.

Late Monday morning, I entered the Camden County Sheriff Department's Peach Coast Station. The experience brought back vivid recollections of every time I'd broken a speed limit or jaywalked. Could the deputy on duty in the department's lobby read those violations in my eyes?

"Mr. Spence, good morning." The young man trembled as though he was greeting a pop star. I thought he'd ask for Spence's autograph. Instead, his expression dimmed with concern. "Is there a problem, sir?"

"No, Billy, everything's fine." His deep voice was soothing. "This is Ms. Marvella Harris. Marvey, this is Deputy Billy Green."

Billy's soft chin dropped and his eyes grew as wide

as saucers. "Yes, ma'am. I've heard a lot about you. You're from New York City." He made it sound like, *You're from outer space.*

"It's nice to meet you, Deputy Green."

"Yes, ma'am. Why, Deputies Whatley and Cole, they've been telling us all about you and ..." Billy flushed beneath an abundance of freckles. The color clashed with his near-burgundy red hair.

I tilted my head, struggling to suppress a smile. "I'm sure they have, Deputy."

Billy squirmed, sending Spence a beseeching look. Spence didn't seem amused so I jumped into the silence to keep things moving. I only had an hour for lunch.

"We'd like to speak with the deputies, please?"

"Why, yes, ma'am." Billy seemed thrilled at the prospect of getting out of the awkward exchange. He pointed toward the hallway behind him. "Y'all can just go straight back. You cain't miss 'em."

The Peach Coast Station must have been one of the cleanest law enforcement facilities in the country. I found the scent of lemon disinfectant welcoming. The white linoleum flooring leading into the bullpen probably glowed in the dark. The beige paint on the space's perimeter walls looked fresh. Long, rectangular windows hung bare against the walls, giving the room's occupants an almost three-hundred-and-sixty-degree, unobstructed view of the building's immediate surroundings. The aromas of fresh coffee and warm pastries reminded me it was almost lunchtime.

Four desks pressed against the far wall, two on either side of a window overlooking the parking lot. Each station had two computer monitors and a headset attached to a desk phone. Was that the station's dispatch team? Three women and one man, who looked like veterans of the department, were shooting the breeze. It must've been a slow morning.

Spence and I located Jed and Errol toward the rear of the long, narrow room.

Errol sprang from his chair. His eyes glittered with pleased surprise in his tan face, and he greeted us with a warm smile. "Hey, Ms. Marvey! Mr. Spence! It's sure nice of y'all to stop by."

Jed rose reluctantly to his full height, a few inches taller than me, and adjusted the waistband of his olive green polyester pants. His cool gray eyes gave us a wary scrutiny. "Ms. Marvey. Mr. Spence. What can we do for y'all?"

I squared my shoulders and got to the point. "I have information I believe is connected to the homicides you're investigating."

Errol looked interested. He crossed his arms over his short-sleeved white shirt and narrow black tie.

Jed looked from Spence to Errol before turning his skepticism toward me. "Let's get this over with."

Ignoring his lack of graciousness, I followed him into the sheriff's department's version of an employee break-room. The older deputy indicated one of the dark faux wood tables.

I started to take the chair opposite Jed when I noticed Spence holding the back of it. "Do you want that chair?"

He gave me a patient look. "I'm holding it for you."

"Oh." Whatever that meant. I sat and he took the chair to my right. Jed and Errol sat across from us.

The vending machine was intriguing. If I wasn't mistaken, the companies that produced several of those

treats were headquartered in the South, if not specifically in Georgia. Hometown pride on display.

Realizing I was on borrowed time, I handed Jed the
original list. I had a copy of it in my purse. I explained
when and where I'd found it, and why I believed it mattered. Once again, Errol was intrigued. Jed looked at
me as though I'd just walked off that spaceship Deputy
Green thought I'd arrived in.

"Why would someone make a list of people they intended to kill while they were at some fancy event?"

The muscles in the back of my neck tightened with
impatience. "I never said the person created the list *during* the kickoff. It's possible he or she already had the
list in their pocket and it fell out."

"I can see that." Errol nodded his agreement.

"I can't." Jed's tone was flat. "Lemme start over.
Why would a serial killer make a list of their victims?
Seems like to me that's something they could keep in
their heads rather than creating more evidence against
them."

"How did Hank and Nelle die?" Spence watched Jed
closely as though he was trying to read the older man's
thoughts.

But Jed had an excellent poker face. "You know we
can't discuss ongoing investigations, Mr. Holt."

Aha! Jed's slip gave me a surge of adrenaline—and
satisfaction.

I pounced. "Are you saying you believe *both* deaths
were murders, not just Hank's? Deputy Whatley, you
told the *Crier* the two deaths aren't connected, yet you
and Deputy Cole have been assigned to lead both investigations and the victims' names are on this list."

Jed dragged his right hand over his thinning snow

white hair. "I don't know what kind of law enforcement training you have, Ms. Marvey, but generally killers don't go around writing their victim's names on a paper like a Christmas card list, then drop it off at the library."

I started to respond, but Spence spoke before me. "How would you explain two people who died under mysterious circumstances being on this list?"

I blinked. I'd asked Spence the same question when he'd tried to debunk my theory.

Jed cocked an eyebrow. His gray eyes gleamed. "Mr. Holt, I saw your name on that list, too. Do you have any reason to believe someone's out to get you?" He'd framed his question to box Spence into contradicting me.

Unfair.

I schooled my features into the expression I used on the No. 5 train in Brooklyn. But inside, my stomach churned and my muscles were so tight, I feared I'd snap in half. Regardless, I wouldn't give up my inquiry. If I was correct about this list—and I suspected I was—then Spence was in danger. I didn't care about looking silly or feeling foolish. I cared about keeping a friend safe. A very good friend.

Spence inclined his head toward the sheet of paper on the table. "If Marvey's concerned about that list, so am I. Her instincts were correct on the last homicide investigation. I think you should look into it."

My muscles sighed with relief. Satisfaction warmed me from the inside out.

Jed picked up the paper and scowled. "It's not much to go on."

"It's more than we had when we started the day." Errol's glass-half-full rejoinder earned him a glower from his veteran partner.

Spence looked from Jed to Errol. "What leads do you have?"

Errol shrugged. "What we have right now don't amount to a hill of beans."

"We're not supposed to discuss ongoing investigations with civilians, *deputy*." Jed sounded like he was crunching glass.

Errol smiled unrepentantly. "It's not much of an investigation right now, though, is it, JW?"

I coughed to mask my laughter. "Then I don't think it would do any harm to see whether there's a connection between the people on the list, would it?"

Spence nodded his encouragement. "Marvey and I couldn't identify a connection, but with your experience and jurisdiction, you'd have better luck uncovering something."

Errol shrugged again. "I don't see the harm in it."

Jed still looked resistant. "Fine, but we're only doing this to keep you from getting involved in this case."

I stood away from the table. "I'll leave this information in your capable hands."

I hoped they wouldn't realize I hadn't actually promised to stay out of their investigation. How could I make a promise like that when a friend's life could be hanging in the balance?

CHAPTER 7

"Who'd want to hurt Spence? He's a prince." Jo's fingers flew over her keyboard as she entered catalog information into a computer screen I couldn't see.

It was shortly after five o'clock on Monday evening. I'd stopped by Jo's bookstore, To Be Read, on my way home from the library. It was something I did on those occasions when I needed a sounding board who'd respond in complete sentences rather than the inscrutable expressions Phoenix gave me.

"I agree. But why else would his name be on a list with two homicide victims?" I regarded Jo from one of the padded green chairs on the opposite side of her desk. She sat in front of her laptop, surrounded by University of Florida paraphernalia: orange and blue stress balls, coffee mug, mousepad, pens, and pencils. A pennant was tacked to the wall behind her.

I thought confiding my concerns about the list with Jo would make me feel better. After what we'd gone through during our investigation into Fiona's murder, I'd expected her to be open to the possibility that the seemingly innocent sheet of paper could be a hit list. Instead, she displayed the same skepticism as Jed, Errol and even Spence.

"You've gotta be wrong about that list." Her ponytail waved behind her shoulders like a wagging finger as she looked back and forth between a stack of papers and her monitor.

"Believe me, Jo. I hope I am." I rubbed my forearms to warm them up. Jo's office was always chilly. I suspected she kept it that way so she could wear her orange and blue University of Florida cardigan.

"Spence is well-liked, admired, and respected in this town." The *click-click-click* of her keyboard punctuated Jo's every word. "Just as his mother is and his father had been. His family's companies employ a lot of people, and those businesses contribute a ton of revenue to the community. Not to mention their philanthropy. No one would want to hurt him. That's just crazy."

Jo's arguments for Spence's sainthood raised valid points. They also made my heart sigh. He was a special person, caring and considerate. Smart and funny. Handsome and humble. The woman who claimed his heart would be so lucky...provided she could handle falling in love under a spotlight. I couldn't. My heart sighed again.

I nudged aside these distracting thoughts and returned to brooding about my theory. "The deputies don't believe me, either."

"I'm sorry, Marvey." Jo shrugged and kept typing. "It's just too far-fetched. Spence is a really nice guy. There's no motive for anyone to want to harm him."

I cocked my head, considering Jo's words. "People

said the same thing about Hank. That he was a really nice guy. Nelle was nice, too."

"I suppose." *Click-click-click.* Jo's typing provided sound effects for my thoughts. "She was always pleas-ant when she came into the bookstore. Always polite to my team, which I appreciate. I don't tolerate rudeness toward the people I employ." She frowned at the thought of such discourtesy.

I'd once witnessed a customer snap at one of To Be Read's staff members. Jo had made the hapless person apologize.

"I wonder if the other person on the list, the bike shop owner, is also well-regarded."

"Brittany Wilson? What're you thinking? That the serial killer's going around taking out all the nice people in town? Then the list would be a lot longer and you'd be on it as well."

"So would you." I sent her a sly look. "And Nolan."

Jo's fingers stumbled on the keyboard. Her softly rounded face pinkened. "Nolan *is* nice. That must be why he and Spence have been such good friends for so long."

Yeahumm...

I shifted impatiently on the cushioned seat. "The deputies don't have any leads on either Hank's or Nelle's deaths, and they don't want me investigating."

"That didn't stop you last time, but the list isn't much to go on." Jo sent me an apologetic look.

No, I hadn't let the deputies dissuade me from inves-tigating Fiona Lyle-Hayes's murder, but the memory of how close Jo and I had come to tragedy still shook me. If we hadn't been so close and able to work together, we would've been added to the body count. But I couldn't let that hold me back.

"Spence and Brittany are in danger. I have to do something."

Jo spread her hands. "But you don't have anything. How're you even going to start investigating?"

"I'll start where we started last time." I stood to leave. "With the librarians."

The text from my older brother, DeAndre, came Monday evening: *Mom Dad worried hope ur not sleuthin again.*

A guilty flush heated my cheeks. Seated at my honey wood dining table, I nudged aside the index cards I was using to take notes for my latest investigation and re-read Dre's text. *For pity's sake.* Criminal grammar aside, I'd think a college professor would understand the value of punctuation. What were those students teaching him?

Ignoring his reference to the murder cases, I responded to his text: *Thanks. I'll talk with Mom and Dad. (Notice the complete sentences and punctuation. Proper grammar is another way of saying, "I love you.")*

I hit send before returning my cell phone to the table and minimizing Nelle Kenton's ProNet profile on my laptop screen. ProNet was a social media site that many professionals used to find networking opportunities for their companies and themselves. I told Phoenix, "I think your grandparents are considering moving their visit up again."

Unconcerned, he continued his grooming from his spot beside my chair.

I rose to stretch, allowing my feet to carry me into the living room. I was desperate to see Mom and Dad, but we'd made plans for the end of July. Now just wasn't a good time.

Does that make me a horrible daughter? I asked myself. *Don't answer that.*

I turned to find the photo of the four of us that stood on the Maplewood fireplace mantel. Dre looked so much like Dad—and a little like Mom, too. Like Isaac Harris, Dre had the same warm brown skin and dark brown eyes, chiseled features, and tight dark curls. But he had Mom's smile. I did, too.

I'd seen pictures of Ciara Bennett-Harris in her twenties. It was remarkable how much I looked like her, except she was a little taller. Why was I the shortest in our family?

I looked down to find Phoenix watching me curiously. "Actually, I'm *not* the shortest in the family. You are."

Choosing not to challenge my assessment, Phoenix followed me back to the dining room and settled onto my lap.

I shifted through the index cards, but guilt kept my parents at the forefront of my mind. They must have asked Dre if I'd mentioned the suspicious deaths to him. Dre and I often confided things to each other that we couldn't share with them, or at least not right away. Their divide-and-interrogate tactics worked from time to time. In this case, however, they'd miscalculated. If he knew what I was doing, Dre would worry about me. Besides, it wouldn't be fair to put him in the position of withholding information from our parents. That's why I hadn't told anyone in my family.

I was still patting myself on the back for that decision when my cell rang. My father's number glowed on my screen. I knew my mother would be sitting beside him. How did they always know when I'd finished dinner and was settling in to relax for the evening? Was I that much a creature of habit?

Act natural.

"Hi, Dad. Hi, Mom."

"Are you getting enough sleep?" Mom's question was an odd segue from our greeting.

"I am. I promise. And I hope you and Dad are too." I stroked the soft warm fur along Phoenix's back. "How are things at work?" If they were as busy as I was, they couldn't possibly get away right now.

"Everything's fine." Beneath my mother's words, I heard the familiar sounds of their neighborhood: dogs barking, car doors slamming, and neighbors calling to each other.

My parents must have been speaking to me from their foyer. The front windows would be open to capture the evening breeze. Our family home was old and didn't have central air. Summers in Brooklyn's concrete neighborhoods could be brutal.

"We read about the fundraiser you hosted for the library." Dad sent his concern across the satellite towers. "Sounds like it was a lot of work. Your mother and I want to make sure you're not working *too* hard."

My parents were getting their money's worth from their subscription to *The Peach Coast Crier*.

"This wasn't my first fundraiser. You know that." My parents, Dre, and his wife, Kaylee, had attended all of the ones I'd helped plan when I'd worked for the New York system. Their support always meant the world to me.

"You're used to working with a much bigger staff on those events." Dad had a point.

"The pace of the work is hectic, but I can handle it. And the library team's *amazing*. We feed off of each other's enthusiasm. That helps us accomplish twice as much with less than half the staff."

"Well, that's good." Mom sighed with what sounded like relief.

"Good." Dad spoke at the same time.

Since we'd settled that issue, I moved on to a more pressing topic. "There's a book conference at a local hotel scheduled for the weekend you're here. Would you like me to get us tickets for it?"

"I don't know," Mom said. I imagined them exchanging dubious looks as they considered the idea. "Your father and I have never been to a book conference before."

"This would be something new and different you could do while you're in coastal Georgia doing other new and different things." Was I overselling? Perhaps.

"All right. I'm up for it." My father's game-for-anything tone made me smile. I often thought I'd inherited my adventurous side from him.

"How about you, Mom?"

"I'll do it." She took the verbal plunge. "Go ahead and get the tickets."

I pumped my fist in victory. Phoenix was unimpressed. He sent me an irritated look before returning to his nap.

"It'll be fun. You'll see." My words tumbled over each other.

"All we want to do is make sure you're safe and

happy, sweetheart. Everything else is a distraction." My father's voice was warm, almost wistful. It made me even more homesick.

"You don't have to travel all the way to Peach Coast for that, Dad. I'm sure you can tell by the sound of my voice."

"We'd rather see you." My mother seemed determined. "The sooner, the better. That way, we'll get the full picture of your new life in Peach Coast."

That's what made me nervous. Hopefully, my team and I will have completed our investigation long before my parents' visit.

CHAPTER 8

I GAVE MY PARENTS MY LOVE before wrapping up our conversation. Then, with a small—okay, substantial—amount of guilt, I returned to reviewing Nelle's ProNet profile.

Was I on the wrong track?

Perhaps.

One murder investigation didn't make me an expert. That success could've been a fluke. A very fortunate fluke. But surfing Nelle's and Hank's social media accounts seemed a good place to mine information about and connections between the victims. I continued putting notes on the index cards until my front doorbell chimed.

"Busy evening. Are you expecting someone?" I lifted Phoenix's napping form from my lap.

He stood on the hardwood flooring and sent me a look of grave disappointment.

"I'm not choosing our visitors over you. I just want to see who's at the door. Aren't you curious?"

After checking the security peephole in my front

door, I opened it to welcome Jo and Spence. "What's going on?"

Spence's expression managed to convey both amusement and chastisement. "Good evening, Marvey. How was your day?"

Not this again. The art of Southern small talk was a minefield for New Yorkers. I despaired of ever mastering it.

"It was fine. Thanks." I stepped back, gesturing toward my overstuffed sofa in a silent invitation to make themselves comfortable. "How was yours?"

"Busy, but wonderful." Jo moved past me, her long, heavy ponytail swinging back and forth like a metronome. "Got a shipment of new releases ready to set up for tomorrow. But tonight, we're here to help with the investigation."

I caught a light, flowery fragrance from her. When had she started wearing perfume? And why? Did it have anything to do with Nolan? My inquiring mind wanted to know. I'd give her a chance to volunteer the information, but the clock was ticking.

Jo sank onto the sofa and crossed her long slim legs in her lightweight powder blue pants. Her white collared T-shirt had the University of Florida logo in orange thread embroidered into the upper left corner. Her big brown eyes held mine. "You put your life in danger helping me prove my innocence. I'm not going to leave you to investigate a murder on your own."

I blinked. "Jo, I didn't help you so you'd feel beholden to me. I helped because you're my friend."

"I know." She tossed a look between me and Spence, who stood beside the sofa. "And I'm helping because you and Spence are my friends."

Spence pushed his hands into the front pockets of his gray cargo shorts. "I saw what you went through last time. I don't want you to put yourself in danger for me."

He still didn't get it. My sigh eased some of the pressure in my chest. "I'm not going to bury my head in the sand when I have a very real concern for your safety. You heard the deputies. Jed thinks I'm delusional." The memory of our meeting with the deputies this morning made me grind my teeth.

"If you're determined to protect me, I'm going to protect you." Spence crossed his arms over his chest. He wore a plain short-sleeved black jersey that did wonderful things for his biceps.

I suspected he was standing because I was. I admired his chivalry, but he was going to be standing for a while. My pulse galloped with fear for his well-being, making me far too restless to sit. "Are you saying it's dangerous for me to investigate a threat against you that you don't believe exists? You hear how that sounds, right?"

Phoenix invited himself to the meeting, bounding onto the sofa to curl up on Jo's lap. Both Jo and Spence had formed a friendship with my rescue tabby.

Jo smoothed her right hand over his back. "If you two are done arguing, can we figure out a strategy for our investigation?"

"We're not arguing." Did Spence sound a little rattled? "We're exchanging a difference of opinion."

I arched an eyebrow, correcting him. "We're arguing, and I don't have a problem with that. Would you like some iced tea?"

Without waiting for their response, I went to the

kitchen to get the refreshments. I poured three glasses of the sweet tea brand I saved for their visits and added a plate of pralines to the tray. They were tasty, though not as good as Anna May's.

They joined me at the dining table. As I set the tray behind my laptop, I motioned for them to join me. Reclaiming my seat, I gestured toward Nelle's ProNet profile. "I thought I should start by learning as much as I can about Hank and Nelle. In true crime novels, the investigations start with the victims. To find the killer, we first have to understand the victim. With whom do they associate? What activities, personal and professional, are they involved in? Where have they been and what were they doing there? I'm going to review this information with the librarians in the morning."

"I'm one of Nelle's connections on ProNet." Spence pulled a chair toward Jo before circling the table to sit on my other side. "I also follow her and Hank on Group-Meet and PictureThis.—Followed." A shadow moved over Spence's features and his eyes darkened as he corrected his comment to reflect his friends' passing.

I swallowed the lump in my throat and squeezed his forearm in comfort. He nodded, acknowledging my sympathy. I didn't know either of them well, but they'd been warm and friendly whenever our paths had crossed. And they'd been devoted to the library.

Phoenix sprang onto a nearby chair before climbing onto Spence's lap. It was as though he knew his friend needed comfort. Spence scratched behind Phoenix's ear.

I hadn't gotten to Nelle's more sociable social media platforms. But I'd found Hank's and Spence's connections on her ProNet network. Learning now that he had even more connections with our victims tightened the cold knot of tension in my stomach. "I hadn't realized you were on social media."

Still petting Phoenix, he shrugged. "It's good for journalists. We find interesting news tips there."

"I'm on social media because I like it." Jo leaned forward to look at Spence and me. "You two should follow me."

I shook my head. "I'm only on social media for the library. That account follows your store and Spence's paper."

"*Bor-ing.*" Jo sang the word as she rolled her eyes.

With a long-suffering sigh, I turned from Jo to address Spence. "Is Brittany Wilson in any of your social networks?"

"Not my personal accounts." Spence shifted Phoenix's weight to settle back onto his chair. He set his right ankle on his left knee. "She might follow the paper, though. As you know, we have followers all over the country." He gave me a winning smile.

I ignored his unnecessary reminder that my parents followed the paper on Chirp. Mom and Dad often commented on the posts.

Heaven help me.

"Let's set aside social media for now." Turning away from the computer screen, I collected the stack of still-blank index cards. "What do we know about Nelle and Hank? And what connects them to you and Brittany?"

"As I said before, the only thing I can think of is that we're all from Peach Coast, born and raised." Spence narrowed his eyes, staring across the room as though scanning his memory for something more.

I tapped my computer screen. "According to

Nelle's social media profile, she was born in Nashville, Tennessee."

Spence's lips parted with surprise and recollection. "That's right. She's lived in Peach Coast for so long I hadn't remembered she wasn't born here."

I didn't correct Spence's reference to Nelle in the present tense. "When did she move to town?" Every detail could help our investigation.

Spence was silent as he considered the question. "The summer before her first year of high school, I think. Yes, that's right. She arrived just in time to start school with her graduating class. I started two years later."

On a fresh index card, I noted Nelle was from Nashville. On a separate card, I wrote she'd started high school in Peach Coast. This was another detail that focused on high school. The town only had one high school, though. Still, could this be significant?

Jo leaned forward to claim one of the glasses of sweet tea. "So she's the only one of the group who wasn't born here. That weakens the theory that the two murders are connected."

I turned the latest index card face down on top of the growing stack. "I prefer to think it narrows the possible links."

Jo inclined her head as though conceding my point. "What else do we have?" She gave Spence a considering look. "You aren't neighbors."

Spence shook his head, still stroking Phoenix's side. "We live in different parts of town."

I stared unseeing at my computer monitor. "Which seems to rule out proximity as a connection."

Jo continued down a mental list. "You don't work

for the same company, either. You and Brittany are self-employed."

Brittany owned and operated Coastal Cycles, a bike shop near the beach. She sold new bikes to residents and rented bikes to tourists who wanted to take self-guided tours around town. In addition, Brittany was an attorney, licensed to practice law in Georgia, Florida, and South Carolina. A beachfront bike shop owner with a law degree; there was a story there.

"Nelle worked for Malcovich Savings and Loan, and Hank worked for the public school system." Spence set Phoenix on the floor.

"Which rules out an employment connection." I frowned.

My anxiety spiked with every potential motive Jo removed from our list. At what point would we start ruling things in? We needed to find a connection—fast. That piece of paper wasn't going away, which meant neither was the threat. With each passing moment, it grew larger in my mind. I stood to pace off some of my anxiety, bringing a few index cards with me.

"Hank was on the Grace Takes Action board with me, and Brittany and I are on the art board. I think Hank and Brittany were on the business council." Spence's words gave me a slight reprieve.

Grace Takes Action was a nondenominational, faith-based nonprofit that helped members of the community in need, whether it was the homeless, the hungry, or neighbors struggling with addictions.

Encouraged, I paused in my circuit around the dining table and spun toward him. "Perhaps this has something to do with these volunteer organizations. Nelle was on the library's board of directors. Is there an issue that multiple organizations are addressing that connects back with the suspect?"

Spence frowned. I sensed him searching his memory. "The art board and Grace Takes Action don't have overlapping issues."

I made a face. "I don't think the library board does, either." I grabbed another index card and made a note to double check. "According to the coach's obituary, he'd graduated from the University of Georgia and was an assistant coach at a high school in Athens. I suppose a lot of Peach Coast residents graduated from that university."

"Including Brittany." Spence gave me an ironic look. "She went into law to please her family. Most of her relatives are lawyers, but she wanted to open a bike shop on the beach."

I'd *known* there was a story there.

Jo selected a praline. "Hank had been excited to get the head coaching job with his alma mater a few years ago. He was also the geometry teacher." She bit into the treat.

I settled back onto my seat. "June said she and Hank broke up before he died." I looked from Jo on my left to Spence on my right. Phoenix was grooming himself across the room. "She thought Hank was in love with someone else but she wouldn't tell me who."

Jo's eyebrows arched in intrigue. "Could June have suspected Hank was in love with Nelle?"

Spence shook his head. "I can't see June killing anyone much less two people, one of whom she cared about. Can you?"

"No, not really." Jo sighed. "Besides June wasn't at the event so the list couldn't be hers."

Good point. I was relieved we'd used logic instead of emotion to remove June from our suspect list. "So far, the only real connection the four of you have is your high school. That's where Nelle enters the picture."

"There's only one high school in Peach Coast: Mother Mathilda Taylor Beasley." Jo's tone was dry. "And Spence was in a different graduating class."

"Did you associate with each other in high school?" I turned to Spence. "Did June and Hank date in high school?"

"I don't know." Spence gave a reluctant smile. "I was two years behind them. And I didn't exactly run with the cool kids."

I gave him a dubious look. "That's hard to believe." Spence was easily the coolest person in town. He really was like the unofficial prince of Peach Coast. Why would someone want to kill the prince? "We've made a start, albeit not a very impressive one." I frowned at my small collection of index cards.

"But it's a start." Jo rose to her feet and stretched. "Hopefully, if there's a reason to be concerned we'll come across something during our research. Or the librarians will."

We had to move much more quickly. I didn't know how much time we'd have until the killer struck again. All I knew was that they would.

CHAPTER 9

"**G**REAT JOB, EVERYONE." I SMILED at Floyd, Viv, and Adrian seated around the small conference table in the corner of my office early Tuesday morning. "Saturday's book swap appears to be in great shape."

We'd wrapped up an efficient status meeting on the event, which was another part of our Summer Solicitation Drive. Everything was lined up and waiting for us with three days to go. What a relief. There were carts to display the scores of books contributed to the cause, donation forms for any we received the day of, change for those buying the gently used books, a sign-up sheet for new library e-newsletter subscribers, and library card registration forms.

Hope springs eternal.

"We've been movin' faster than a hot knife through butter to get everything done." Adrian fussed with the rubber band holding his small ponytail. Was growing his hair out more trouble than he'd expected?

I looked at the members of my project team and remembered with gratitude how they'd helped me prove

Jo's innocence last month. "Before you leave, I have another project I was hoping you'd help me with."

Adrian perked up. "Are we going to investigate the murders?"

I needed to try harder to broaden Adrian's reading interests. We could rotate in other genres to supplement true crime and horror.

"In a way." Opening the manila folder I'd tucked beneath my fundraiser project binder, I retrieved photocopies of the hit list and passed them out. "I'm hoping you can help me prevent a murder."

"*Prevent* a murder?" Adrian's voice rose to excited octaves as he accepted one of the copies.

Floyd and Viv studied the paper with almost identical expressions of surprise and concern.

I leaned into the table. "I found this list Thursday evening while I was giving the activity room a final review after the kickoff. As you'll recall, at that time, Deputies Whatley and Cole were suspicious of Hank Figg's death. Then Nelle Kenton was found dead Saturday. The same deputies are investigating her death as well."

Adrian's eyes were wide. His voice was low. "Are you sayin' this is a hit list?"

I hesitated. I didn't like to say it out loud.

Floyd had no such qualms. "Sounds like a hit list to me."

Viv's eyes widened. "Spence Holt's on the list."

Floyd leaned into the table to get a better look at the names. "Who'd want to kill Holt? That's like someone putting a hit out on Mr. Rogers."

The comparison was a stretch, but I understood what he meant. "That's what I want to find out. Jo and Spence are helping me."

"I'd known Hank Figg almost since the day he was born." Floyd's voice was rough. His eyes reddened as they locked with mine. "He was a stand-up kid who'd grown into a better-than-decent man. And Nelle Kenton. I think she was in her teens when she and her family moved to town. All good people." He blinked quickly as though clearing his vision. "If they really were murdered, this community needs to bring their killer to justice. We owe that to their families."

The gruff man's grief shook me. I felt his sorrow like a blast from across the table. My throat thickened with emotion. "Is Hank's family still in town?"

Nelle had told me about her family and shown me pictures of her parents and younger sisters. I grieved for their loss. I didn't know anything about Hank's family.

"An aunt." Floyd cleared his throat. "Think he has cousins out of state."

What a tragedy. And now his aunt was without family to celebrate holidays and other special occasions. A wave of anger threatened to swamp me. Pushing past it, I stood to grab the box of facial tissue from my desk. I set it in the center of my conference table. Viv, Adrian, and I each took one. After a short hesitation, Floyd did too.

"Coach Figg was only a few years older'n me when I took his geometry class in high school." Adrian mumbled the words. "He was a good teacher. I really liked him." He blew his nose. "Hated his class."

Seated across from Adrian, Viv gave a faint smile. "Hank was a flirt, but he wasn't obnoxious or aggressive." Her smile faded. "I didn't know Nelle well, but she was always friendly and courteous when our paths crossed."

That was Nelle, warm and polite. And now she was gone. I swallowed the lump in my throat. It was a moment before I could speak. "Deputy Cole's open to the theory that this list is connected to Hank's and Nelle's murders, but Deputy Whatley doesn't agree. At least they're dusting the original note for prints. It's a start, but not enough. I was hoping you would help me try to track down whoever wrote it. I know you're looking at a photocopy, but does the handwriting look at all familiar?"

Floyd frowned at the sheet of paper for several moments, his expression intense. "No. There's nothing distinct about it."

Viv and Adrian stared at the names a few moments longer before shaking their heads in denial.

"I thought it was a long shot." Disappointed, I rubbed my forehead where a headache had been nagging me since I'd opened my eyes that morning. "All we really know is the four people on this list went to the same high school."

Adrian blew out a breath. "Most of the people in this town went to that high school."

"Do you really think the murders could have a connection to their high school experience?" Viv tapped her copy of the list. "That was thirteen years ago for Spence and even longer for the others. It doesn't make sense that someone would wait that long before committing murder."

Floyd grunted. "This isn't *The Count of Monte Cristo*."

I tipped my head, acknowledging the literary reference. In the Alexandre Dumas story, the mysterious count spends more than a decade plotting his murderous revenge against the antagonists who'd wronged him.

"Will you help me?" I looked at my coworkers—my friends. "I know I'm asking a lot. This adversary is much more dangerous. Last time, we were trying to identify a murderer who'd acted on impulse. This time, we're looking for a serial killer whose actions are premeditated."

Viv straightened on her chair. "If there's any chance we can prevent another tragedy like Hank's and Nelle's deaths, we should take it."

"Especially if someone's trying to kill Mr. Holt." Adrian sounded outraged.

"Count me in." Floyd's nod was decisive.

"Thank you. Thank you so much." My body was weak with relief. The headache I'd woken with eased. "This isn't going to be easy. As I said, I don't have much information."

Floyd grunted. "It's gotta be someone from the event. How else would the list have made it to the activity room? None of us left it. If it'd been there when we were setting up, we'd have seen it."

"So that narrows our potential suspects from almost one thousand people to seventy-six." I look around the table.

Floyd looked at us askance. "Do the deputies know the cause of death?"

"They don't have the coroner's report yet." I gave Floyd a dubious look. "But I won't hold my breath that they'll share it with us, though."

"It would help to know what killed them." Floyd studied the paper. "We need more to go on. Something."

"You're right." I sat back against my chair. "And we're running out of time."

"Well, now, Ms. Marvey, it sounds like you're doing

one of your so-called investigations, but I'm sure that can't be right, can it?"

I looked up at the new voice. Jed stood framed in my office doorway. His expression was less than enthusiastic. Way less.

Busted.

"Deputies, how can I help you?" As casually as I could manage, I hid my list, slipping it back into its manila folder. In my peripheral vision, I watched Floyd, Viv, and Adrian do the same with their copies. Jed and Errol didn't need to know about the duplicates.

Fortunately, they were more interested in my office than my clandestine maneuvers. I glanced around the space, trying to see it through their eyes. The room was tidy, in large part thanks to the custodial staff. The furnishings were probably older than me. I had the impression at least the desks and chairs, if not the cabinets, had been making the rounds through various government offices. Oh, the stories they could tell if they could talk.

Beside me, my desk was well organized. My black wire inbox was full, but the day was young. Photos of my parents, brother, sister-in-law, and nephew were arranged beside my computer. Framed photos of literacy posters hung on the walls around us.

"It's been a while since I've been inside of one of these." Jed turned his attention from the posters to me. I saw a flicker of discomfort in his ice gray eyes.

"A library?" That was a troubling thought. "How long?"

"Don't know, really." Jed's shrug seemed intended to release tension rather than express confusion. He took off his green campaign hat. "If I had to guess, I'd say finals week my senior year of college. I don't like how silent libraries are. It's unsettling."

I blinked. Considering his thinning, snow-white hair, Jed seemed to be saying he hadn't been inside a library in decades. I inhaled a sharp breath, catching the scent of coffee from my teammates' partially filled mugs.

How could someone be apart from the library for so long? The books and periodicals. CDs and DVDs. Presentations and workshops. How. Was. That. Possible?

I pulled myself together before my inner screams became outer screams.

"I invited you to the fundraiser with me." Errol's delivery was chiding.

"I was busy." Jed mumbled his excuse, which made it even more unbelievable.

"Doing what?" I considered him with skepticism.

"I don't remember." More mumbles. Jed's steps were hesitant as he crossed into my office. He looked over his shoulder as though making sure he had a clear path to the exit.

Standing, I looked between the two men. They hadn't answered my question. "How can we help you?"

"We just want to ask y'all some questions about that event." Jed gestured toward us with the mid-sized black notepad he carried. "Since you're all here together, it'll make things easier for us. We can speak with Ms. Corrinne separate."

Errol rocked back on his heels. "We're questioning everyone who attended the kickoff."

"Let me get a couple of chairs for you." I started to circle the table.

"I'll get them, Marvey." Adrian popped out of his seat beside me.

He was barely missed before he returned, dragging two weathered, gray-cushioned chairs that had seen better days. He positioned them side by side in front of the conference table before resuming his seat. Jed and Errol thanked him as they settled down.

Waves of excitement at the prospect of being interrogated by the deputies rolled off of Adrian. I wasn't the only one who sensed his enthusiasm. Viv looked amused. Floyd and I exchanged concerned looks.

I turned back to Errol. "You're going to interview everyone who attended the kickoff? That's a lot of people."

Jed gave us a look of amused condescension. "How many would that be, Ms. Marvey?"

Viv crossed her legs, smoothing the skirt of her suit. "We had seventy-six attendees."

Errol gave his partner a look of exasperation. "I told you it'd been packed."

My teammates and I exchanged smug looks. It would be quite some time before the pleasure of achieving nearly one hundred percent attendance to our event wore off.

Viv turned back to Jed. "The library has a lot of community support."

Floyd inclined his head toward me. "And that's been building even more since Marvey's joined us."

My cheeks heated. Such a generous compliment from the gruff reference librarian was unexpected. "It's a team effort."

Jed lifted his hands. "If we could cut short the mutual admiration and return to our questioning, we'll be able to get y'all back to work that much faster." He looked to me. "I'm gonna need a list of all the people who were there."

I made a note to myself on a fresh sheet of paper from my writing tablet. "I'll run that report for you, but a few people who'd confirmed didn't attend. I'll remove their names before sending you the list."

Errol tossed a smile toward me. "Thank you, Ms. Marvey. That'd be real helpful. And again, it was a real nice event."

Jed arched an eyebrow. "I'm just thrilled that you enjoyed yourself, Errol."

"Thanks, JW." Errol inclined his head. "You know, ever since I got back into reading, I've been a happier person. Maybe reading could help you to be more content, too."

"I'm so pleased to hear that." Viv gave the young deputy an approving look. "You're one of our most enthusiastic patrons, and that's saying a lot."

"Really?" Errol's cheeks flushed with pleasure.

Jed scowled. "Can we focus on the interview now, deputy? If that's not too much trouble."

Errol straightened on his seat. "Sure thing, JW."

Seated across from me, Floyd rested his forearms on the table. "Why do you want to talk with the people who came to the kickoff? Do you think someone from the reception killed Nelle Kenton?"

I waited for the deputies' response, glad Floyd had asked the question. Yesterday, they'd dismissed my concerns. Today, they seemed to be taking them more seriously. Had something happened?

Jed shrugged a little too nonchalantly. "The people who came to your event are some of the last people to see Ms. Nelle alive."

"But Nelle wasn't murdered until two days *after* the kickoff." I looked between the deputies. "Are you reconsidering the list of names I showed you this morning? Do you now think Hank's and Nelle's homicides are connected?"

Jed gave me a quick look, then dropped his eyes to his notepad. A virtual curtain seemed to lower over his flushed features, making his expression unreadable. "We're looking at all angles, Ms. Marvey."

"Have you identified the cause of death?" Adrian leaned toward the veteran officer.

Jed held up a hand again. "I know y'all probably have never been interrogated by law enforcement before—except you, Ms. Marvey, but that was during the last homicide investigation. You see, the way this here process actually works is *we* ask the questions." He gestured between himself and Errol. Then he waved a hand toward us. "And y'all answer them. Understood?"

"Why wouldn't I understand?" Adrian gave the deputy a confused look. "But do you know how they died?"

Jed squeezed his eyes shut, then opened them again. He regarded Adrian in befuddlement. It was obvious he'd never encountered the combined intellectual curiosity contained within a roomful of librarians. He turned toward me and glared as though the situation in which he found himself had been my fault. "Figg was poisoned. Looks like Kenton was poisoned, too. The M.E. wants to do more testing."

Adrian's jaw dropped. "Poison is typically a woman's weapon."

Viv, Floyd, and I exchanged curious looks.

"Can you cite your source?" Floyd sounded impressed yet skeptical. He was going to be a tough sell. On the other hand, I could be convinced—depending on his source material.

"The FBI." Adrian spread his arms. "Its Supplemental Homicide Report says men and women both prefer to kill with guns, but women use poison more often than men." He shrugged. "Poison's not a popular weapon, though. I think it's used in half of one percent of all murders."

He'd had me at FBI.

"Nelle and Hank were killed and their murders are connected." My voice was breathless. My mind went blank. My body grew cold.

"Yes." Jed was grim. "There's a serial killer in Peach Coast."

And Spence was on their list.

CHAPTER 10

"Hⁱow's Spence doing?" Viv cut into her chicken during our lunch break Wednesday afternoon. Wisps of smoke floated up from the dish.

My librarian team and I were back at my small conference table, this time discussing the investigation. I noted Viv's chicken and dumplings, Adrian's chicken and sausage jambalaya, and Floyd's fried chicken. The mouthwatering scents of sauces and spices rose from their containers to disperse across my office. They all looked so delicious. In contrast, my plastic bowl of homemade chef's salad seemed so...disappointing. Should I ask Spence to teach me some simple Southern dishes?

I dragged my greedy gaze from Viv's entree. "Spence is finding it hard to believe someone would want to kill him. It doesn't seem real to either of us, but we can't explain away the list."

Floyd straightened his beige and blue striped tie, which he'd paired with a beige shirt. "He's a newspaper man. He's bound to have twisted a few shorts into knots."

An interesting if uncomfortable visual.

"Speaking of who'd want to kill Spence, I'll share my key suspect first." Viv turned her notepad to a page covered in neatly written notes. "Delores Polly."

"What did Ms. Delores do?" Adrian sounded incredulous.

Floyd grunted. "Didn't see that coming."

Neither had I. "I don't want to believe Delores could be a serial killer, either. But, Adrian, you know true crime novels often quote detectives as saying we can't allow personal feelings to prevent us from following the evidence."

Adrian nodded glumly. "But what d'you have on Ms. Delores?"

Viv trailed an index finger down her page of notes. "Delores was very upset when the Town College Scholarship Committee passed over her godson. She'd accused the judges of favoritism. And do you remember who was on the judging panel?"

The due date for the scholarship applications was April 1st, Fool's Day, which seemed an odd deadline for an academic scholarship application. The three-member judging panel was tasked with awarding full, four-year scholarships to five high school juniors who'd be entering their senior year. The winners were announced May 3rd.

"Hank Figg, Nelle Kenton, and Spence Holt." Floyd pushed aside his empty dish. "But what's her motive to kill Brittany Wilson? She wasn't a judge."

I lifted a hand, palm out. "We agreed we just needed a few names to start with. Additional research will either reveal more motives or rule them out." I wrote Delores's name on an index card. "Thanks, Viv. Who's next?"

"I'll go." Floyd raised his hand. "Reba McRaney. Last month, she lost the mayoral race. Spectacularly."

"Mayor Flowers got almost four and a half times as many votes as her," Viv said with a grimace.

I winced. "I remember that. It was bad."

Adrian nodded. "The mayor may think the sun comes up just to hear him crow, but Ms. Reba, well, she was just scaring people."

Floyd continued, "A few days after she made her concession speech, which was comical, she came into the library. I overheard her claiming her campaign—and I quote—'had been sabotaged by the mayor's supporters.' She specifically named Nelle Kenton and Brittany Wilson. She also said the *Crier* had taken an interview she'd given them out of context." He arched an eyebrow. "There was no way Reba McRaney was gonna become mayor."

I knew Floyd didn't care much for the mayor, but he didn't seem to like his previous challenger, either. "Why not?"

He cocked his head. "Let's just say common sense isn't a flower that grows in everyone's garden."

I added that Southernism to the notes I'd been collecting in my phone, then turned to Adrian. "Do you have any ideas about possible suspects?"

Adrian scattered an uncertain look around the table. "I was thinking maybe it could be Ms. Philomena Fossey. She owns Shoreline Souvenirs."

I was familiar with the business and its owner. "Why her?"

He frowned. "Her motive for killing the coach could

be unrequited love. Ms. Philomena had dated the coach before the coach went out with Ms. June. And I think Ms. Philomena also has a motive for killing Ms. Nelle and Ms. Brittany. The court's website confirms that Ms. Brittany filed a lawsuit against Ms. Philomena on behalf of Ms. Nelle."

Viv's well-shaped eyebrows knitted. "For what?"

Adrian referred to his notes. "She claims Ms. Nelle made a defamatory statement against her business that caused Malcovich to reject her business loan application."

I straightened on my chair as Adrian's words jogged my memory. "Philomena and Nelle were arguing about a loan during the kickoff. I'd asked them to leave the room, but instead Philomena dropped the disagreement. Before she left, she said something like, 'It's not personal. Right?' And Nelle responded, 'Of course not. It's strictly business.'"

Floyd grunted. "And two days later, Nelle's murdered."

"That's chilling." Viv rubbed her hands up and down her arms. "I hate thinking any of my neighbors could be serial killers."

We murmured our agreements. As hard as it was for me to imagine friends, colleagues, and associates as cold-blooded murderers, how difficult must it be for Floyd, Viv, and Adrian? Many of their neighbors were people they'd seen grow up or grown up with. By virtue of their shared history, you'd think the town's residents wouldn't be inclined to bump each other off.

Setting aside the layers and complexities I was starting to unearth in this Southern small town, I refocused on our meeting. "This is all good information, and the possible motives are connected to recent events."

But how did they tie back to the local high school? Maybe they didn't.

I added everyone's notes to my manila folder, which I was beginning to think of as a case file. None of the potential suspects had a connection to all four victims. Philomena and Reba had connections to three of them, though. But again, this list was our starting point.

Floyd settled back against his seat and crossed his arms over his chest. "What do we do next?"

"Jo and I'll do some more research, then try to subtly question Delores, Reba, and Philomena."

A wave of discomfort washed over me. It was one thing to say we need to keep our personal feelings out of our investigations. But how do you ask friends and neighbors whether they're a serial killer?

Spence picked me up after work Wednesday evening so we could interview Brittany Wilson, owner of Coastal Cycles and the third name on the hit list. I got in his gray hatchback, which smelled like him, sandalwood and peppermint. It looked like he'd never eaten in it, not a single French fry.

He handed me a plain white business-sized envelope. He'd written my name on it.

"What's this?" I asked.

"It's Ms. Delores's email." He waited until I'd fastened my seat belt before pulling out of the parking lot and merging into the meager traffic.

"I'd thought you'd deleted it." I unfolded the paper. His decision to delete what had been described as a threat had puzzled me. Maybe it was a Southern thing. I would've at least confronted Delores.

"Our legal department requires IT to archive emails in case they're needed in future legal proceedings. I asked them to print me a copy." Spence checked his blind spot before changing lanes. He was such a careful driver, even when his was the only car on the street.

I read the heading first. Delores had sent it to Hank, Nelle, and Spence at the same time. *Efficient.* "It's dated May third at 9:07, the day the scholarship winners were announced. Delores didn't waste any time sending it."

"Hank was upset. Right after I deleted the email, he sent a reply to all of us."

When he didn't continue, I prompted him. "Do you remember what he wrote?"

His lips curved in a half smile that eased my growing tension and made my heart skip. "Not verbatim. He wrote something like for two years, her godson did the bare minimum to pass his classes and that his magically producing a solid essay for the competition wasn't enough for him to be awarded a full, four-year scholarship."

Ouch. "If that's true, Hank was right. How did Nelle respond?"

Spence shrugged his broad shoulders under his cream cotton shirt. His suit jacket and tie were folded on the back seat. "She didn't, and we never mentioned it."

"Hmm. I wonder if she deleted it, too." Wanting to be objective, I cleared my mind before reading Delores's email. But by the second paragraph, I saw red.

How do you think the town will view you once I reveal how biased and unfair your decisions were? You'll feel the pain of losing something important to you. I'll make sure of it. You're going to hurt like he's hurting. You took away a promising young man's future and I can take away yours.

"I can see why legal insists on archiving emails. This is horrible." My cheeks were warm. My pulse kicked up. I had to force myself not to crumple it into a ball. The email was lengthy, angry, and bordering on unhinged.

"That's why I deleted it." He flexed his shoulders in a restless movement. "You know Ms. Delores. In her right mind, she'd never carry on like that. This was an emotional response to a disappointment."

I gaped at him. *An emotional...*"This is a textbook threat. I wish you'd reported it to the deputies. Why didn't you?"

He slid a look at me before returning his attention to the road. "Do you really think Delores Polly would plot to kill me because her godson didn't get a scholarship?"

"That's what I'm going to ask her." With shaking hands, I refolded the message and shoved it back into its envelope.

"Marvey—"

"No stone unturned, Spence. No stone unturned." Delores had threatened someone I cared about very much. I was going to get to the bottom of it.

Brittany Wilson rode into the indoor customer display area of Coastal Cycles Wednesday evening on a pink and black road bike. I backpedaled on my own two legs as she cycled toward me. Was she going to stop? I looked at Spence. He looked at me. Finally, she braked with a little more than an arm's length of space between her and Spence and me.

"Hi, Spence. How've you been?" She straddled the cycle. She was outfitted from her helmet to her shoes in pink and black gear that matched her bike.

"I've been fine, Brittany. And you?" Spence gave her a polite smile.

"Can't complain." Her eyes assessed me as she responded to Spence.

Brittany looked like who she was: a competitive amateur athlete. She was perhaps as tall as Spence at a little more than six feet, and fit with lean, well-developed muscles. My research had turned up articles on her previous events: marathons, biathlons, and triathlons. Six years ago, she'd finished her first Ironman Triathlon in Hawaii among the top twenty-five competitors. She'd been climbing up that chart ever since. The event consisted of swimming two-point-four miles, cycling one hundred and twelve miles, and running twenty-six-point-two miles. But she'd never competed in the Peach Coast Cobbler Crawl. *Hmm.* What was the story there?

She removed her helmet, revealing tight dark curls that emphasized her wide ebony eyes and high cheekbones in her dark brown angular face.

Spence settled his hand on the small of my back. "Brittany, this is Marvella Harris. She's from New York. Marvey, Brittany owns Coastal Cycles."

"It's a pleasure to meet you. Your clerk said it would be okay to wait for you." I tried to appear casual as I surveyed the racks of bikes and biking gear on display around us. "I've just moved to Peach Coast and Spence has been kind enough to show me around to help me get acclimated to my new home."

Hitting the five-month mark of residency, my *I'm New In Town* act was starting to strain credulity.

"Welcome to Peach Coast, Marvella. It's good to meet you." She tucked her helmet in the crook of her arm.

"Please, call me Marvey."

The store had a strong but not unpleasant cinnamon scent. The space was bright, made even brighter by the white walls that reflected the light from fluorescent bulbs. Colorful bikes—racing, touring, mountain models—in every style and size were displayed on the walls and arranged in floor racks all over the interior. Biking accessories, including helmets, clothing, shoes, and water bottles, stood on shelves.

Brittany led her cycle to the customer service counter. Impulse buys such as energy bars, bubble gum, and bike chains had been stacked near the register.

"You were in the paper last month." She spoke over her shoulder as she circled the counter. "You solved Fiona Lyle-Hayes's murder."

"I had a lot of help." It made me uncomfortable that people thought I'd single-handedly cleared Jo's name. Spence's paper was responsible for that perception. I sent him a chiding look. He gave me an innocent shrug, but his eyes twinkled and his lips struggled against a smile.

"Before Fiona, we'd had maybe one murder in two years. Now, we've had three in two months." Brittany shook her head in disbelief.

She'd opened the door to the perfect opportunity for me to find out what she knew. "Do you have any thoughts on these recent murders?"

Brittany's sharp look swept between me and Spence.

I'd have withered beneath that stare if I hadn't felt so desperate to protect Spence.

"Now how would I know anything about them?" She asked as though she thought I'd lost my mind.

If she thought a show of temper would make me back down, she was mistaken. First, Spence's life was at stake. Second, I'd taken New York City public transportation seven days a week for more than twenty years. It took a lot to rattle me.

Spence spoke before I could respond. "You socialized in similar circles with Hank and Nelle. Do you know whether they had conflicts with anyone?" His calm, measured tone reduced much of Brittany's agitation— but not all of it.

"I've already given a statement to the deputies." She gave me a pointed look. "The *real* deputies, not pretend detectives."

"I prefer the term 'amateur sleuth.'" Perhaps I shouldn't have interrupted.

She ignored me. "Like I told the deputies, I wasn't close with Hank or Nelle, not even in school. I didn't get involved in their personal issues."

"What about you, Brittany?" I tried to read her body language. Her arms were crossed and she avoided eye contact with me. Was she trying to hide something? "Have you had trouble with anyone? Is anyone giving you a hard time?"

She gave me a narrow-eyed stare as though she was trying to read my mind. "What's going on?" She turned to Spence. "Why're you asking me these questions?"

I pulled the list I'd found in the activity room from my purse and set it on the counter in front of her. She scanned the short list. Her eyes widened and her head shot up.

"What is this?" Her voice trembled a bit. "Is this some kind of joke? If it is, you're sick."

Spence shoved his hands into his pockets. "We don't think it's a joke."

I waved a hand toward her. "Based on your reaction, you're making the same connections we've made about the list."

Brittany set her hands on her slim hips and angled her chin. "Who wrote it?"

"We're trying to find out." I spoke gently. "I found it after a library event last Thursday evening, twelve days after Hank was killed. Then last Saturday, Nelle was killed. It seemed like too much of a coincidence. That's why I brought it to Spence and the deputies. Now we're bringing it to you."

Her eyes wavered before she looked to me again. "Are you saying this is some sort of hit list and that someone's trying to kill me?"

I really disliked that term. It sounded like a gimmick from a Mickey Spillane mystery. This was real life and my friend was in actual danger. "Isn't that what you thought when you saw your name on a list with two people who've already been murdered? Why else did you have that reaction?"

Brittany waved a dismissive hand over the paper, but she seemed unable to look away from it. "What do the deputies think?"

I hesitated. "They're starting to ask questions. Both Hank and Nelle died under suspicious circumstances."

"This is ridiculous." She pushed the paper back toward me. The act was short and sharp, almost violent.

"Just because you found a piece of paper with my name on it doesn't mean someone's trying to kill me."

Spence frowned. "Then what do *you* think it means?"

She crossed her arms again and glared at me. "I think it means you're trying to stir up trouble or cause a panic."

I stared at her in silent amazement. "Why would I do that?"

"How should I know? Maybe you want attention." She shrugged, her movements stiff and jerky. "What I don't understand, Spence, is why you'd go along with this. I'd think you'd know better."

"I'm concerned by the implications of that list." He nodded toward it. "You should be, too."

"Well, I'm not." Brittany remained stubborn even as the blood drained from her face. "You might as well shred it or recycle it. Just get rid of it. There's no reason for anyone to want to harm me."

Methinks the lady doth protest too much.

Brittany was smart. Like Spence, she'd been the valedictorian of her high school graduating class. According to her ProNet profile, she'd graduated magna cum laude from Harvard University undergrad and had earned her juris doctorate from Harvard Law School. Then why wouldn't she at least consider the possibility that someone wanted to kill her? Either the idea was too frightening to face, or she knew more than she was admitting. Which one was it? Could it be both?

"Thank you for your time." I put the list back in my purse and gave her a copy of my business card. "If you recall anything that could help us understand why someone would want to hurt Hank or Nelle, please call me."

Brittany nodded curtly. I felt her eyes on my back as Spence and I left Coastal Cycles.

I broke our silence as we entered the shopping center's parking lot. "Was it my imagination, or did she seem nervous for someone who doesn't believe herself to be in danger?"

"More than a little bit."

I glanced over my shoulder toward the bike shop. "We need to find out why."

CHAPTER 11

*C*OACH WAS SUCH A SPECIAL *person.*
He really cared about those kids.
He was the role model young people need today.

The comments I overheard during Hank Figg's memorial Thursday evening filled me with regret. I wished I'd known him better. Even though this was a wake and people were expected to say nice things about the deceased, these comments weren't polite platitudes. They were heartfelt testimonials.

Who'd want to kill someone so beloved?

I felt like a monster, knowing the main reason I was attending the wake was to find information to keep Spence safe. Hopefully, Hank's spirit would understand.

I tugged on Jo's shirt sleeve. "We should split up. See what we can find out. We'll compare notes afterward."

On the other side of the small funeral parlor, Spence was speaking with the young reporter assigned to cover the event for the *Crier*. The recent college graduate's wide brown eyes circled the room. I could almost hear him chanting in his mind, *I can't mess this up. I can't mess this up.* Based on the level of anxiety he displayed, I wasn't confident he'd be a good source of information for my inquiry.

As I weaved through the crowded lobby, the smell of incense followed me. Frankincense, maybe? It was one of the most popular scents for grieving, thought to provide a sense of soothing comfort. Jed and Errol stood near the front of the room. I turned my back on Jed's grumpy gaze and proceeded in the opposite direction. With each measured step, I strained to catch conversations, listening for any small clue. Friends, neighbors, coworkers, student-athletes, students and their parents had come, seemingly eager to pay their respects and share their grief.

"His teaching style made my daughter like math."

"He rearranged his schedule to meet with my son, so he could get additional help when he needed it."

Pulling a tissue from my handbag, I paused to dry my eyes. These testimonials were really getting to me. In addition to keeping Spence safe, I needed justice for Hank and Nelle.

Through the crowd, I saw Anna May Weekley talking with Lucas Daniel. Trudie Trueman, who'd recently returned to Peach Coast after her mother's death, stood close to Nolan Duggan as they spoke. Philomena Fossey, June Bishop, and Reba McRaney were deep in conversation, their voices hushed and urgent. I started to move in their direction when I was interrupted.

"Did you know my nephew?" The question came from a woman whose dainty white collar eased the solemnity of her black mourning dress. Streaks of gray highlighted her dark brown bun.

Hank's aunt, the last member of his family in Peach

Coast. The idea of losing a relative to natural causes was like a knife to the heart. My world would fall apart if I later learned someone had killed them.

I turned to give her my full attention. "My deepest condolences on your loss. I'm Marvella Harris. I work for the Peach Coast Library. Your nephew organized the Class of 2006's donation to our summer fundraiser."

"I'm Eudella Figg Bidwell. I taught at the high school with Hank." My new acquaintance used her peach handkerchief to dry a tear from her round porcelain cheek. Her cornflower blue eyes were red, puffy, and swimming in unshed grief. "He was always so kind to others, even when he wasn't in the best mood. Just like his father, my brother. God rest their souls. I always thought he'd be there. I never imagined a time when... he wouldn't."

Her words broke my heart. "I'm so sorry. It sounds like you and Hank were close."

She nodded, wiping her cheeks again. "He was like another son to me. My son and two daughters have all grown and moved away. They should be here tomorrow. Hank, he'd check on me and take me out for my birthday. His being here kept my kids from pressuring me to leave Peach Coast and go live with them."

"That was lovely of him." My mind raced to capitalize on the opportunity to speak with someone who'd known Hank so well. I gestured to the room at large. "He was obviously very well-liked. It seems everyone in town cared about him."

"Not everyone." Eudella looked over her shoulder. I followed her gaze to the trio of women, standing in a corner of the room. "Hank loved the ladies. He dated each of them shortly before he died."

I pulled my attention from Reba, Philomena, and June, hoping Eudella could add new information. "Did he call the relationships off, or did they?"

Eudella gave me a wry look. "He always said the breakups were mutual, but I saw the way the exes looked at him. And he was never without a girlfriend." Her eyes twinkled. "Hank was a warm and wonderful person, but he was a ladies' man. I told him you can't treat people that way, especially in a small town. People have feelings. And you young women always think you're going to be *the one* to change a wanderer into the settling-down type. You can't *make* Mr. Right. You have to *find* him."

Finding Mr. Right. The older woman had a point.

Without realizing I was scanning the room for him, I located Spence. He was still trapped in that same corner. His cub reporter had moved on, and a member of the school board had taken his place. Poor Spence. He was always gracious and patient. His kindness was one of his most attractive qualities. But it must have been exhausting to have so many people demanding your attention. The minute he, Jo, and I had entered the funeral parlor, he'd been waylaid by one person after another who'd wanted "a moment of his time."

Was that the reason he didn't date more? Not only would it be nearly impossible to go out in public, but people would speculate about your relationship. People wondered about Spence and me now, and we were just friends. Imagine if we were a couple. I'd lose my mind. My privacy was important to me, and in Peach Coast, Spence was very much a public figure.

I pulled my attention away from the handsome newspaperman and made myself refocus on the investigation. I asked Eudella, "Do you know whether he dated anyone special in high school?"

"High school?" Her eyebrows jumped up. "Now that's been a minute. It was hard enough keeping track of his current girlfriends."

"I'm sure, but perhaps you remember one or two names? Someone special?"

She frowned as she seemed to try harder to bring the past forward. "Now that I think about it, I seem to recall he dated Nelle Kenton for a while back in high school. Yes, that's right. They were in the same graduating class. They broke up right before their senior prom, though. Isn't that a shame?"

I didn't know if it was or not. "Yes, it is."

"They seemed to move on. But recently he said he'd found the courage to ask her out again and she'd said yes. And now poor Nelle has also passed." She gave me another considering look. "They're saying they were both murdered."

I grabbed the opening before it closed. "Do you have any idea who would've wanted to kill Hank or Nelle?"

She looked over her shoulder toward Philomena, Reba, and June again. "You know what they say about a woman scorned. And Philomena had been scorned twice."

"Twice?"

Eudella nodded. "She and Hank had dated in high school just before he started dating Nelle. And they dated again after college."

Interesting. But could jealousy be the right motive for Philomena possibly killing Nelle? After breaking up with her, Hank had dated Reba and June before reuniting with Nelle. And I still didn't have a motive for her wanting to murder Spence and Brittany.

"Had Hank confided any concerns to you or conflicts he'd been having with anyone?"

"No, but why are you so insistent? Are you investigating these murders, too?" She smiled at my surprise. "I know who you are, Marvella Harris. I read about you in the paper."

Of course she had. The *Crier* was required reading in Peach Coast. But now I had to give a reason for my interest in the case, one that wouldn't cause a panic in the community the way my theory about a serial killer would.

I spread my hands and managed an apologetic smile. "I'm from New York."

"Ah!" Eudella nodded as though it all made sense now. "Well, Hank got more and more quiet during the fundraising for the class gift. When I asked him about it, he made some strange comment about not keeping secrets because they always came out in the end."

My muscles trembled. Was this a break in the investigation?

"Did he tell you what the secret was?"

Eudella sighed, linking her hands in front of her hips. "No, I'm sorry, dear. He didn't offer and I didn't ask. An aunt must know when to push and when not to."

I had a feeling this would've been a really great time to push. I didn't tell her that, though. Instead, I thanked her for her insights, then turned to search for a restroom. My bladder was reminding me of the quantity of coffee I'd had this morning. But despite this discomfort, my mind raced with excitement. Was it possible Hank's secret was the key to the murder cases? If so, how was I going to discover it?

I had the restroom all to myself. Apparently, other people hadn't consumed as many cups of joe as I had. I made a beeline for the farthest stall in the room just in time. Crisis averted, I started to rise, when two women in a loud and very energetic conversation burst into the room. I'd heard them open the door, but I hadn't heard them close it.

Urgh! Why do people do that?

It was discomfiting, to say the least, to be in the stall of a public restroom when people were holding the main door open. I settled back down, grinding my teeth to keep from shouting at them to close the door.

"I heard she was real, real upset when he broke up with her, you know?" Speaker One said. Was she the one holding the door open?

"Yeah, but June musta known Hank would never marry her. Hank was *not* the marrying kind. But he'd been mooning ovah Nelle for years. The whole town knew it."

Wait. What? I leaned forward, straining to hear their conversation.

"Jenna May, will you close the door if you're going to be *using names*?"

Thank you!

"Don't go flying off the handle, Lora Lee. You don't have to shout."

Lora Lee was Speaker One, then. Jenna May was the violator of Restroom Door Etiquette.

With their identities determined, my thoughts turned to my next move. My current position was awkward for sleuthing, but if I made my presence known, they'd stop talking.

A friend's life could be at stake, Marvey.

Awkward it was, then. Ladies, please continue.

"The *Crier* reported the deaths were murder." Jenna May was speaking. She lowered her voice before continuing. "Do you think June could've killed 'em?"

"June?" Lora Lee's laugh sounded genuine. "I've known June Bishop for years. She doesn't have a mean bone in her body. She probably apologizes every time she clips a rose." She laughed again as though enjoying her own joke.

I was pleased by their unwitting confirmation that the librarian team and I were right not to put June on the suspect list.

"I don't know." Jenna May's response came slowly. I wished they'd speed things up. My legs were starting to cramp. "Love makes some people act like they ain't got the good sense God gave a rock."

Lora Lee laughed again. "In that case, my money's on Reba MacRaney. That woman came unhinged during the mayoral race last year. Bless her heart."

"Hmm... And didn't he break up with Philomena right before he started datin' June?"

Lora Lee corrected her. "No, it was Philomena, Reba, and *then* June." They crossed the white tile flooring, then opened the door. "And remember, no names. We don't want to be caught gossiping *at a wake.*"

Silence. I exhaled in relief as I hurried to rejoin Jo and Spence. I needed to get their reaction to what I'd just heard. Putting the information I'd gathered from Eudella Figg Bidwell together with the impressions I'd overheard from Lora Lee and Jenna May, perhaps jealousy was the motive for Hank's and Nelle's murders. The killer could have been one of Hank's alleged many scorned former girlfriends. These homicides might not be connected to Spence at all. Maybe there was an innocent explanation for his name appearing on the list.

At least that's what I wanted to believe.

"So you think Nelle and Hank were murdered by a jilted girlfriend?" Jo's seat belt prevented her from leaning too far forward on the backseat of Spence's black SUV.

"Based on what I'd been able to find out." I sat sideways on the passenger seat so I could split my attention between Spence and Jo. The smell of frankincense had followed us from the funeral home. It had probably hitched a ride on our clothing. "Hank was a ladies' man. And it may not have been Philomena, Reba, or June. It could've been someone who wanted his attention. What did you two learn?"

Jo threw up her hands. "The same thing you did. Everyone believed Hank was a wonderful person with a weakness for the ladies."

"I heard the same." Spence's attention was glued to the nearly nonexistent traffic traversing Peach Blossom Boulevard. "From his students, players, colleagues, neighbors."

I frowned. "His aunt was the only family member I met at his wake."

Spence glanced my way before returning his attention to the traffic. A trace of a smile hovered around his lips and gleamed in his eyes. "Hank was an only child. His parents were much older when he surprised them."

"I know Hank was a genuinely nice person." Jo shrugged. "But even if he wasn't, would you expect someone to bring up his faults at his wake?"

Good point.

The evening was growing late, dragging shadows across the broad asphalt road and wide red brick sidewalks. A few couples meandered along the boulevard as though walking off their dinner.

Bulbs in the tall brass antique street lamps glowed gold in the textured glass panes. It added to the charm of the town's main business area. A slight breeze ruffled the leaves of the majestic old sugar maple trees that stood along the sidewalk. It was the kind of evening in which you could feel the universe breathing. The world slowed, giving you time to reflect on family, friends, neighbors, and murder.

"I really want the motive for Hank's and Nelle's homicides to be unrequited love—"

"So do I." Jo interrupted me.

"Me too." Spence again gave me a quick sideways glance before shifting his eyes back to the road.

"But what about the other names on that list?" I clenched my hands together on my lap and shifted to face forward. "I won't feel safe until we know why your name was included."

"But, Marvey, what if it *isn't* a hit list, and you're looking for threats where none exist?" Jo's quiet question broke the brief silence.

"Until we have a definitive answer, I can't stop asking questions." It wasn't easy being the lone voice of dissension, but I had to follow my conscience. How would

I feel if I disregarded the little voice in the back of my mind and something—heaven forbid—happened?

CHAPTER 12

A LOOK OF RESIGNATION CROSSED JED'S face when I entered the sheriff's office late Friday morning. But even though that was far from welcoming, the scents of Anna May's peach cobbler and fresh coffee sent a different message. I fought the urge to pour myself a cup.

Was my coffee habit getting out of control? I made a mental note to address that once I was assured of Spence's safety.

"Ms. Marvey, it's nice to see you this morning." Errol's enthusiastic greeting more than made up for Jed's sour expression. "Hey, thanks again for recommending that Western series to me. I sure am enjoying it."

I beamed at him. "I'm glad."

His words brightened my day more than chocolate, and that was saying something. Viv and I had been certain the Western historical crime fiction series would appeal to the earnest law enforcement officer. I'd have to share this latest triumph with her when I returned to the library.

Jed grunted, standing slowly to address me. "What brings you in, Ms. Marvey?"

"Are there any updates on the investigation?" I looked from Errol to Jed and back.

Jed wiped his upper lip. "Now, Ms. Marvey, the public can read any information we can share about the investigation in the paper. Until then, your stopping by—especially unannounced—is just impeding our investigation."

I looked at Jed's and Errol's desks. Neither officer appeared to have been steeped in the case. In fact, all the work stations in the sheriff's office looked fresh and clean, as though they'd been unpacked from boxes that recently arrived from a European furniture store.

"Deputy Whatley, I've expressed to you why I'm so concerned about this case." I folded my hands in front of my hips and held on to my patience. "A dear friend and prominent member of this community could be in danger."

He glowered. "And you're basing your hypothetical on a scrap of paper with a couple of names on it. We're investigating two homicides, ma'am. Not some fantasy game."

"Those victims were my friends, Deputy. Their names are on that scrap of paper, too." I was proud of my calm, steady delivery. On the inside, I was shaking with impatience. Like Spence and Jo—and apparently Jed—I wanted to believe that list was unimportant. But until I knew its purpose, I couldn't take the risk of burying my head in the sand. "Did you find any prints on the letter?"

"Yes, ma'am." Errol spoke before Jed could blast me again. "We've excluded your fingerprints, but we couldn't identify the other sets. They're not in our database."

Multiple sets of unidentified prints; that was less than helpful. "Did you learn anything useful at the wake?"

Errol gave me a look of empathy, as though he could feel my worry. "No, ma'am. I'm afraid not."

"Errol!" Jed snapped.

"C'mon, JW." Errol spread his arms. "I'm not goin' to give away anything that's goin' to jeopardize our investigation. But if you had a friend in danger, wouldn't you want the investigating officers to give you *something*, good, bad, or otherwise?"

"Thank you, Deputy Cole." My grateful smile felt weak. Most of my energy and all of my strength was invested in challenging his partner.

Errol inclined his head. "Don't mention it, ma'am. I've got friends, too."

Maybe that was the difference between him and Jed. I gave the older officer a quick look before returning to Errol. "I wish I could find something to prove the list has nothing to do with these homi—"

"Deputy Whatley!"

I turned at Brittany's shout. The owner of Coastal Cycles bike shop marched down the aisle toward us. Her steps were jerky with temper. Every line of her body in the lightweight peach track suit was tense with anger.

"Morning, Ms. Brittany." Jed's tone was cautious. "What's on your mind, ma'am?"

Brittany stopped an arm's length from us and drew what I thought was supposed to be a calming breath. I don't think it worked. "Deputy Whatley." It seemed a struggle for her to moderate her tone after her initial outburst. She nodded toward Errol. "Deputy Cole. Marvey?" She gave me a curious look.

"It's good to see you again, Brittany." I searched her face for some clue to the reason of her upset. "What's wrong?"

She faced Jed. Her expression was a mask of determination. "Someone broke into my store last night. I don't know how they got in. The door was still locked when I opened up this morning."

Errol reached for his notepad. A rare scowl creased his youthful features. "Did they take anything, ma'am?"

Brittany shook her head, calmer now that she had the attention of someone in authority. "No. I searched my entire shop. Nothing seems to have been taken. Nothing was disturbed. But I feel as though I've been violated."

Jed shook his head. "Excuse me, ma'am, but what makes you think someone broke into your shop if the doors were locked and nothing was stolen?"

Her cheeks were flushed an angry red. "Because they left this on my checkout counter." She shoved her arm forward. A blue pennant with the gray logo of the Mother Mathilda Taylor Beasley High School was clenched in her fist. "It wasn't there when I locked up last night. They left it behind like they were marking their territory in my store."

I nodded toward the item. "That logo's different from the one on the stationery Hank used for the Class of 2006's gift."

Brittany shook the pennant. Her dark brown eyes sparked with temper. "This is the old logo. They stopped using it a few years after I graduated."

The silent exchange between Jed and Errol spoke volumes.

"What is it?" I prompted them. "Why is this significant?"

Errol lifted his gaze from the pennant. His reluctance to answer was palpable.

It was Jed who finally responded. His tone was somber. "We found a pennant like that one with Hank's body and another with Nelle's."

It was like someone had dumped ice water over me. The blood had drained from Brittany's face. The pennant fell from her fist as though her hand had gone numb.

She took a step back. "What're you saying? Is this some kind of threat? Is someone telling me I'm supposed to be the next one to...die?"

Errol guided her to his chair. Jed spun on his heels in a movement so abrupt it startled me. He crossed the room, moving more quickly than I'd ever seen him move. He filled two paper cups from the water bottle beside the coffee station. Long strides carried him back to us.

He pressed one of the cups into Brittany's shaking hands and helped guide it to her mouth. "Slowly now."

Brittany was the third name on the four-name list. Spence's name was the last. I collapsed onto the chair beside me. It was Jed's. My head swam. My thoughts scattered. Blood pounded in my ears. I forced myself to keep breathing.

Think! Think! How can I keep him safe?

We had to find this killer.

Errol looked at me. "Ms. Marvey, looks like you were right about that list."

"That list!" A hint of hysteria strained Brittany's

voice. She turned a faint shade of green. Was she going to be sick? "That's it. I want round-the-clock protection."

My thoughts snapped back together. If they gave Brittany protection, I wanted Spence to have it too.

Jed crossed his arms. "Ms. Brittany, you know we don't have that kind of budget." He held out a hand when she started to protest. "But what I will promise you is increased patrols at your home and store, so whoever may be trying to hurt you will know we're keeping an eye on you." He glanced at me. "We'd better do the same for Mr. Spence."

I breathed a sigh of relief. "Thank you, Deputy Whately."

Brittany settled back against the chair. Jed's words seemed to have calmed her. "All right."

Errol stepped back to lean against his desk. "We'll also make sure all the deputies know you've received this threat. Everyone will be watching out for you and Mr. Spence. We promise."

"Thank you." Brittany and I spoke at the same time.

I caught her eyes. They were still wide and scared. "Do you have any idea why this pennant is significant?"

"No." Brittany seemed to be trying to focus. "It's old. No one even uses it anymore. The only reason it was significant to me is that I knew it didn't belong there."

I sighed. "You said your store was still locked when you arrived. Do you have an alarm system?"

She shook her head. "But believe me, I'll be getting one."

I did believe her. She was still shaking. "Who else has a key to your store?"

"Ms. Marvey." Jed's voice was sharp. "Would you mind very much, ma'am, if I conducted the interview?"

I gestured toward Brittany. "Not at all, Deputy What-ley. I apologize."

He leaned back against his desk. "Ms. Brittany, who else has a key to your store?"

She flexed her shoulder blades as though trying to ease her tension. "The only other person with a key is my assistant manager. He swears he didn't return to the store last night and he's never seen this pennant before. He's not from Peach Coast." She turned to me. Her voice was muted. "I guess you were right. You did find a serial killer's hit list. I'm sorry I didn't believe you when you came to my store."

Jed glowered at me. "You kept a copy of the list, then went to show it to Ms. Brittany—"

I opened my mouth to explain, but Brittany spoke before me.

"And I'm glad she did." She straightened on her chair to confront Jed. "Why didn't you?"

I arched an eyebrow at Jed, waiting for his response.

He stammered, searching for a defense. "Because this is a sensitive matter in an active case."

"And I'm involved in that case." Brittany pressed a finger into her chest.

Jed went silent. Perhaps he'd realized no matter what he said, the fact remained a third target from the list had been confirmed. We could no longer deny there was a serial killer in Peach Coast. And they weren't done yet.

"Have you found a pennant?" I strode into Spence's office and right up to his desk. It had been a quick, albeit tense, drive from the sheriff's office to the newspaper. I'd driven into work since I'd wanted to go into the sheriff's office on my break. My nerves would've benefited from a long walk, though.

Spence's brow furrowed with concern. He stood and circled his large dark wood desk. "Marvey, what's wrong?"

My fingers dug into the hard muscles of his upper arm. I forced myself to speak slowly. "Spence. Have you found a pennant? A Mother Mathilda Taylor Beasley High School pennant with the old logo, circa 2006?"

"No, I haven't." He guided me to one of the visitor's chairs in front of his desk before stepping away to close his office door. When he returned, he settled onto the chair beside me and took my hands. "Do you need help finding it? Where last did you see it?"

"What?" I was horrified until I remembered he had no idea what I'd just learned. I took a steadying breath and explained what had happened to Brittany. I described the exchange we'd had at the sheriff's office. As I spoke, Spence's expression transition from bewilderment, to surprise, and finally concern.

"Brittany's all right?" His hands tightened on mine.

"She's badly shaken, of course. But physically, she's all right. She seemed reassured that the deputies will be watching over her."

He stood to pace. "This doesn't make any sense. Why would anyone want to hurt Brittany?"

I popped out of my seat, aggravated that he still wouldn't acknowledge the danger he was in. "Why would anyone want to hurt *you*?"

"Or Hank or Nelle?" He looked over his shoulder toward me. "What are we supposed to have done? And to whom?"

"We have to figure this out, Spence. This isn't a drill. It's the real thing."

He settled his hands on his lean hips. "I'll assign a reporter to write an update on the investigation."

I gaped at his back. "Seriously? Spence, I need you to focus right now. This isn't a *scoop*. A serial killer is planning to *kill* you."

He turned to me. "Marvey, I'm focused. I promise. Running this update will let the killer know we're on to them."

"And they'll be more careful." I clenched my hands at my sides. "But if we keep this quiet, they might become overconfident and make a mistake that'll lead to their arrest."

Spence crossed his arms over his white shirt. "What am I supposed to do in the meantime? Look over my shoulder until this person's caught?"

"Yes! And the deputies are going to schedule additional patrols at your home and the paper." I stepped closer to him. "I can see how this would be frustrating. You're not the type to run and hide, but I need you to be aware of your surroundings so that you can stay safe. I will lose my mind if anything happens to you."

Spence hesitated. My heart punched my chest at the look in his eyes. "Marvey—" A knock on his door interrupted him. He sighed. "Come in."

Jed and Errol walked in. They didn't seem surprised to see me. I tried to return Errol's smile of pleasure.

Jed gestured toward me with his notepad. "I suppose Ms. Marvey filled you in on the goings-on?"

Spence shoved his hands into the front pockets of

his black pants. "We've been discussing it, but I'm afraid I don't have any ideas that could help the investigation."

"Perhaps if a professional asked you some questions, it might spark something." Jed opened his notepad to a blank page.

I caught Spence's gaze and rolled my eyes. I saw the twinkle in his eyes before he looked away.

"Please have a seat, deputies." He gestured to the three of us to join him at the mid-sized conference table in his office.

What followed were fourteen of the most frustrating minutes of my life.

Had he received any threats?

No.

Did he have any enemies?

None that he knew of.

Has he had any arguments with anyone?

Not heated arguments.

Frustrated, I interrupted. "Spence isn't the only name on that list. These questions aren't going to help us find the connection between Spence, Hank, Nelle, and Brittany."

Jed reared back against his chair and angled a wide-eyed look at me. "Well, what would you have us ask, Ms. Marvella, since you seem to think you're the professional?"

I clenched my teeth. I couldn't allow Jed's fragile feelings to hamper the investigation. "Three of the four people on the list received a pennant. Two of them are now dead."

Errol frowned, shaking his head. "Why's the pennant important?"

I met his eyes. "That's what we need to find out."

CHAPTER 13

"GOOD MORNING, SPENCE. DID YOU sleep well?" I infused as much Southern charm as I could manage via cell phone while sitting at my dining room table early the next morning.

"Good morning, Marvey. Indeed I did. How 'bout you?" Spence sounded like he'd been up for hours. Apparently, I needn't have waited as long as I had before calling him.

I smiled in response to the humor lacing his words. I'd half expected him to ask after the welfare of my mama. That seemed to be a top priority question, at least here in Peach Coast. "Yes, I did. Thanks for asking."

"Of course." The pinging of metal tapping against porcelain sounded in the background. Like me, Spence must have been making his morning coffee. "As delighted as I am to hear your voice this morning, we just spoke last night."

"I know."

"Are you going to make a habit of this?" He chuckled. That was a good sign. It meant he wasn't irritated. And he had a nice laugh.

"A habit of what?"

"Calling to wish me good night every night and good morning every morning. Not that I'm complaining. In fact, I could get used to it."

Was he flirting with me? Whatever he was doing was making me tongue tied. A first.

I cleared my throat. "Yes, actually, I am. I thought that, if you aren't able to have round-the-clock protection—"

"Marvey—"

"And I do understand the Camden County Sheriff's Office doesn't have those kinds of resources—"

"Marvey—"

"Then the least I could do as your friend is check in periodically. Say two or three times a day."

"That's a lot."

"That way, I could know as soon as possible if the unthinkable happens."

"Marvey?"

"Yes, Spence?"

"Please don't do that."

"With respect, Spence, I think it's necessary." A change of subject was in order. "Are you attending the library's Big Book Swap today?"

"That depends." His tone was dry. "Are you going to have me under surveillance?"

The thought had crossed my mind that it would be a lot easier to ensure his safety if he spent at least some time at the library. "I'll tell you what. I'll keep it to a visual surveillance. I won't actually handcuff you to me."

"I'll hold you to that." He laughed again. He really did have a great laugh.

I struggled against my fear for his safety. If anything happened to him, I would be devastated. I had to stop this serial killer before tragedy struck again.

But how?

"Your usual, Marvey?" Anna May's comfortable welcome greeted me early Saturday morning.

"Yes, please, Anna May. And a slice of your delicious peach cobbler to go." The tempting aromas of sweet pastries, warm breads, and strong coffee embraced me as I crossed to the front of the café. Along the way, I exchanged greetings with several familiar, friendly faces.

Most of the regulars expressed excitement for the library's first-ever book swap. Several of them weren't ready to part with their own books but were willing to spend a few dollars for gently used ones. With luck, a robust turnout for this event would convince the library's board of directors to support the swap as an annual activity. It also would benefit Lonnie's pet shop. Success was just around the corner. I could feel it. My blood pumped with exhilaration. I might not even need my usual small doctored café mocha.

Ha! Who was I kidding?

After exchanging pleasantries with Anna May, Dabney and Etta, I paid for my order and turned to leave. That's when I noticed Trudie Trueman. She was sitting alone at a corner table for four near the front of the cafe. A white porcelain coffee mug was inches from her right hand. Dressed in a faded red V-neck T-shirt, she glared at a thin black notebook laying open on the table in front of her. Puddles of papers and manila folders surrounded her. It seemed like she'd been sitting there, swimming in aggravation for hours. Frustration rolled off her like waves. If anyone needed a hug, it was her. Besides, I wanted to check out Jo's potential rival for Nolan's affection.

"Excuse me, Ms. Trueman. I'm Marvella Harris, the library's director of community outreach."

Startled, she looked up. Confusion receded from her striking dark brown eyes and was replaced by recognition. Her frown melted into a warm smile. "I know who you are. Please call me Trudie. I enjoyed the kickoff."

"I'm glad." My heart warmed. "I'm sorry I didn't introduce myself that night."

"There were a lot of people at the event." She pulled her paperwork closer to clear a spot at her table. "Will you join me?"

I settled onto the seat across from her. "I didn't mean to interrupt. You look very busy."

She sent me a wry look. "You probably heard I inherited my family's construction company."

"Yes. My condolences on your father's passing."

"I appreciate that. I miss him and my mother very much. Before his death, I didn't have any involvement in the business. I worked in administration for a health care provider." She scrutinized the rivers of papers and folders. "I'm beginning to regret that. There's a lot to learn."

I grimaced, looking at the paperwork strewn across the table. "Do you have any siblings or other family members who could help you?"

"Nope. It's just me, although Nolan's been wonderful, explaining the accounting system and reviewing the ledgers with me." She laid her palms flat on the piles of folders. "I spend every Saturday at this table. Somehow it doesn't feel like working when I'm surrounded by such wonderful smells."

"I understand." Laughing, I rose to leave. "I've taken enough of your time. Good luck. I hope you're able to keep the company going for your family."

"Thank you. I intend to." She inclined her head. "I'll probably see you later at the swap. My parents were both voracious readers, but some of their books have too many memories. I'd like to donate them to your fundraiser."

My heart ached for her. Losing both of your parents and not having any family left to share their memories with must have been so painful. "We appreciate your support. I look forward to seeing you then."

At the condiments counter, I stopped to grab a few extra napkins—then froze. Delores Polly had walked through the door. This would be the perfect opportunity to pull her aside and question her about the threatening emails she'd sent to Spence, Nelle, and Hank after her godson had been denied the Town College Scholarship last month.

But Delores as a serial killer? She was an organist at my church.

Don't let personal feelings get in the way of an objective homicide investigation.

Reminding myself that Southerners preferred to ease into a conversation, I crossed to her. "Good morning, Delores. Have you been well?"

Her gray eyes were wide behind large glasses that masked half of her small face. "Good morning, Marvey. I've been fine. And how are you?"

With my hand on her shoulder, I drew her away from the door to a quieter corner of the cafe. "Well, since you've asked, these latest murders in Peach Coast have made me uneasy."

"Really?" Delores tilted her head and frowned at me. She'd styled her dark brown hair in a simple bun at the nape of her neck. "Being from New York, I'd think you'd be used to murders."

Why did people in Peach Coast think there were dead bodies every day on every street corner in every borough of New York?

"Actually, before moving to Peach Coast, I'd never seen a homicide victim."

"Is that right?" Her eyes grew even wider with amazement. "Well, I for one am glad you were able to help the deputies uncover the truth about Fiona Lyle-Hayes's murder."

I considered the petite woman. She'd dressed in a modest gray dress with cap sleeves and a mid-calf hem. "Delores, do you have any thoughts on who might have wanted to kill Coach Figg or Nelle Kenton?"

Her thin brown eyebrows knitted. "Well, no. Why would I?"

"Hank, Nelle, and Spence Holt were judges for the Town College Scholarship."

"That's right." Her voice slowed and her expression grew wary as though she was trying to determine where this conversation was going.

I hoped my next words wouldn't turn the organist against me. Again. "Is it true you were upset your godson wasn't awarded a scholarship?"

She pressed her palm to the neckline of her dress. Her voice was a harsh whisper. "Are you accusing me of killing them and plotting to kill Spence Holt because of that silly competition?"

"You didn't think it was silly when your godson lost. It's a full, four-year scholarship. In response, you sent the judges a long, angry email, threatening to make them feel the pain of losing something important to them."

Her pale cheeks bloomed like a Campari tomato. Grabbing my arm, she pulled me out of the café and didn't stop until we were in its parking lot. Her lips trembled as she glared at me in silence for several seconds. "Where did you hear about that? From Spence Holt?"

Taking a page from my favorite journalist, I refused to reveal my source. "Delores, I'm sorry. This is hard for me. I like you a lot, despite our bumpy start when you tried to stop my investigation into Fiona Lyle-Hayes's murder."

"*Like* me?" Breathing heavily, she crossed her arms over her thin chest and raised her pointed chin. "You New Yorkers are a strange bunch. How can you *like* me when you think I'm capable of killing people?"

"If I didn't like you, I'd be having this conversation with the deputies instead of asking you to help me understand why I shouldn't be suspicious of you."

Slowly, her postured relaxed. The flush faded from her cheeks. "You know, if I was the killer—which I'm *not*—this would be the second time you're putting yourself in harm's way for a friend."

I gave the small woman a suspicious look. "I suppose you're right."

"That shows how much you value your friends."

"I do value them, very much. I can't sit on the sidelines, doing nothing when they could be in danger."

"They're very lucky to have your friendship." She relaxed her arms. "And I'm not offended. Well, not much. In fact, there's something I should've gotten off of my chest a long time ago. Yes, I was angry. Very angry. My godson's a good boy. I love him like he's my own son. I was disappointed that he wasn't awarded any of those scholarships. There were *five* of them!"

"But sending that email wasn't the best decision you could've made."

"It was a *terrible* decision." Her hand wringing caused her gray purse to slip from her right shoulder. "I've regretted it ever since. Truth be told, the judges were right. It took me a couple of weeks to admit what I should've known at the time." She sighed and adjusted her purse. "My godson hadn't earned a scholarship. His grades have always needed work, and I practically wrote that entire essay for him."

"Delores! That's cheating. He was supposed to write it by himself."

"I know." She wrung her hands again, faster this time. "I must have been out of my mind. I never really wished any harm to come to Coach Figg, and if anything ever happened to Spence Holt I'd just lose my mind."

That would make two of us. "Delores, I want to believe you didn't have anything to do with these murders, but I keep going back to the email you sent. It's really mean."

"I know. I was wrong. The Good Book says you're supposed to treat others the way you want to be treated. I shouldn't have done what I did." Her gray eyes swam with regret.

Delores couldn't be our serial killer. I wasn't basing this on her being a church organist or looking as though she couldn't hurt anyone. It was alleged motivation. Granted, her email had been mean and unhinged, but she hadn't threatened Hank's, Nelle's, or Spence's lives. She'd planned to damage their reputations. And what about Brittany? If Delores's motivation was the committee's rejection of her godson, the bicycle shop owner hadn't had anything to do with that.

I removed her from our main suspect list, but we still had an unresolved issue. "It's too late to make amends with Hank and Nelle, but it's not too late to speak with Spence."

Delores nodded, her eyes downcast. "It's past time I made things right with him. Even after I sent that disgraceful email, he's been all that's cordial and gracious toward me. And I've gone out of my way to be kind toward him and his mama. But you're right. I need to ask for his forgiveness."

I reached out to squeeze Delores's shoulder. "I know where you can find him this afternoon. Why don't you stop by the library?"

CHAPTER 14

"THIS IS THE BEST TURNOUT we've *ever* had for our pet adoption." Lonnie's pale round face was suffused with joy. He'd all but skipped to my station in the Peach Coast Library's parking lot late Saturday morning.

Since the library was closed on the weekends this summer, we were hosting the book swap—as well as the pet adoption—in the parking lot. Large, colorful signs bracketed by orange cones directed guests to the neighboring municipal parking lot to give the dual events plenty of room. The strategy also protected our furry friends in case any broke free of their fenced areas.

"I'm so glad this has worked out." I surveyed the area.

It was hot—mid-June in Georgia. What else would it be? But a soft breeze floated across the crowded lot, nudging aside fluffy white clouds and dancing with sugar maple and sweetgum trees. Their vibrant green leaves shimmied and wiggled against the jewel-blue sky. The air smelled like summer, swollen with the scents of rich soil, healthy grass, and the abundance of flora from the library's landscaping.

The lot was crowded with guests from toddlers to seniors. Solo visitors in search of their next novel adventure, couples sharing their love of reading and each other, and parents passing on their literary interests to their children. Guests with books to swap had stopped to play with and pet the animals. Adoptive pet parents lingered among the gently used books. The smiles, laughter, and animated conversations—of both the two-legged and four-legged attendees—made me forget the stress and anxiety of planning the event. And how hot and sticky I felt.

Lonnie looked around with a dazed expression. "I can't thank you enough for suggesting we combine our efforts to get me out of a bind. I'm beginning to think the mix-up at the community center was a blessing in disguise. Perhaps we should consider making this joint event an annual thing."

"Corrinne had mentioned that also." My attention drifted over Lonnie's shoulder where I could see her approaching us.

She, Viv, Floyd, Adrian, and I were wearing powder blue Peach Coast Library Big Book Swap T-shirts. I smiled at the memory of Floyd's horror when we suggested peach or pink T-shirts. Powder blue was the closest he'd get to a compromise. There was a holdout in every group.

Corrinne stopped beside Lonnie. What was it about her that turned a simple discounted T-shirt into haute couture?

"Marvey's right. I love the idea." Corrinne swept out an arm, encompassing the people and pets playing on the other side of the books. "Your adoption day adds a lot of good energy and interaction to the event."

Lonnie tripped over his tongue as he attempted a reply. "Well. Then. That's great. Yes. Thank you."

Corrinne gave the pet shop owner her Serene Highness smile. "Let's get together next week to talk about what we need to do to build on our success while the events are still fresh in our minds."

"Well. Then. Yes." Lonnie shuffled his feet. "Thanks, Corrinne. We'll talk later."

I watched Lonnie scurry back to the safety of his volunteers and pets. His brief encounter with Corrinne seemed to have rattled him.

A female voice interrupted my musings. "Half the town must be here."

I turned to find Jo, Nolan, and Spence. "Not half. Closer to a fifth. Thank you for coming." I included Spence and Nolan with my smile. "I'm so glad you made it."

I gave Spence a quick once over, looking for signs of tension, stress, bruising, and/or impending illness. He seemed fine.

Nolan tore his attention from Jo. "It was Jo's idea we check out the swap. I have to admit, I was surprised she'd suggest it. Y'all are selling books for a dollar and less. That seems like competition for her bookstore."

Jo and I exchanged an indulgent look. Not everyone understood the synergy between libraries and bookstores. In Nolan's defense, his protective instincts toward Jo might be distorting his perceptions, whether either of them was ready to admit to those feelings or not.

"Our event actually helps Jo's store." I gestured

toward the crowd. "When people find a book here they like, they'll go to To Be Read to find more books by that author or more stories in that genre."

Jo rested her hand on Nolan's forearm. "My sales have increased since Marvey's been promoting the library and reading. Remember?"

"Excuse me." Trudie joined our group, wheeling a small handcart behind her. "Hi, Nolan, everyone." Her bright smile dimmed as her eyes dropped to Jo's hand on Nolan's arm. She cleared her throat. "Marvey, where should I take these books?"

Her handcart balanced a large brown cardboard box that must contain close to fifty books.

"That's quite a haul you've brought us." It was a struggle to keep from diving into the container and scoping out the titles. "You can swap for an equal number of books, if you'd like."

"I'd better not tempt myself." Trudie's eyes lingered on Nolan. "I already have so much reading to do to learn about my family's business. Nolan understands what I mean."

Based on the lingering looks and flirtatious smiles Trudie directed toward Nolan, Lisa May was correct in her assertion that she was interested in him. The question was, did Nolan know? And what effect, if any, would her infatuation have on his budding relationship with Jo?

Time for an intervention. "Let me help you take this box over to the swap area. Why don't you three look over the books and play with the pets? Enjoy yourselves."

Trudie's lips parted. Her eyes widened with panic. "Um, Marvey, perhaps if you could point me in the right direction, Nolan can help me. That way he and I can review some questions I have about the company accounts."

"This is a library event." With my hand on the small of Trudie's back, I escorted her to the book area. "It's my responsibility to assist you, not Nolan's. And I take my responsibilities very seriously."

I nudged Trudie along, maneuvering the obstacle course of racing children and meandering parents, many of whom were guiding their pets around the displays.

"My family's construction company did the library's renovations." There was pride in Trudie's voice as her eyes lovingly examined the library's facade.

"Your company did a wonderful job." Those simple words couldn't convey the true depths of my admiration. The Peach Coast Library was a magical place. "I love that they kept the original woodworking. I can feel the history."

"Thank you. My parents didn't think of their work as just building things. They were leaving a legacy." She dragged her attention from the building. "The town's changed a lot since I left. It used to be a lot safer. Now we've had three murders in less than two months. And I heard a tourist was murdered two years ago. It's crazy. What's happening?"

"I think everyone's asking that question." I brought us to a stop beside the sorting table. "Did you know Hank or Nelle?"

"We went to high school together." She shrugged as she opened the box. "We were in different graduating classes, though, so I didn't know them well."

She scanned the parking lot. Was she looking for Nolan? Following her gaze, I found my friends. Delores was speaking with Spence. Was she apologizing for her flaming email? I hoped so.

"Excuse me."

I turned toward the male voice and found Lucas. He wore baggy running shorts and a blue short-sleeved pullover with the high school logo on his left upper chest. "Coach Daniels, thank you for coming."

"Where do I pay for this?" His head swiveled as he looked around the parking lot. He was holding a heavy hardcover volume on clay sculpting. There was a story there.

"I can help you. That'll be one dollar. Would you like a receipt?"

He gave me a dubious look. "No, thanks."

I accepted his cash. "Thank you again for coming. I hope to see you at the library."

He nodded, glanced at Trudie, then strode away.

"He's new to Peach Coast too." Trudie watched him disappear into the crowd. "It must be so unsettling to move to a new town, start a new job, and then a month later, your boss is murdered. People are scared. I hope the deputies find the killer soon."

"So do I." Then I could be assured of Spence's safety and start to put this nightmare behind me.

Trudie lowered her voice. "In high school, Hank had a reputation of dating multiple women at the same time. I wouldn't be surprised if Hank and Nelle were killed by a jealous woman—or two jealous women working together."

Working together.

Maybe we didn't have to find *one* suspect with a grudge against the four people on the list. Maybe we needed two who'd be willing to collaborate.

"June, the floral arrangements in your windows are gorgeous." I stopped in front of Petals Palooza Florist Shop early Monday morning. The dramatic colors of the dahlias, roses, daffodils, and elephant ears displayed in the storefront windows mesmerized and cheered me.

"Thank you, Marvey." June added another bouquet of roses to the display in front of her store before turning to me. Her floral dress billowed around her slender frame every time she moved. "You're always so complimentary of my work. Other people don't even comment on the window displays. I think of you each time I work on it."

I beamed. "Really?" Turning back to the window, I studied the display with a fresh perspective. "Then you absolutely know what appeals to me. This display is breathtaking."

June laughed. She crossed to adjust a nearby bouquet. "You have great taste."

"Thank you." Her comment was such an honor. It also left knots in my stomach because of what I was about to ask her. "June, you'd mentioned you and Hank ended your relationship because you'd suspected he'd fallen in love with someone else. Was that other person Nelle?"

June froze. Her hands fluttered among the pink and white dahlias. "How did you know that?"

"I overheard a couple of women at Hank's wake, talking about the coach's dating history. They said he'd recently asked Nelle to dinner."

June rolled her tawny brown eyes. "I can just imagine what else they were saying about me." She forced a laugh, but I heard the hurt in her voice.

I pressed a hand against my stomach to ease the knots building there. *Focus on Spence and keeping him safe.* "If one of the women from the wake brought her suspicions to you directly, how would you respond?"

June arched a thin honey-blond eyebrow. "Like if that person was *you*, for example?"

"I don't think you're a killer, June, but two people already have been murdered and there could be others." I know there are. "I want to help stop this before someone else is hurt or worse. Whatever you tell me could help me figure this out."

June sighed, shoving her hands on her waist. "Why can't you let the deputies figure it out? That's their job."

"I have my reasons. Please, June."

She considered me closely before finally answering my question. "Yes, you're right and so are the women from the wake. Hank was in love with Nelle. I don't think he got over her from high school. Figuring that out was like a scene from some romance novel."

"I'm sorry, June. That must have hurt."

"Yeah, well, it didn't feel good." She shrugged a shoulder, but I saw the shadows in her eyes before she lowered them. "I mean, you've seen her. Never a hair out of place. Makeup always perfect. And her clothes. I knew I couldn't compete with Nelle. God rest her soul. So I told him we were through."

Or had he broken up with her? It made more sense the rumor mill was wrong and June had called things off. In any event, I couldn't see Hank asking Nelle out while he was still dating June. Peach Coast was a very small town. Besides, everyone said Hank was nice and a nice person wouldn't do something like that.

Then why would Trudie claim Hank had dated multiple women at the same time? Curious.

"How did Hank take your ending things with him?"

June returned to her vase of dahlias. "He acted like he didn't know what I was talking about, like he wasn't interested in Nelle. He wasn't interested in anyone but me." She rolled her eyes. "I may've been born at night, but it wasn't that night. I told him he was free to lie to himself but he wasn't gonna lie to me. I'd seen the way he looked at her. And she was looking back."

"I'm sorry, June." I felt like a broken record, repeating the same three words.

She raised her hand as though dashing away tears. "It hurt. For a while. A good, long while." Her laugh wobbled in the middle. "But it was the right thing to do. You know, when you care about someone, you just want them to be happy. If not with you, then with someone they truly love. And Hank had loved Nelle since high school."

And now they were both dead. It was one of the saddest stories I'd ever heard. High school sweethearts kept apart, then murdered before their happily-ever-after.

But what did Hank and Nelle's tragic love affair have to do with Spence and Brittany?

CHAPTER 15

T O BE READ WAS CROWDED during Monday's lunch hour. There wasn't an empty aisle in sight, and the little café area was standing room only. Foot traffic in the independent bookstore was even better than before Fiona Lyle-Hayes's murder. Some of her staff had worried customers would avoid the store for fear it would be haunted. A haunted bookstore. Let's hope not.

The soft, powdery scent of air fresheners mingled with the subtle, sweet fragrance from the bouquets of flowers strategically set around the store. Over it all were the enticing scents of savory soups and freshly baked breads from the café counter.

Natural sunlight flooded the store, casting a warm glow over the blond wood bookshelves and fluffy, colorful armchairs nearby. Ignoring their silent beckoning, I turned toward the customer counter in search of Jo and Spence. We'd planned to order lunch from the bookstore café's soup and sandwich menu before retreating to Jo's office.

I found Jo helping one of her young employees. "Are we waiting for Spence?"

I glanced around in case Spence had followed the call of literature deeper into the aisles. I'd lost myself among those shelves a time or eleven.

"Yes, but you're early. He'll be here." Jo stepped from behind the counter.

My attention shifted to the employee, a slender young woman with a mass of reddish-gold curls and big brown eyes. I had a good feeling for Blanche's future. Not only was she learning critical job skills and responsibility at Jo's store, but she also had a library card that she used often. She was especially fond of self-help books.

"Hello, Jo. Marvey. Jo, may I speak with you?"

I turned and was surprised to find Trudie at To Be Read. I thought she was too busy at the moment to read.

"Sure, Trudie." Jo gave her a polite smile. "How can I help you?"

Trudie gave me a hesitant look before addressing Jo. "What's going on between you and Nolan?"

Whoa! I hadn't seen that coming.

I faced Jo, interested in her response.

Her smile faded to be replaced by confusion. "Me and Nolan? I don't know what you mean."

Give me a break. I sensed Trudie's discomfort and reluctance. It must have taken a lot of courage for her to broach this subject with Jo. "Why do you ask?"

Trudie gave me an uncertain look. "I was just wondering." Her cheeks filled with faint pink and she shuffled her feet again before returning her attention to Jo. "The two of you seem to spend a lot of time together.

And he mentions you. Often. Is your relationship with him platonic or is it...more than that?"

Jo spread her hands. "Nolan and I are just friends. That's all."

"Are you sure?" Trudie didn't seem to be buying that answer any more than I was.

"I'm positive." Jo's smile didn't reach her eyes. Fibber. "We're just very good friends."

"All right." Trudie's face glowed. Her eyes glittered as she looked from Jo to me and back. She looked like she'd just taken first place in the Peach Coast Cobbler Crawl: happy and relieved. "Great! Thank you! Enjoy the rest of your day."

I watched Trudie as she practically waltzed to the exit.

"Trudie's not the right person for Nolan." Jo's voice was a blend of smug and insecure.

"Is that because you and Nolan are more than *very good friends*?" It was time we confronted the relationship fibs in the room.

"What?" Jo avoided eye contact. "What are you talking about? I told Trudie, Nolan and I are just friends and that's the truth."

"I don't believe you. And *you* don't believe you, either. I've seen the way you look at him. And the way he looks at you. There's enough chemistry flowing between the two of you to require FDA approval."

"Stop it." Jo bent over with a startled laugh. She clutched my arm for balance. "That's not true."

"Oh, yes, it is."

As Trudie arrived at the exit, the door was pulled open from the other side. Incredibly, her smile grew even brighter for the person holding the door for her.

I waited to see the beneficiary of her exuberant mood. Spence. Of course.

I raised my hand in greeting as I continued speaking with Jo. "When're you going to tell Nolan how you feel?"

"When're you going to tell Spence?" Jo turned to our friend.

I almost swallowed my tongue.

"Tell me what?" Spence came to a stop beside us.

I felt like a deer in headlights. "That I need to know whether you've received a pennant."

"I haven't, but I promise to tell you right away—*if* I receive one."

Jo shot me a disgusted look before leading us to the café. Service was fast and efficient. We carried our soups, sandwiches, and iced teas into Jo's office. After catching up on each other's day and well-being, I brought us to the point of the meeting.

"Our investigation's moving in circles."

Jo started to bite her fingernails. She lowered her hand when she saw my scowl. "During our last investigation, we had trouble gaining traction too. We're still learning about the victims and the possible suspects."

Spence nodded. "Jo's right. It's even more complicated this time because we're looking for a serial killer; more victims, more motives, more suspects. And we aren't trained investigators."

Everything they said made sense. Still... "We're running out of time. In fact, we don't know how much time we have before the killer strikes again."

Spence swallowed a bite of his sandwich. We'd all requested the spicy chicken. "Brittany and I are being careful."

I hoped so. "As long as you're taking this seriously."

I struggled to shrug off my unease. "Instead of looking at one suspect with a grudge against four people, is it possible we should be looking for two suspects working together?"

Jo's eyes sharpened with interest. "You mean like Delores Polly working with Philomena Fossey?" She referred to her notes. "They both resented Hank and Nelle. And Delores has a grudge against you, Spence." She sent him an apologetic look before turning again to her notebook. "And Philomena has a reason to be angry with Nelle and Brittany."

I held up a cautioning finger. "Maybe not Delores. I think we can rule her out."

Spence inclined his head toward me. "She said you're the one who convinced her to apologize for the email she sent Hank, Nelle, and me."

"She would've apologized eventually even if I hadn't said anything." I refocused on the case. "June's definitely off the list. I spoke with her again this morning. It's true that, if she'd had an accomplice, she wouldn't've had to be at the event. But she really cared about Hank. She'd ended their relationship so he could be happy with Nelle."

"Aww." Jo's lips formed a perfect circle. Her eyebrows knitted. "That makes me so sad."

"I don't think June's involved, either. She seemed genuinely upset at Hank's wake." Spence consulted his notepad. "With her and Delores off the list, that leaves only Reba and Philomena."

My mind spun. I struggled to corral my thoughts. "Reba may still be angry with you and Brittany because of her failed mayoral bid. That scandal is also threatening her reelection to town council. If she isn't reelected to the council, she may feel that she can't try again for the mayor's office. She may hold you and Brittany responsible for destroying her political career."

Jo's eyes were wide with concern and anxiety. She glanced at her fingernails before fisting her hands. "And in addition to Philomena's jealousy of Hank and Nelle, she's angry about Brittany filing that lawsuit against her."

We were quiet as we digested the enormity of our current situation. My muscles were weighted with fear and frustration. We couldn't lose sight of the fact one of us was in mortal danger. This wasn't a puzzle game. It was life and death.

Jo shattered the silence. "So we have potential motives. Now we need to find out if Philomena and Reba have been seen together more often."

Spence put away his notes and checked his watch. "And whether they had the opportunity or means to kill Hank and Nelle. We won't know the means until the deputies get the coroner's report, though."

"And we may not even know then, unless we can convince the deputies to tell us." I gathered the refuse from my lunch. "I'm not giving up on the high school connection, either."

Spence and I said our goodbyes to Jo. I accepted his offer of a ride back to the library.

He pulled out of the parking lot, merging with the traffic. "I have a meeting at the high school after work this evening. The summer academic program coordinator wants me to talk to his students about careers in the media."

From the passenger seat, I stared at him, fighting my natural urge to smother. I lost. "Are you going to the high school alone? With a serial killer stalking you? Is that a good idea?"

He gave me a quick glance. "I'm telling you about the meeting so you don't worry if I miss your evening check-in. The meeting starts at six. I promise to be careful."

"Not good enough." My jaw felt stiff with obstinacy. "I'm coming with you."

"Marvey—"

"We agreed to protect each other, remember? I'll be ready at five-thirty." I sat back against the seat and scowled through the windshield. I allowed the silence to grow.

After several moments, Spence sighed his surrender. "If you insist on attending this dry, dull meeting with me, then I'll pick you up at five. We'll get dinner first."

"Fine."

I felt Spence's impatience. He'd get over it, but I wasn't going to risk his life to avoid an argument. As a bonus, this evening, I'd get a peek into Spence's past. Perhaps I'd even pick up some information that could help resolve whatever's happening in his present. Sort of like a time travel mystery. I loved those.

CHAPTER 16

“**I**T LOOKS MORE LIKE A small college campus than a high school.” I looked over Mother Mathilda Taylor Beasley High School as Spence guided his sedan to the parking lot on the side of the building.

I'd passed the high school numerous times with Jo. She gave me guided tours of my adopted town during our weekly jogs. A silver gable-and-valley roof topped the two-story, red brick building. Its cupola was white vinyl with a red cap.

The school sat in the middle of meticulous landscaping. A defense line of thick, old American Elm trees stood behind the building. Privet hedges bordered two sides of the vivid green lawn. In the center of the grass, surrounded by small hedges was a sign that read, *Mother Mathilda Taylor Beasley High School, Home of the Saints, Est. 1975.*

It was after five o'clock Monday evening. A small team of groundskeepers was maintaining the grass, trees, and bushes. What looked like a handful of administrators and students were strolling the school.

I heard Spence's long-suffering sigh as I let myself out of his car. He didn't like me opening the door on my own. Fair enough. I didn't like having my door opened for me. We remained at an impasse.

I paused in front of the school's sign. "The landscaping's beautiful."

Spence circled the car and stopped beside me. "The school was originally named Peach Coast High School. It was renamed and dedicated to Mother Mathilda in 2002."

"That was two years before she was named a Georgia Woman of Achievement."

"You know about Mother Mathilda." He'd left his garnet tie and gray suit jacket in the car. The top two buttons of his soft gray shirt were unbuttoned.

"I looked her up. I figured she had to be important since the high school, recreational center, and park are named for her." I gestured toward the school's sign. "She was an amazing person."

"Yes, she was." His attention left me and circled the school's grounds. "Knowing her legacy in education, it made sense the school would be named after her."

Mother Mathilda Taylor Beasley's contribution to education was just one of her accomplishments. Records indicate that by 1859, she'd been operating a secret school in Savannah. This was during a time when it had been against the law to teach free or enslaved Black people to read. The punishment was a fine and a whipping. I found her commitment to educating children despite the great personal and physical risk inspiring.

"What was it like going to school here? How were your teachers and the other students?" A deep breath filled my senses with the scents of the grass and foliage surrounding us.

Spence's shrug was more of a flexing of his back muscles. "Everyone was nice. The teachers were dedicated. My classmates were...adolescents. It helped that I was from a prominent family," he added dryly.

"You don't give yourself enough credit." I sent him a wry look before setting off for the school's entrance. "People aren't nice to you because of your family. They're nice to you because you're a nice guy."

"How can you tell the difference?" He fell into step beside me.

"First, you didn't complain when I asked you to drive me home to feed Phoenix before coming here. Second, Phoenix likes you. He *really* likes you."

"And I really like Phoenix."

"Besides, if people didn't like you, they'd avoid you. The fact that people gravitate to you whenever you're in public is a sign they genuinely like you."

"I guess you have a point."

"Of course I do." I jerked my chin toward the activity around the school grounds. "I thought the academic year had ended. Why are so many people here?"

"The school offers summer programs for students all over the county, academic and athletic."

"What a wonderful idea. I wonder if the library could partner with the school on those programs. I'll check with Corrinne." I reached for the doorknob, but Spence caught it first.

"Just this once. Please." He pulled the door open, stepping back to allow me to precede him.

"Thank you."

"Come with me." He escorted me through the school.

"I want to get something out of the way before the meeting."

"All right." *Mysterious.* I hustled to keep up with his determined strides.

The school was pristine, well-maintained, and bright. High ceilings made the hallways seem vast and airy. Smooth, white walls reflected the natural light streaming through large, spotless windows. Light danced on the slate gray tiling like sunlight on water. My low-heeled pumps tapped softly against it.

He brought us to a stop in front of a highlights showcase for the Class of 2008.

"This is your graduating class." I excitedly searched the long Plexiglas case. "Where are you?"

"Upper left." He inclined his head in that direction. "I was the newspaper editor."

"That's fitting." I lifted my gaze and grinned. "There you are."

They'd taken the photograph in a classroom. Several desks had computers. The banner above the wall behind them read, "The Messenger Newspaper."

The photo had captured an adolescent Spence, standing in front of a small group of students around his age. He looked so determined. He stared straight at the camera, his shoulders squared and his arms crossed. Intelligence as well as mischief brightened his dark eyes. I wished I'd known this Spence. I was certain we would've been friends.

"You were a good-looking kid." I turned my smile to him. "I bet you had more than a few admirers."

"You'd lose that bet." His response was dry. "I was a heavy, awkward teen who preferred books to people."

"Then our high school selves had that in common." I

gave him an amused look. "You'd mentioned your struggle with healthy eating because of your cooking hobby, but you gained control over it."

"You're good for my ego."

I chuckled as I turned back to the case. "What's your strongest memory of working on the paper?"

"My parents always told me to report the truth, good, bad, or indifferent. People want and deserve the truth. Unfortunately, that didn't always serve the school administration's objectives. Mama and Daddy got a lot of calls about the articles I printed and the questions I asked."

I laughed at the image of a young, rabble-rousing Spence. Yes, we definitely would've been friends. "Since your parents are newspaper people, I'm sure they were proud of you." I searched the case for another glimpse into Spence's past. "You were on the debate team and senior student government. I'm impressed."

"I was the son of public servants. My parents were on the town council and school board. They inspired me." Spence paced over to another graduating class display. "What student activities were you part of?"

"I was on student government, too, and the yearbook committee and track." I joined him in front of the Class of 2006 display. "Our track meets didn't require us to eat peach cobbler."

"Your loss."

"Ah! There's a photo of Hank and Nelle as homecoming king and queen." My smile froze. I pointed to a different picture in the display. "Brittany was editor of your school paper in 2006?"

"I remember that." Spence's words were hesitant as though the memories were starting to fill in. "She was

really good. She pushed for real news, not the fluff pieces the administration preferred like trends in student
fashion and cafeteria food preferences."

I stared hard at the photo of the newspaper committee. It was a similar pose to the one of Spence with his
staff. "Hank and Nelle were on the paper with her."

"Yes, they were two of the best reporters the paper's
ever had. I'm sure their parents got a lot of calls, too."

"Could that be the link we're looking for?" I turned to
him. "Is the school newspaper the connection between
you, Brittany, Hank, and Nelle?"

Spence frowned at the display. "You think someone's
killing us over a story that appeared in a high school
newspaper more than ten years ago?"

"You were all involved with the paper."

"But at different times. I didn't work on the paper
with them."

"That's a good point." My surge of excitement dwin-
dled. I rallied. "Could we get old copies of the papers
from 2006, '07, and '08?"

"Spence, taking a trip down memory lane?" Lucas
appeared out of nowhere to stand beside Spence.

"Lucas. You've met Marvella Harris." Spence brought
me into the conversation.

Lucas nodded his greeting. He was about Spence's
height. His track suit was in the high school's blue
and white colors and hung a little loose on his slender,
almost-thin build. "Yeah, at the library event and the
swap. I don't have a library card yet, but it's on my to-
do list."

I gave him an encouraging smile. "Let me know if
you need help completing the application. And thank
you again for attending the kickoff and book swap. We
appreciate your support."

"Sure." He looked pleased with himself. "Several of my players' parents were there. It was good to talk with them away from school."

He was the interim head coach. Of course, he'd talk with his players' parents. There wasn't anything suspicious about that, unless... "Do you want the head coach's position?"

"I'm qualified for it." Lucas sounded more than a little defensive. "Hank was a good coach, but I have more experience."

"You do have a lot of experience." Spence's tone was diplomatic. "But Hank was more than a coach. He also taught math. The *Crier*'s article didn't mention whether you had teaching experience."

His eyes flashed. "I taught art, but a lot of schools dropped their art programs because of budget cuts. The board hasn't made a decision about my teaching yet."

I remembered the book he'd purchased at the book swap, a hardcover tome on clay sculpting. That was one mystery solved.

"They probably want to wait a respectable amount of time before naming the next coach. He has a lot of history with the school." Spence's theory made sense.

I nodded my agreement. "The community's going through a lot, losing him and Nelle Kenton so suddenly and so close together. Did you know Nelle?"

A cloud swept across his features. "I actually did. I met her when I opened my accounts with the bank. She was a real nice lady. I was hoping to get to know her better. But I suppose she and Hank were always destined to be." He jerked his chin toward the photo of Hank and Nelle during homecoming.

How had he known Hank and Nelle were getting

back together? According to Hank's cousin, Eudella, they hadn't started dating again before Hank was killed. "Were Hank and Nelle seeing each other?"

Lucas jabbed a thumb over his shoulder toward the back of the school. "I assumed they were. I saw them kissing in the parking lot. Hank was a lucky guy; until he wasn't." With that last cryptic comment, he ambled away.

I watched him disappear down the hallway. "Did his comment seem spiteful to you?"

"Yes, it did." Spence sounded as troubled by the exchange as I felt.

"From the article the paper wrote about him, he's from North Carolina. What else do we know about him?"

"Chauncey Bell, the reporter who wrote the story, said Lucas didn't seem excited about the job. He had the impression Lucas was resentful, his word. Lucas worked with Hank, but what's his connection to Nelle, Brittany, and me?"

"The connection may not be a what, remember?" I looked at him. "It could be who."

CHAPTER 17

T HE MEETING WITH THE SUMMER academic program director had been suspiciously short.
The information could have been covered in
a five-minute phone call. I suspected the director had
requested the meeting to get face time with one of the
town's luminaries. Did that ever get old?

On the way home, Spence and I decided to take a
detour to the sheriff's department for any updates on
the case. It was almost six-thirty Monday evening. The
pastries were all gone but the coffee still smelled fresh.
And, as I'd suspected, Jed and Errol were still at work.
Did they sleep here?

"Good evening, deputies." Spence offered them a
courteous smile.

I hoped his hail-good-fellow-well-met manner would
take the edge off of Jed. It didn't.

Jed's greeting was even worse. "Evening, Mr. Spence.
Ms. Marvey. Is there anything we can do for you outside
of discussing an ongoing investigation?"

Errol stopped rocking his chair, and set it firmly
on the ground. "Well, now, JW. Since Mr. Spence is a

potential victim of the suspected serial killer, don't you think we could be a little lenient on that rule? I mean, it could help keep him safe."

I sent Errol a grateful look. "You have a good point, Deputy Cole. Thank you." I did a quick ten-count before facing Jed. "This is a matter of life and death, Deputy Whatley. Please. Any information you could provide could protect my friend."

Jed rubbed his eyes with his thumb and forefinger. "All right. All right. We do have an update." He sighed, lowering his voice. Errol, Spence, and I moved closer to him. "The M.E.'s confirmed that both victims were poisoned with the same drug, tetrahydrozoline."

Errol gestured for Spence and me to take the visitors' chairs near his desk. "It's one of the active ingredients in over-the-counter eye drops."

"Why does tetrahydrozoline poisoning sound familiar to me?" Spence studied the white-tiled flooring as though he could find the answer under our feet. "I remember something about that in the news recently."

Jed sat back on his seat. "Couple years back, a man in North Carolina used eye drops to kill his wife for the life insurance money."

North Carolina? Spence and I exchanged a look. This was another piece of information that put Lucas in the spotlight. As far as I was concerned, he was now on the list.

Errol continued the update. "At first, it looked like Coach Hank died of a heart attack. But that didn't make much sense to his family. His aunt said Coach was healthy as a horse. And, since Ms. Marvey found that note, we asked the M.E. to dig a little deeper, focusing on stuff that could mimic a heart attack."

"He's doing the same test for Nelle Kenton," Jed added. "But remember now, we're only sharing this information with *you* because, like you said, Spence here's name's on the list. Y'all can't share this information with anyone. That means not Jo Gomez and not any of the librarians. No one." With the memory of our high school visit still fresh in my mind, Jed's stern look made me feel like I was in the principal's office.

"I understand your concern, Deputy Whatley, but Jo and the librarians are very well read." I spread my arms to emphasize my point. "They might be able to provide additional insights on the investigation, especially armed with the method of the murders."

"If you tell all of those people, we would've gone from just two people knowing, me and Errol, to eight," Jed grumbled, but I could tell he was leaning toward my point.

"We can be trusted to keep the information secret. I assure you." I held my breath as I waited for his determination.

He scowled. "Not one person more."

I exhaled. "Promise."

"Thank you, deputies. We appreciate your time." With his hand on the small of my back, Spence nudged me out of the bullpen and toward the parking lot.

"Are you thinking what I'm thinking?" He lowered his voice to ask as we crossed to his car.

"That depends. Are you asking about Jed warming up to us or Lucas being from North Carolina?"

"I'm talking about Lucas." Spence held the passenger side door for me. "Maybe we shouldn't rule him out yet."

I settled onto the passenger seat and waited for

Spence to get behind the wheel. "I don't think he would've killed Hank to get the head coaching position, do you?"

"No, killing Hank wouldn't guarantee him the job. The school still needs a math teacher. And what's his connection to the rest of us? There has to be something more. I'll contact some sports reporters, see if they have any ideas, off the record."

"Great idea. Thank you." We had a murder weapon and a fresh suspect. I felt hopeful.

"And Marvey?" Spence started the car. "I'm sorry, but Jed's not warming up to you."

"Were you followed?" I asked as soon as Spence answered his cell phone Monday night. I'd timed the call for when he entered his home, which I'd estimated to be thirteen minutes after he'd taken me home.

However, Spence greeted my question with a silence that had a tinge of disbelief. It reminded me of the dubious expression he'd given me when I offered him the toll-free number for the national poison help hotline.

"Marvey? Why are you calling? Is something wrong?"

"I want to make sure you got home safely." I paced circles in my living room. "At the very least, I want whoever's targeting you to know people are watching over you."

Spence sighed. In the background, I heard a jingling sound from metal hitting metal. Was he putting away his keys? "I appreciate your concern, but I think the killer's getting that message from the increased police patrols around my house."

I nodded my satisfaction although Spence couldn't see me. "I'm glad to hear about the patrols. And I hope the killer's noticed. The sooner this is done, the sooner my parents can relax."

He chuckled softly. "I've been meaning to tell you, I'd like to invite your parents to dinner with my mother and me when they come to visit. I'll make a regional entrée that'll give them a taste of Georgia."

I dropped onto my sofa. Phoenix leaped onto the cushion beside me, then made himself comfortable on my lap. "Spence, that would be wonderful. They'd absolutely love it. Thank you."

"It's my pleasure. And thank you for being so assertive with the investigation. I appreciate your concern for my safety."

"We're friends, Spence. Of course I'm going to hunt down whoever's threatening you." I stroked Phoenix's back as I tried to picture Spence in his home. Was he sitting on his sofa too? His living room was modern and comfortable. "Tons of people care about you. In fact, Jo's scheduled an appointment with Reba McRaney tomorrow afternoon to see if we can find anything to link her to the murders."

Surprised laughter escaped him. "She's getting her hair done as cover for the investigation? I appreciate her sacrifice."

His humor was contagious. "She's excited. She says it's been a while since she's treated herself to a salon day."

"Then I'm glad the investigation has given her the opportunity."

I cuddled Phoenix closer. "I hope it proves fruitful. Just continue to be careful, Spence. Be aware of your surroundings, and don't take anything ingestible from people you don't know. Or even from people you do know." Spence didn't know any strangers and the killer could be anyone.

"I promise, Marvey. Please don't worry so much."

It was hard not to worry when the days were flying by while our investigation stood still. The killer had murdered Hank and Nelle two weeks apart. This Saturday would be two weeks since Nelle's death. If the killer stayed true to schedule, either Brittany or Spence could be in danger this weekend.

"We haven't seen any updates about the murders in your paper. What's happening?" My mother's greeting would've resulted in chastisement from my new friends, but it made me homesick.

My parents' late-night call Monday had caught me in the middle of my pre-bedtime ritual, which included brushing my teeth and curling up on the sofa with a good book. I had to think fast.

I couldn't lie to them. Not only was that disrespectful, they'd also see right through it. Parents were human lie detectors. However, I couldn't tell them I was investigating serial murders, either.

I stalled. "Everyone's on edge. I can sense their heightened anxiety as I walked and jogged around town."

In houses along my jogging route, more curtains and

blinds shifted as though neighbors were paying closer attention to each other and activities on their streets. It made me sad.

My father made a hum of understanding. "Why isn't the *Crier* providing regular updates? People would feel reassured if they had more information on the cases."

"The deputies aren't ready to provide updates." I played and replayed my response in my mind. It was honest, but what I'd left unsaid made my stomach churn with guilt. "How're you both? How was your day?"

There was a short, surprised pause accompanied by familiar traffic sounds in the background. After five months, I'd finally gotten used to falling asleep without it.

"We're fine, sweetheart." Dad's tone brushed aside my questions. "You're the one with a serial killer in your town."

"I'm safe, Dad." I swung my legs off the sofa and sat up. "My alarm system's set even when I'm home. And I'm always aware of my surroundings. You don't have to worry."

"Aren't you friends with the newspaper editor, Spence Holt?" Mom asked. "Can't you find out from *him* whether the deputies have any updates?"

"Mom, I wouldn't impose that way on our friendship. It would put him in an unfair position, if the deputies have sworn him to secrecy."

"Sweetheart, your mother and I need answers." Dad's concern carried down the line. I felt it as though he'd put his arms around my shoulders.

"Mom, Dad, I'm sorry there isn't more I can tell you."

"Then we'll have to come down there and assess the

situation ourselves." Mom's decision struck fear into me. I didn't want my parents in town while a serial killer was on the loose.

"What? Mom, that's not necessary." I stood to pace my living room. Wandering past my blond wood fireplace, I let my eyes linger on the photo of my parents snuggled together on their sofa. Thirty-five years of marriage and they still behaved like newlyweds. "I'm fine, except that I miss you both very much. But let's stick with our plans for July."

"Marvey, honey, of course it's necessary." Mom's voice softened. "You're a thousand miles away—"

"Nine hundred and eight point four," I absently corrected. My feet carried me into my kitchen to my stash of chocolate-covered peanuts. Should I or shouldn't I?

Mom continued as though I hadn't spoken. "—without family nearby to look out for you or stay with you until this murderer is caught. Or maybe you should just come home where your father and I could keep an eye on you."

I closed my eyes briefly, shaking my head. Now they were getting extreme. "There's crime in New York as well. Remember? You can't watch me twenty-four-seven-three-sixty-five." I closed the cupboard and left the kitchen. Retrieving the chocolate-covered peanuts required both hands. "If you came here now, what would you do?" I tried reasoning with her, but getting Ciara Bennett-Harris to change her mind wasn't easy.

Dad took that question. "Your mother and I want to see how safe this town really is and whether the local law enforcement is capable of protecting you."

"But, Mom, Dad, you have a subscription to the paper and you have me to tell you what's going on." *Or as much as I can tell you.* "I can't take time off to visit with you now. I'm in the middle of a big project."

The silence lasted a little longer this time. They were probably whispering with each other, trying to identify weaknesses in my argument. Well, there were weaknesses all over the place. That didn't mean I was backing down.

Finally, Mom responded for them. "All right, honey. We'll wait until July. But you'll let us know if anything happens between now and then, right?"

I released the breath I'd been holding. "I'll let you know as soon as they've caught the killer."

CHAPTER 18

"I THINK WE NEED TO TALK. Don't you?" Cecelia Holt's greeting carried an uncharacteristic urgency. She strode into my office Tuesday morning, her tan stilettos clicking with elegant purpose. Her sage green skirt suit complemented her complexion and emphasized her slim figure. The faint scent of her magnolia perfume accompanied her to a guest chair in front of my desk. She set her tan clutch and black faux leather briefcase on the one beside her.

From her demeanor, she could only be referencing one issue: The threats against her son. My heart plummeted into my stomach where it lay like a stone. How had she found out? Had Spence told her or had she overheard something? More importantly, why was she here in my office instead of speaking with him in his?

Urgh!

I didn't want to be in the middle of a family debate. My initial reaction was to respond with a whiny, *Do we have to?* But I sensed the library board chair wouldn't tolerate that.

"You and Spence must have spoken already."

"He tried to hide this situation from me, but I could tell something was wrong." She crossed her legs, stacking her well-manicured hands on her right knee. "A mother always knows."

I'd tried to warn him. But with the secrets I was keeping from my parents, who was I to judge? Families were funny that way. Our parents spent the first part of our lives trying not to worry us. We spent the second part of our lives trying not to worry them.

I settled back against my chair. "I can't add anything to what I'm sure Spence has already shared with you."

"Let me be the judge of that." She pinned me in place with her direct stare and extended her hand. "May I see this...list, please?"

Hadn't Spence shown her the copy I'd given him?

Oh, Spence. By withholding information from your mother, did you know you were putting me in the middle?

I assessed Cecelia's tense features. Her jawline looked taut as though she was clenching her teeth. The lines bracketing her mouth were deeper, and the shadows in her dark eyes broke my heart. I couldn't turn away an anxious mother.

. I pulled my purse from my bottom desk drawer and fished my copy of the list from one of its compartments. I handed the sheet to her. Cecelia's hands shook as she read the four names: Hank Figg, Nelle Kenton, Brittany Wilson, and Spencer Holt.

"I knew he wasn't lying. He wouldn't lie to me about something like that. But I couldn't believe he was telling the truth. I needed to see it for myself." Her tortured brown eyes lifted to mine. "Who'd want to hurt my son?"

I swallowed the lump in my throat. "I don't know. But I intend to find out."

"I know that you do." She handed back the list. The hem of her narrow skirt fell just over her knee. "Spence told me you've been watching out for him and pushing the deputies with their investigation. Thank you for being such a good friend to my son. You're one of the best friends he's ever had."

I blushed at the compliment. "I feel the same about him."

There was silence for several moments before Cecelia spoke again. "He's worried about you. I am too. I want my son to be safe, but I don't want you to be in danger."

"Then we want the same things." I leaned into the table and sent her an encouraging smile. "Did Spence ask you to talk me out of this investigation? Because I'm not going to curl up on my sofa with Phoenix and a good book when I know someone's trying to kill a friend."

Her features brightened with the hint of a smile. "You're both very stubborn. You'll have to figure out a way to keep each other safe."

"I'm working on that."

"I appreciate your loyalty to my son, but he's worried and I don't like to see him like that." She gave a self-deprecating chuckle. "He's thirty years old, lives on his own, and manages four very successful enterprises. But I still worry about him today the way I have since his birth."

My lips curved in a partial smile. "I can't imagine Spence as a baby."

She laughed. "He's always been a handful, always wanted to do things on his own and in his way. His father was proud of him because of that. He was excited to see what Spence would do next. I was the overprotective parent." Cecelia abruptly stilled. From across the table, I felt the fear crushing her. "I wanted to make things easier for him. Remove everything and anything that could harm him. So learning that a serial killer has put him on some kind of hit list is like a waking nightmare."

A cold hand seemed to grip me and her anxiety became mine. "Do you have any suggestions of who might want to hurt him?"

"Spence said you thought it could be connected to the high school they all attended." She reached into her briefcase and retrieved three hardbound books. One was black, another blue, the third cream. "These are the yearbooks for each of the years Spence was at Mother Mathilda High School. There may be some clue here that could help with the investigation."

I reached for them eagerly. "That's a great idea. Thank you."

"You're the best person to review them. The people and places are new to you so you'll pay closer attention."

I let my eyes drift from hers as I recalled the tour Spence had given me. "He doesn't think there's a connection, and I can see his point. He wasn't in the same graduating class. And for him, high school was thirteen years ago. Too much time has passed."

"I disagree." Cecelia leaned forward as though to emphasize her words. "Remember the saying, 'Revenge is a dish best served cold.'"

"But how cold? Fifteen years seems like a deep freeze."

Revenge is a dish best served cold.

Cecelia's words still lingered on my mind when my desk phone rang a short time later. The clock on my computer monitor read a few minutes after nine Tuesday morning.

"Peach Coast Library. Marvella Harris speaking."

An officious voice responded. "Ms. Harris, Chet Little, vice president for corporate giving for Malcovich Savings and Loan."

Chet's introduction caught me off guard. "Vice president?"

It had only been ten days since Nelle, Malcovich's previous vice president for corporate giving, had died. Had they already named her replacement? Wasn't that kind of insensitive? Hank had been killed three weeks and three days ago. The school system still hadn't named a new head coach for the high school boys basketball team.

Chet sniffed. The abrupt sound seemed defensive as though my question knocked the wind from his officious sail. "Yes, well, technically, I'm the *interim* vice president for corporate giving. But, Ms. Harris, I'm calling about the bank's donation to the library's Summer Solicitation Drive."

"Thank you again. The library appreciates the bank's support in ensuring everyone in our community has equal access to knowledge."

"We're withdrawing our donation." His words were rushed.

Had he said what I thought I'd heard? "You're withdrawing your support?"

"That's right."

Oh, no! Oh, no! Oh, no!

I tightened my grip on the receiver and gathered my scattered thoughts. "May I ask why?"

"Well, Ms. Harris, there are a great number of charitable organizations that support Peach Coast and we'd like to fund them. We've decided one of these other groups would be a better investment of our charitable deductions—dollars." Chet seemed to enjoy delivering that set down. What had books ever done to him?

"I submitted the library's application for your bank's donation in March. Nelle approved it in April. Why has the bank decided to revoke its gift?"

"Our corporate leaders have taken another look at your application in light of certain recent changes." His tone was defensive. "There are other options for people to get books. The library isn't as critical to the community as, say, a medical facility, for example."

I unclenched my teeth. "Is that the organization you've decided to support instead of the library?"

There was a short hesitation. "Yes. Yes, it is. Nelle was the only member of the executive team who supported the library."

With Nelle gone, apparently there wasn't anyone on the Malcovich Savings and Loan executive team to speak for the library. I couldn't begrudge donations to the medical facility, though. It also was a worthy cause.

In the background, I heard a tinny sound as though he was nervously tapping his pen against his desk. Had he expected me to accept the bank's decision to withdraw its gift without asking why? The library's future was at stake. I wasn't going to pretend that didn't matter just because my questions made him uncomfortable.

"I disagree with your characterization of the library's value to its community." I spoke slowly so the corporate bean counter could understand my every syllable. "The library's contributions are *different* but not of lesser importance. Our services include job search support, homework assistance, voting information, and the summer reading program. Malcovich Savings and Loan could be a part of helping the library expand its programs and offerings even further."

"I'm afraid you're wasting your time, Ms. Harris. The bank will not change its position on this matter. We're no longer donating to your fundraiser."

Desperation drove me. "It's unfair of you to take back your gift now, Mr. Little. You've made the financial commitment. The fundraiser's already started."

"Ms. Harris, the simple fact is it's our money and we can choose to do whatever we want with it. Enjoy the rest of your day." And on those bitter words, the line went dead.

"Urgh!" I cradled the receiver and slumped back on my chair.

Enjoy the rest of my day? How would that be possible when I now had to find a donor with deep enough pockets to replace Malcovich Savings and Loan?

"We've lost our lead donor." After breaking the news to Corrinne first, I didn't waste time bringing the librarians up to speed on Malcovich Savings and Loan backing out of their donor sponsorship commitment for our fundraiser minutes ago this Tuesday morning. It was like tearing off an adhesive bandage: quick, simple, direct.

"What?"

"What happened?"

"Are you kiddin' me?"

The trio spoke as one voice. Their reactions under-scored the devastating blow of the bank's defection.

"I'm afraid I'm not kidding, Adrian. I wish I was." We sat in our usual seats around the small conference table in Corrinne's office. Corrinne was at the head of the table. Floyd was on my left. Viv sat across from me with Adrian on her right.

"What happened?" Viv repeated her question. She appeared to be struggling with anger and disappoint-ment. So was I.

I recapped the call I'd had with Chet Little as I dis-tributed copies of a printout to the four other librarians. "This is a list of possible substitute donors. I've indi-cated the ones who haven't responded to our solicita-tion yet. I've also noted the ones who've already declined to contribute. I want to invite them again. Looking over this list, can you identify any other big donors to replace Malcovich?"

Corrinne circled a name on the list. "Logan Financial Investment's already made a generous contribution, but perhaps they could be convinced to increase their gift. I'll ask Cecelia Holt to contact them."

I recalled that Cecelia's little sister, Charlene, was the investment company's president. "Thank you, Cor-rinne. Let me know if Ms. Holt needs any information to help with her pitch."

Floyd tapped the sheet he held in his hands. "Peach Coast Savings isn't on here."

"They've already donated." I admitted to myself to being tempted to approach the bank again. "And they were our lead donor for the winter solicitation. I don't want to wear out our welcome by asking them to be lead donor for every campaign."

"You raise a good point, Marvey." Viv lowered her printout to the table. "I'm uncomfortable always asking people for money."

Floyd's grunt conveyed his empathy. "I agree. At some point, people are going to head in the other direction when they see us coming."

I understood their discomfort. I really did. People think fundraising is fun and glamorous. In reality, it's extremely stressful.

I looked at each of the librarians in turn. "Remind people that when they support libraries—and medical centers and schools—they're strengthening their community."

Viv extended her right hand toward me, then Corrinne. "But can't we manage without a big donor?"

Corrinne shook her head. "We're better positioned now that Marvey's set up multiple donor streams, but our costs increase every year: subscriptions, new books, educational resources, software upgrades, as well as our utilities."

"And jobs?" We'd been skirting the issue of additional budget cuts. It was time to face it directly. Could the library be facing layoffs if the summer drive doesn't turn a profit?

Silence was deafening as we waited for her response.

"Neither the town council nor the board have made a decision, you understand?" Corrinne waited for our nods of confirmation before continuing. She exhaled a heavy breath. "Candidly, I'm concerned. If this fundraising campaign isn't effective, we'll be forced to cut summer hours again next year. And it's possible that we'll also have to furlough staff. We may even have layoffs."

My stomach muscles knotted. I felt sick. Corrinne continued speaking, but I couldn't process any of it. I wasn't alone. Floyd, Viv, and Adrian also were frozen in shock. We were librarians in a town with only one library. What would we do, where would we go if our jobs were eliminated? Well, Floyd could retire. He was supposed to retire last year, but the rest of us would be in bad shape.

I'd left my home and family in Brooklyn, bought a house in Peach Coast. I'd been putting down roots, becoming a part of the community, developing a routine and making plans for the future, but by this time next year I could be out of a job.

Fighting off my panic, I brought my attention back to Corrinne.

"Several board members believe fundraising distracts libraries and our patrons from our primary mission." She played with the string of pearls accessorizing her blush sheath dress. Her clear coat nail polish was subtle. "To get their approval for this to be an annual event, we have to prove it's worth everyone's effort."

"But isn't fundraising a major part of my job?" Another blow to my job security. I massaged the back of my neck, trying to ease the growing tension. "How does the board think we'll raise money without fundraisers?"

"It would be a lot easier to focus on our mission if we didn't have to constantly worry about our budget." Floyd's tone was gruff.

"But we do, so we need to start brainstorming." There was too much at stake for us to give up at the first sign of trouble.

"Tetrahydrozoline? Like eye drops?" Adrian seemed disappointed the poison used to kill Hank and Nelle wasn't more exotic. Perhaps tetradotoxin from pufferfish or ricin from the castor oil plant, dubbed the deadliest plant in the world, would have excited him more.

Adrian, Viv, Floyd, and I were sharing a late lunch in my office Tuesday afternoon. My door was closed. I imagined hours later, I'd still be able to smell the spicy aromas of Adrian's chicken and sausage gumbo. The air was swollen with the scents of Viv's blackened chicken salad and Floyd's fried chicken and okra. My ham and cheese on multigrain sandwich couldn't compete.

I slid a look toward the large blue plastic bowl that contained Adrian's gumbo. Would he be amenable to a trade, half of my sandwich for half of his gumbo? Probably not. I stifled a sigh and went back to my sandwich. Next time, I'll dress it up with some oil and vinegar, salt and pepper. A tomato slice. Something. I had to stop fixing my lunches on autopilot.

I wiped my mouth. "That's right. Tetrahydrozoline's used in regular, over-the-counter eye drops. Anyone can purchase them."

Floyd drank his sweet tea. "Then there's nothing about the poison that could help identify the killer."

"I have eye drops in my medicine cabinet." Viv shrugged as she cut into her salad. "I haven't used them for years, though."

"So do I." I pursed my lips in thought. "I don't even notice them in the cabinet anymore, which brings us to another complication. Our suspect may not have purchased the eye drops recently."

"So where do we go from here?" Viv fed herself another forkful of salad.

I told the librarians about the murder trial of the North Carolina paramedic who used tetrahydrozoline to kill his wife. "I did a search and found two other cases of tetrahydrozoline poisoning in Charlotte alone. In those cases, women were charged with poisoning their partners."

"Isn't Lucas Daniel from North Carolina?" Viv's voice bounced with excitement. "Maybe he heard about those trials and that's where he got the idea."

"Spence and I had the same thought. He's doing more research into Lucas's background, trying to find motives or at least connections with the people on the list."

Adrian nodded as he swallowed more gumbo. "I still think we're looking for a woman as the killer, though. Poison's—"

"A woman's weapon." Floyd finished that thought. He shifted his attention from Adrian's ponytail. "We heard you the first fifty-eleven times. Did *you* hear Marvey when she said the paramedic killed *his* wife? Obviously, men poison people, too."

Adrian returned his attention to his half-full bowl of delicious-smelling gumbo. "One man to two women. I guess we'll see who's right."

"This isn't a competition." Viv nudged Adrian's arm with her elbow.

"Nelle was killed two weeks after Hank." I gathered the remains of my lunch. "This Saturday, four days from today, marks two weeks since Nelle's death. Another person could be killed—either Brittany or Spence. We're running out of time."

Floyd moved aside his now-empty plate and turned to Adrian. "How does tetrahydrozoline work?"

No one seemed surprised that Adrian had the answer. "From what I've read, tetrahydrozoline can make you feel like you're having a heart attack."

"That's probably one of the reasons the killer chose that drug." I gestured toward him with my diet soda. "It's hard to trace back to them and it mimics death by natural causes. Medical examiners don't typically check for tetrahydrozoline."

"How does it kill you?" Floyd asked.

"It's absorbed through your digestive system into your main blood circulation. I think that's why poison control tells you not to throw up. That would make the poison absorb even faster." Adrian frowned in concentration. "It travels to your heart and central nervous system and'll slow your heart and blood pressure by a lot. It'll also drop your body temperature. You could end up in a coma, and if you don't get help real quick, you'll die."

Floyd shook his head. "Sometimes you scare me."

"How long does it take to work?" Viv asked.

Adrian spread his hands. "It depends on the dosage. I'd think the killer would've given Coach a much bigger dose than Ms. Nelle. She was a lot smaller than him."

I made a mental note to share Adrian's information with Spence. "The killer probably poisoned Hank's and Nelle's food or drink. It would be easier than trying to inject it."

Viv started to pack away the remnants of her lunch.

"It sounds as though the killer's someone the victims were comfortable enough to leave alone with their food."

Floyd looked around the table suspiciously. "For me, that wouldn't be a long list."

High school yearbooks: A treasure trove of angsty poetry, promising short stories, and limitless possibilities.

Curled up on my armchair Tuesday evening, I combed through the Class of 2006 yearbook Cecelia had given me. Nothing jumped out at me, nothing of any significance. The senior photo pages listed each graduate's extracurricular activities, intended college, and ambitions. The ambitions were fun—and revealing.

June Bishop: To be governor of Georgia.

Hank Figg: To be a shooting guard with the Atlanta Hawks.

Nelle Kenton: Work on Wall Street.

Philomena Patterson (now Fossey): Star on Broadway.

Reba Reilly (now McRaney): Develop an exclusive line of cosmetics.

Brittany Wilson: Win the Tour de France.

This trip down other people's memory lane had raised more questions than answers. Like Hank, Nelle, and Brittany, Philomena had worked on the high school paper. Had she and Nelle competed for stories as well as Hank's attention?

They were both also in the drama club. With these shared interests, had they ever been friends or had they always been competitors?

Reba also had been in the drama club. According to the yearbook, that's the only extracurricular activity she shared with Nelle.

The advertiser section in the back of the yearbook conveyed best wishes from several familiar companies, including all the Holt family holdings, *The Peach Coast Crier*, Peach Coast Inn, Peach Coast Community Bank, and the Camden County Hotel; Trudie's family's business, Camden County Construction Company; and Malcovich Savings and Loan. Fortunately, they hadn't changed their mind about supporting the high school. These same advertisers were among those in the 2007 and 2008 yearbooks.

The yearbooks hadn't been as helpful as I'd hoped. Perhaps I'd learn more from the high school newspapers Brittany and Spence were tracking down for me.

I exchanged the 2006 for the 2008 yearbook, Spence's graduating class. His senior photo appeared in the graduating class section alphabetically. He'd worn a dark suit and tie, and stared directly into the photo with determination and intent.

Spencer Holt: newspaper editor; student government; debate team; to earn the Pulitzer Prize for International Reporting; Stanford University.

What happened to that dream, Spence? Have you replaced it, or are you still chasing it?

The doorbell rang, stirring Phoenix from his nap. "Go back to sleep." For once, he listened.

Checking the peephole, I recognized Jo on my porch. At least, I thought it was Jo.

CHAPTER 19

*T*HE '80S CALLED. THEY WANT *their hairstyle back.*
Like totally.

The thought sprang into my head, but friendship kept the words off my tongue.

"Wow. Your hair looks...It's really big." The shadows had lengthened but the sun was still bright enough to identify the misdemeanor masquerading as her hair. I stepped back, drawing the door open wider to let her into my home.

"I just asked for a wash and set." Jo's voice was so faint. Was she speaking to herself? Her movements as she crossed the threshold into my living room were uncertain as though she was on autopilot.

How had she navigated traffic on her way here? Oh, right. Peach Coast didn't have traffic, at least not compared to New York.

"What happened?" I put my arms around her shoulders and guided her to my overstuffed sofa on the left side of the room. The raspberry scent of the hairspray hit me from an arm's length away. I felt as though I'd plunged into a pitcher of fruit punch.

My palms itched to touch the raven sculpture to see if it felt as durable as it looked. The style was so different from Jo's usual long, vibrant ponytail. Her glossy hair was molded into a crown of tiny curls that added at least six inches to her five-foot-six-inch height. The rest of her hair was curled and teased into a mane that extended past her shoulders and hung almost to her waist. She looked like one of the cosmetology mannequins in Reba's display window come to life.

Jo's eyes were wide and unfocused. "She just kept spraying and spraying and spraying."

"Do you want to wash your hair?" I asked gently.

She turned wide, sorrowful eyes to mine. "Yes, please."

I took her upstairs and gave her two towels and my hair care products. They weren't tailored to her hair, but this was an emergency. "Take your time."

She took me at my word. About thirty-minutes later, she returned to the living room. Her hair was still damp, but it flowed over her shoulders and down her back, making her look almost like her old self. She charged into the living room with her usual energy.

I laughed, clapping my hands. "Welcome back!"

She exhaled. "It's good to be back. Thank you."

"I feel responsible for your traumatic experience." I offered the somber apology.

Jo settled onto the sofa across from the matching armchair Phoenix and I occupied. She lifted a hand and waved away my words. "I don't blame you. I should've left. But I wanted to ask Reba about Hank and Nelle."

I leaned forward. "What did you learn?"

Jo slumped back against the sofa. "I learned that people really open up to hairstylists. She got me to tell her a lot of things about me and Nolan. She asked questions about you and Spence, too."

I gaped at her. "What did you tell her?"

She shrugged. "That the two of you would make a great couple and I didn't understand what was taking you so long to realize it."

My heart stopped. The town was speculating about us while we were just friends. What kind of pressure would our relationship be under if we pursued something more? "Jo—"

She ignored my interruption. "Overall, I didn't learn as much as I'd hoped. We knew she blamed the news story for igniting the scandal that cost her the mayoral election, but when I asked her about it, she criticized the reporter, not Spence."

"Then why's Spence the one on the list?"

"Beats me." Jo threw up her hands. "She didn't have any quarrels with Hank at all. And she liked Nelle. If fact, they'd been friends since middle school. Nelle encouraged Reba to go into politics and was a huge supporter of her town council campaigns." Jo sniffed in disdain. "Reba said Nelle never let her do her hair. I bet that's why they were friends for so long."

I battled back a smile and gave Jo an empathetic look.

Through my research, I'd learned that Reba had spent two terms—a total of eight years—on the Peach Coast Town Council, rising from at-large member during her first term to town council president with her re-election. Impressive.

"It doesn't sound as though Reba could be the second half of our theoretical serial killer duo. She wouldn't agree to having anyone kill her friend and she didn't have a grudge against the coach." Ignoring Phoenix's frown, I shifted him from my lap and crossed to the fireplace.

"But Reba does have a suspicion about who *might* be holding a grudge."

"Who?" And why hadn't she started the story with the action?

"Philomena Fossey. She said Philomena believes Nelle was the reason she didn't get approved for a business loan. And I saw Philomena having dinner with Lucas Daniel on my way to my hair appointment tonight."

"Philomena and Nelle were arguing about a loan during the kickoff event." I set my hands on my hips as my thoughts raced. "And it's interesting how often Lucas shows up in our investigation. Now if we could just identify a motive or four."

"Rumor has it you're playing amateur sleuth. Is that true?" Lucas joined me on the line in On A Roll early Wednesday morning.

I turned to the interim head coach. He wore a Mother Mathilda blue wicking shirt and black track pants with double white strips down his pant legs. "Why are you asking?"

He shrugged, shifting his dark gaze to the menu behind me. The simple black acrylic sign displayed the café's items in metallic changeable white letters. Most people in Peach Coast didn't need to consult the menu. They either had it memorized like Dabney and Etta, or they always ordered the same thing, like me. But Lucas was new to town. I was willing to give him more time.

"Playing amateur sleuth is a risky game. Aren't you afraid you could get hurt, chasing after a killer?" His words were casual. Too casual? Was he threatening me?

The mouthwatering scents of strong coffee and sweet pastries had put me in a good mood. I'd play along. "Are you worried for my safety?"

Not waiting for his response, I stepped forward for my turn at the counter. Anna May's red T-shirt read, *Decaf? Don't Mocha Me Laugh.* She presented me with my doctored café mocha, a slice of peach cobbler to go, and a wink.

In return, I gave her exact change and a smile. I loved our morning ritual. "Thank you, Anna May." I moved aside while Lucas placed his order.

"Black coffee, please."

Anna May waited a beat. When he didn't add anything to his request, she set her hands on her full hips. Never a good sign. "That's it? Just coffee? Black?"

"Yes, please. Small." He pulled out his wallet in anticipation of payment.

I held my breath. Tension was building around Anna May like a pending tropical storm. Couldn't he sense it? I stepped back.

"You came here for a *small. Black. Coffee?*" She repeated his order. "Is your coffee pot at home broken or something?"

Lucas looked bewildered. "Excuse me?"

Anna May leaned forward over the counter, putting her almost nose to nose with Lucas. "I don't go to the trouble of getting out of bed and opening this café just to pour black coffee. That's not what gives my life meaning."

"But I—"

"I run a respectable café."

"Yes, but I—"

It was like watching a car collision in slow motion. I couldn't just stand there. "I bet Lucas would love a couple—no, three—of your delicious pralines."

He turned his frown on me. "I would?"

"Yes, you absolutely would." I gave him a pointed look.

Lucas got the signal. He turned back to Anna May. "Yes, I would. Absolutely. Three of them. Thank you." He paid for the order in advance, then accepted the coffee and treats. Anna May's expression was marginally warmer.

I led Lucas from the counter, paraphrasing his earlier comment to me. "Ordering only black coffee from On A Roll is a risky game."

"I've learned my lesson." He laughed, shaking his head as he walked with me to the exit. "Thank you for rescuing me. I owe you one."

I sobered. "Tell me why you moved four-hundred-and-twenty-eight-point-one miles from Raleigh to take an assistant coaching job you didn't want in Peach Coast, Georgia?"

He used his back to push through the exit door, balancing his coffee in one hand and his bag of pralines in the other. "I'm on your suspect list, aren't I?"

I searched his expression. "That doesn't offend you?"

His lips curved reluctantly. "If I were playing detective, *I'd* put me on the list. On the surface, I have motive. It's a stupid motive, but you're only *playing* detective. I don't know what the murder weapon was, so I don't know if I'd have means or opportunity, though."

I led him away from the customer traffic in the café's doorway. "So let's play. What would you say to clear your name?"

He smirked. "I don't have to explain myself to you."

A warm breeze perfumed with the salty scents of the nearby wetlands swept over me. "*You* approached *me* about the investigation."

He lowered his voice. "That's because if people think I'm a murderer because of your investigation, you'll cost me the head coaching job."

Now *I* was offended. "I'm *not* gossiping or spreading rumors. I'm just trying to find whoever's responsible for killing my friends."

His eye roll was uncalled for. "You'll notice I haven't been named Hank's replacement. Besides there are much less dramatic ways to get a head coaching job. And what would be my motive for killing Nelle Kenton?"

I started walking toward the library. The broad red brick sidewalk was sparsely populated with other pedestrians, which allowed us to walk beside each other. "I don't know. Perhaps jealousy? You were interested in a relationship with her but she rejected you in favor of Hank?"

At that, Lucas burst into laughter. Was he amused or simply mocking me?

He managed to control his hilarity. "You think I kill every woman who turns me down? That would be a lot of dead bodies. Someone would've noticed long before you came along."

"I'll take that into consideration." I assessed him out of the corner of my eye. He was attractive. I doubted he'd been turned down that often. Although, his personality could use some work.

"I'm not a murderer. Take me off of your list, and stay out of my business." He gave me a tight smile and a nod before turning away.

I watched him retrace his steps to the café. I never confirmed whether he was on my list. So why was he convinced he was?

CHAPTER 20

"TRUDIE, WHAT'S WRONG?" MY BROW furrowed as I searched the other woman's delicate features.

We'd run into each other in front of the library's entrance Wednesday afternoon on my way back from lunch with Spence. The brisk walk and summer-scented breeze had helped me collect my thoughts. Now Trudie's obvious distress had scattered them again. Her eyes were pink and shimmered with unshed tears. Her cheeks were flushed. She was almost vibrating with tension. I offered her the packet of facial tissues from my handbag.

Accepting it, she murmured her thanks and pulled a tissue from the pack. "I'm so embarrassed. I'm being ridiculous. Nolan dumped me. As a client, I mean."

This was unexpected. My eyes grew wide. I wasn't certain how to react. Of course I didn't like seeing anyone upset. At the same time, I wanted to applaud Nolan. He must've realized Trudie had feelings for him, which he didn't return. Why else would he end their business relationship? Under the circumstances, it seemed the kindest thing to do.

But my heart ached for Trudie. She looked miserable. "I'm sorry you're upset. Did he give you a recommendation for another accountant?"

Trudie returned the packet of tissues to me. "Someone in his office, but it won't be the same. He's been the accountant for my family's business for more than ten years. He knows the books better than anyone."

"And he'll be on hand to help if your new accountant has any questions." I squeezed her shoulder. "I'm sure everything will be fine."

Trudie's eyes scanned the landscaping, but I sensed she didn't see the Sugar Maples, dahlias, magnolias or sunflowers in the landscaping around us. "Do you think Jo Gomez told Nolan not to work with me anymore?"

My jaw dropped. "Of course not. Why would you think that?"

Trudie sighed, shaking her head. "I don't know. Maybe she's jealous of the time Nolan was spending with me."

I felt a spurt of irritation that she would blame my friend for Nolan's decision. "Nolan makes his own choices. I'm confident he didn't consult Jo before deciding not to work with your company any longer."

Trudie scanned my expression with narrowed eyes. "You're very protective of her. I heard you risked your life to help prove her innocence when the deputies suspected her of murder last month. She's lucky to have a friend like you."

"I'm lucky to have her friendship."

"You're good for this town." She smiled, turning toward the library's entrance. "I hope the deputies solve these cases soon. I don't like being by myself in my parents' huge house when there's a killer—or *killers*—on the loose. I'm thinking of hosting old friends for rotating sleepovers."

Her words reminded me of the yearbooks Cecelia had loaned me. "Speaking of old friends, I saw the high school's class of 2007 graduation photos. That was your class, wasn't it? But you weren't in any of the photos."

"My parents thought I'd do better at another school. So in 2006, despite my protests, they sent me to a boarding school." Her shrug was stiff as though she still bore at least some resentment.

I felt a twinge of empathy for the adolescent Trudie. "So you graduated with students you hadn't grown up with? That must've been hard."

"It wasn't easy." She gave me a rueful look. "But I'm back now. In some ways, it's like I've gone back in time. There're the same cliques and petty jealousies. Nelle and Philomena arguing at the kickoff was just like high school."

My face warmed with embarrassment that a guest had witnessed the disturbance. "Have they always had a contentious relationship?"

"They were jealous of each other all through high school. I don't know about after since I wasn't here. But Nelle liked a fight. She got into an argument with Lucas Daniel in the parking lot that same night."

Argumentative? Nelle? That didn't sound like her. "I hadn't heard about another argument. Did anyone else hear it?"

She spread her arms. "I was by myself, walking to my car. I didn't notice anyone else around, but I know what I heard. Nelle and Lucas were arguing."

Maybe she was exaggerating. But why? For attention? "What were they arguing about?"

She frowned as though trying to remember the exchange. "I didn't catch everything, but I heard Nelle threaten to take *it* to the sheriff."

I frowned. "What's *it*?"

Trudie spread her arms again. "I have no idea, but it sounded like Lucas was involved in something Nelle disapproved of."

"Did you tell the deputies what you'd heard?"

"No." Trudie's eyes widened as though the idea horrified her. "Honestly, I didn't hear enough of the conversation. This seems more like gossip than evidence."

"Trudie, this is a homicide investigation." I leaned closer, hoping to emphasize the urgency. "That information might help the deputies stop the killer."

"I'll think about it. Promise." She took a step back. "But I'd better let you get back to work."

I watched her stride toward the book stacks. Why was she reluctant to tell the deputies about Nelle's argument with Lucas? Unless she was lying. And why would she do that? But if she wasn't lying, was it possible Hank told Nelle about Lucas's NCAA violations?

There was one way to verify Trudie's story: Ask the librarians.

"Good morning, deputies. Did Nelle Kenton meet with you the week she was killed?" I ignored Jed's expected scowl as I entered the bullpen at the sheriff's department late Thursday morning. The scents of doughnuts and fresh coffee were more welcoming than he was.

The silver-haired deputy made a sound between a grunt and a growl. "Y'all must not be aware of our rule against discussing an open investigation. I coulda sworn I'd told you a time or ten, but I must not've been clear. What else would explain your constantly coming around here, asking about an investigation that's open?"

"Morning, Ms. Marvey." Errol stopped rocking his stationary desk seat. He stood to offer me a smile and a chair.

"Thank you, Deputy Cole." I settled onto it, crossing my legs and laying my handbag on my thigh. I held Jed's eyes. "You're stalled, aren't you?"

He gave me a stony stare in response.

"Why're you asking about Ms. Nelle, ma'am? What're you thinking?" Errol resumed rocking his desk chair. The action made me motion sick.

I returned my attention to Jed. "Trudie Trueman claims she overheard Nelle arguing with Lucas Daniel in the library parking lot the evening of the kickoff."

Errol exchanged an interested look with Jed. "And then Saturday, two days later, Ms. Nelle was murdered."

Jed leaned back against his seat, resting his right ankle on his left knee. Despite his relaxed pose, I sensed his increased attention. "She say what they were arguing about?"

"Nelle threatened to give sheriff's deputies information she had about him." I spread my hands. "Trudie said the two were shouting at each other. Nelle said she was going to take 'it' to the deputies. I didn't hear the argument. Neither did Viv, Floyd, or Adrian. But we were in the library on the other side of the building. Corrinne was near the entrance, thanking our guests. She'd heard raised voices, but the disagreement she heard didn't last long."

"Ms. Kenton didn't come to see me." Jed turned to Errol. "She speak with you?"

"No, JW." Errol looked from me to Jed. "Come to think of it, I wonder why Ms. Trudie didn't tell us about overhearing this argument herself?"

They both looked to me.

I held up my arms. "She thought it seemed more like gossip than evidence. But you could ask her about the argument. She might remember something else that could help."

Jed crossed his arms and shrugged. "Since Ms. Nelle didn't come see us, whatever 'it' was must not've been important after all."

Seriously? That was it? I clenched my fists around my purse as my disappointment and frustration built. "Then you can ask Lucas. He could tell you about his disagreement with Nelle. It might've had something to do with Hank."

"What makes you think that, Ms. Marvey?" Errol finally grounded his chair.

"Lucas had been fired from his previous job for NCAA violations. Hank found out. Maybe he told Nelle." I lowered my voice. "Maybe Nelle was suspicious about Lucas and accused him of killing Hank. She may even have had proof, which she threatened to take to the deputies. That could give Lucas motive for Hank's and Nelle's murders."

Jed scowled. "How d'y'all know all this?"

I shrugged. "Research."

Jed rolled his eyes. "Ms. Harris, we know how to do our jobs. We don't need you directing our investigation."

I held onto my patience with both hands. "I'm not directing you. I'm giving you information you didn't have before, hoping it will help identify the killer and keep Spence safe."

A shadow of uncertainty moved across Jed's face before his features settled back into his scowl. "We've already interviewed Lucas Daniel."

"But he didn't tell you about his argument with Nelle." I tightened my grip on my purse even more to keep from reaching over and shaking him. "He knew it would make him a suspect in her murder. That would give him a connection to both homicides. Why are you being so stubborn about speaking with him again?"

Jed grunted again. "How 'bout you do your job and I'll do mine?"

"How about it, deputy?" I adjusted my purse strap and marched out of the bullpen. If he wasn't going to do his job, I had no choice but to do it for him. Whatever it took to keep Spence safe. Granted, based on our last encounter, Lucas probably wouldn't speak with me. I had to try.

CHAPTER 21

I T WAS FOR TIMES LIKE this that I needed my car. I checked the time on my cellphone after leaving the sheriff's office Thursday. There was no way I'd be able to speak with Lucas at the high school and return to work in what was left of my hour-long lunch break. I didn't want to wait until the end of the day to meet with him, knowing interviewing him could save Spence's life. I needed to see him now. I called Corrinne to let her know I'd be late getting back to work.

It was a brief but pleasant exchange. Her unspoken message was clear: She didn't care how long my break was as long as I got my work done. Guilt over my inability to find a replacement lead donor increased. But Spence's life was more important.

By the time I got to the high school, I was perspiring. A lot. My ice blue short-sleeved blouse clung to my torso. June afternoons in Peach Coast were humid despite the intermittent breeze from the nearby wetlands. I wasn't looking forward to the walk back to the library.

I used the high school's main entrance, tossing a casual smile toward the custodians and administrators nearby and generally acting like I was supposed to be there. It took a few redirects to locate Lucas's office again via memory. My directional challenges weren't limited to driving. I often got turned around walking on the street. My parents believed it was because I was too impatient to get to my destination to pay attention to directions. That was as good a theory as any.

Outside of Lucas's office, I smoothed my blouse and used the back of my wrist to remove the perspiration collecting above my upper lip. I felt hot and sticky, which didn't do much for my confidence. I raised my fist to knock on his partially open door. Smooth jazz whispered across the threshold. Above the music, a cellphone rang with a tone similar to mine. I lowered my hand.

"Yeah, hi." Lucas's greeting sounded as though he was continuing a prior conversation. I couldn't see him and didn't want to risk moving closer to the door in case I gave myself away. Did he recognize the caller ID?

"I haven't spoken with anyone." His words were terse. Who was on the other end of the call?

"They didn't ask about it." He sounded dismissive. There was another pause as he seemed to listen. "I'm on my way. Give me ten minutes."

I swallowed a gasp. *Hide!*

Frantic, I looked up and down the empty hallway. It's not as though I could disguise myself in a crowd. School was out for the summer. The office behind me was locked. I sped down the hall and ducked around the corner. If Lucas came my way, I'd just have to Bogart it out.

Peeking around the corner, I witnessed him striding in the opposite direction. I closed my eyes briefly in relief, then followed. Where was he going? With whom was he meeting? And why? He referenced ten minutes. Was that a ten-minute walk or a ten-minute drive? If he got into his car, I was sunk.

To my relief, he bypassed the school's parking lot. I trailed him for two blocks to an outdoor restaurant. Philomena was waiting for him. *Aha!* Jo had seen Lucas and Philomena having dinner a few nights earlier. Was this a romantic entanglement—or a much more nefarious partnership?

I needed a place to hide that would still allow me to observe their meeting. I couldn't exactly blend in with the other patrons and pedestrians. Peach Coast wasn't nearly as diverse as Brooklyn. Spotting a boutique across the street, I hurried toward it, then slipped in to watch the couple from behind an arrangement of little black dresses in the display window.

"May I help you?" The saleswoman, a middle-aged redhead who looked like she'd stepped out of a clothing catalogue, offered an encouraging smile.

I matched her expression. "I'm just looking."

"Of course. Let me know if you have any questions." She crossed back to the counter and returned to the task she'd been working on before I arrived.

With one eye on the dresses—they were really cute— I kept the other on Lucas and Philomena. They were having a very animated conversation. Philomena was waving her arms and gesturing toward him. Lucas kept shaking his head and jabbing a thumb over his shoulder as though indicating the high school. If only I could hear them or even read their lips.

What are they saying?

I squinted and found myself leaning closer to the

display window. Catching myself, I looked over my shoulder at the saleswoman. She gave me a curious look, a faint smile, then looked away.

I turned back to the scene across the street in time to see Lucas stand, then shove a small paper bag toward Philomena. Shoulders slumped, she shook her head. She stood as she accepted the bag. They had one final exchange, then walked off in different directions.

What had they talked about? What was in the bag? And was any of this connected to the murders?

"Have you found anything you like?" The saleswoman asked.

After spending so much time in the shop and behaving so bizarrely, I couldn't just walk out. And these dresses really were cute. After a quick search through the rack, I discovered an attractive style in my size.

"Actually, I have." I plucked the garment from the rack and held it against me. "I'll take this one."

"Lucas Daniel met with Philomena Fossey about half an hour ago." I spoke with Spence via cellphone behind my closed office door. Then why was I whispering?

The pause that greeted my announcement made me wonder whether Spence had put his cell phone on his desk and walked away.

"How do you know that?" He finally spoke. His slow Southern drawl seemed more pronounced.

"I followed him."

Another significant pause. "You followed someone you suspect of being a serial killer?"

When he put it that way, I had second thoughts about my actions. "I took your advice and told the deputies about Trudie overhearing Lucas and Nelle arguing. Jed didn't think the tip was significant enough to re-interview Lucas or follow up with Trudie. So I decided to do it."

"Marvey, you can't do that." Spence's voice was taut with concern. "You can't confront a suspect on your own."

"But the deputies weren't going to do it."

"You agreed we'd investigate this case together." He'd gone from incredulous to annoyed. "You broke your promise to me."

Wow. That stung. I sat back on my chair and imagined Spence in his office. He was a pacer when he was agitated, just like me. We'd literally walked circles around each other before. Was he pacing now?

"That's not fair, Spence. I didn't make that promise. In fact, I told you it wouldn't be wise for you to accompany me to interview people who might want to kill you."

"Then you could've asked Jo to go with you." He exhaled a heavy breath. "She would've dropped everything to make sure you were safe."

He was right. Jo would've left the bookstore under one of her assistant manager's care while she'd accompanied me. And she drove to work. "It was a spur of the moment decision."

"That was reckless. And you're right. I *am* upset. I can't stand the idea of you being in danger."

"And I can't stand the idea of *you* being in danger." I was sorry to be the source of his upset, but I did what I had to do for his safety.

"How does your rashly charging into danger make the situation better? Hmm?" He prompted when I didn't answer.

I hated that I didn't have a sensible response to his question. "I don't need a protector, Spence."

He burst out laughing. It sounded genuine. "That's really funny coming from you. You launched your investigation to protect me. You think *I* need a protector but *you* don't?"

It was obvious he was referring to the fact that he was about a foot taller and at least fifty pounds heavier than me.

I sighed. "You'd have done the same thing, and you know it. If our roles were reversed, you'd be doing exactly what I'm doing."

He paused, seemingly unable to deny the truth of my words.

"I care about you, Marvey."

"I care about you too."

"No. Listen to me." His voice was low. He seemed to struggle with his words. "Neither one of us wants the other hurt—or worse. I'm doing my best to be careful so you don't worry unnecessarily. I need you to do the same."

Those words hit me harder than his failed attempts to chastise me. He was right. I wasn't being fair to him. He was putting up with my morning, noon, and night safety calls. The least I could do was be more rational in my investigation.

"You're right, Spence. I apologize. I was thoughtless."

He sighed again. "Thank you, Marvey. I appreciate your understanding. So, tell me what you've learned."

With our tense but needed exchange behind us, I explained what I heard, what I saw, and how I interpreted those behaviors.

"How big was the paper bag?" Spence asked.

"It seemed pretty small." I considered my palm and extended fingers. "Maybe a little larger than my hand. But my perspective may be skewed because I saw it from across the street. And, of course, I have no idea what was in it or whether any of this is connected to Hank's or Nelle's murders."

"But if we put it in context of your theory of two people working together, it's an interesting development." Spence sounded as though he was mulling over this information.

"I hope to add his meeting with Philomena to the other questions I want to ask Lucas—when Jo and I interview him."

"Good." There was a smile in his voice. "And I'll be safe at home, waiting patiently for your update."

I rolled my eyes. "That's spreading it a little thick."

We ended our call, then I selected Jo's personal number. I needed to let her know about her new plans for the evening.

"I thought you'd been to Lucas Daniel's office before? *Twice* before." Jo stopped me with her hand on my arm as I turned to once again retrace my steps down the high school's second floor hallway after work Thursday evening.

"It's coming back to me. Just be patient." I led her

back to the main hallway. "There aren't that many offices to check."

"He's expecting us at five. Tonight," she groused. "You really have the worst sense of direction."

"Tell me something I don't know."

"Marvey, are you sure we should be doing this? Suppose Lucas is the killer?"

I stopped to face her. "I'm nervous too, but Spence is in danger. If our questions seem to agitate him, we'll back off."

"All right." She still sounded as nervous as I felt.

I turned down another side hallway. This looked familiar. "What did you say to get him to meet with us?"

Jo shrugged. "I told him I wanted to carry bookmarks promoting the boys basketball schedule. He seemed interested."

I frowned at her beside me. "That's it? How'd you know that would work?"

"Oh, please." She gave me a dry look. "It plays to his ego."

"You're good. And here we are."

Jo knocked on the door. At Lucas's invitation, she led us into his office.

The coach's welcoming smile faded, becoming quizzical when he noticed me. He turned to Jo. "Did you set me up?"

I lifted my right hand, palm up. "I asked her to. I apologize, but I need to ask a couple of questions. Please."

Lucas stood over me, arms crossed. "I've already spoken with you, and I've given a statement to the deputies. How much talking do I have to do before you remove me from your list?"

"This isn't a game, Lucas. I'm trying to save lives; lives that are very important to me. And you may have information critical to the investigation." As I continued to hold his gaze, I sensed him relax by degrees.

Finally, he gestured toward the blond wood chairs in front of his desk. "Ask."

I settled onto the narrow, blue cushioned seat closest to the beige wall, leaving the one on the end for Jo.

A quick scan of his cramped office revealed details of a long and successful amateur sports career. His shelves and walls displayed awards, framed news clips, and trophies he'd received as a player and a coach. He'd participated in multiple events, including basketball, track and field, and swimming. His book case also displayed beautiful sculptures of people, animals, and vases. The collection reminded me of the book he'd purchased during the library's book swap. Had he made those pieces?

I returned my attention to Lucas, studying his expression and body language. So far, he seemed relaxed and somewhat resigned. I decided to ease into our interrogation. "Have you and Philomena Fossey known each other long? I noticed you having lunch together earlier today."

He frowned, shifting his attention between me and Jo. "What does that have to do with Hank's or Nelle's murders?"

I tried a nonchalant shrug. "I was just surprised. I didn't think you'd known anyone before moving here two months ago."

Without taking his eyes from mine, Lucas gestured to the bookcase behind him. His response snapped with impatience. "Mena's agreed to sell my sculptures in her souvenir shop."

Mena? How close were they?

I looked again at the shelves behind him. "You're very talented."

"Yes," Jo agreed. "They're very beautiful."

He grunted. "Thank you."

It didn't bode well for the rest of our interview if he was this snippy when answering questions about his lunch with a friend. I took a deep breath and moved on. "Had you noticed whether Hank seemed distracted or concerned about anything before he was killed?"

Lucas's sigh seemed resigned. He rested his right ankle on his left knee and slouched back on his chair. "As I told the deputies, Hank had seemed preoccupied. I kept having to repeat things. It was annoying."

"Did you ask what was bothering him?" Jo crossed her legs. She leaned closer to his desk as though she didn't want to miss a word.

"No, I thought he'd straighten himself out. I guess he ran out of time." Lucas let his gaze slide from Jo's as though he was ashamed he hadn't done more to help his colleague. There may not have been anything more he could've done.

I shook off my own regrets and exchanged a look with Jo. *Get ready.* "Is it possible he was distracted by your history of NCAA violations?"

Blood drained from his features. His jaw dropped. Then just as quickly, his face filled with color and his lips thinned. "How do you know about that?"

"Research." He didn't need to know what type or that it wasn't my own. He was still slouched on his seat. He was angry, but I didn't feel threatened. Jo didn't seem nervous either. "Did Hank confront you about the violations?"

Lucas narrowed his eyes, glaring at me. He was silent for several beats. I was beginning to think he wouldn't answer when he finally spoke. "You really are nosy, aren't you?"

I held his eyes. "Is that what you told Hank?"

He blew out a breath. Pulling his chair under his desk, he straightened his posture. "Hank wanted to know if the board knew. They do. The past has a way of catching up with you. Like Hank, I was coaching at my high school alma mater. After they fired me, I applied for head coaching jobs with other high schools in the area. Everyone wanted me, until they found out about my violations. Then it was, 'Don't let the door hit you on your way out.' So this time, I was upfront. The board hired me, but with a longer probationary period."

Jo's voice was breathless. "Did Hank believe you?"

Lucas shrugged his broad shoulders under his Mother Matilda blue short-sleeved jersey. "Yes. It's the truth."

And easily verified. Spence had friends on the school board. "Do you think he told Nelle?"

Irritation glittered in his eyes. He fidgeted on his chair. "How should I know?"

"The night of the library's kickoff, you had an argument with Nelle in the parking lot. What was it about?"

He shook his head, furrowing his brow. "We didn't argue."

I looked at Jo before returning to him. "Someone heard you arguing with her after the event."

His confusion cleared. "*We* hadn't been arguing. Nelle was upset, but not with me."

My eyebrows knitted. "Then with whom?"

"That's the thing. She didn't know." He shrugged broad shoulders under his navy blue wicking jersey with the school logo. "Someone had broken into her home and left a pennant behind. She'd asked me if the school had any more like them. I think she was trying to figure out where it came from. I didn't know anything about it."

"A pennant?" My voice was thin as shock rolled over me. I glanced over at Jo. She was staring at Lucas. Her body was as still as a statue. "Did she show it to you? What did it look like?"

"Yeah, she had it with her." Lucas spread his hands above his cluttered desk. "It was old, an outdated version of our school pennant. It was blue and orange, and in navy blue text, it read, 'School Spirit.' I think Hank had one, but as far as I know, they aren't in circulation anymore. I couldn't help her. She was going to take it to the sheriffs. You should ask them."

A chill raced down my spine. The description matched the pennant Brittany had found in her store. The deputies had found a similar one near Hank's body, but since they hadn't found one at Nelle's crime scene, they'd assumed it wasn't significant. They'd been wrong. Very wrong. Each victim had received one before he or she had been poisoned.

What was the connection to the pennant?

CHAPTER 22

E ARLY FRIDAY MORNING, I STOOD at my desk in my library office. My hands were fisted in the pockets of my slate gray slacks as I contemplated the plain sheet of paper centered on its surface. It hadn't been there when I'd left last night. I'd have remembered it. The note printed in black type on plain white paper reminiscent of the hit list read, "You and Spence looked good together at the cocktail party. It would be just as easy to kill both of you as it would be to kill one. Mind your business or you'll be added to the list."

I swallowed again to ease the dryness in my throat. My heart pounded against my chest in equal parts anger and fear. This threat had taken advance planning. The serial killer had figured out a way to break into the library and my office to deliver a message intended to scare me into dropping the investigation. I was definitely frightened. But to go to that much trouble meant they were afraid also. I had to be getting close.

Jed scooped the note from the desk with a gloved hand and dropped it into an evidence bag. "We'll see if we get any prints off this and whether they match the ones from the list of names we have."

Fortunately, I'd taken a photo of the note with my cellphone before I'd called the sheriff's office. I scowled at the evidence bag as I rounded my desk. That note wasn't going to stop me from protecting Spence. I pulled my fists from my pockets and pressed them against my hips.

In addition to Jed and Errol, two younger deputies had arrived with crime scene kits. They'd printed the other librarians and I for exclusionary samples. Now they were dusting my door, chair, and desk. I didn't have much hope of their turning up anything. A killer with the talent to slip in and out of the library's locked doors would've worn gloves. Still there had to be some-thing—some small clue—from this event that could help advance our investigation. I just had to recognize it.

I joined the other librarians who were observing the activity in my office with various reactions. Floyd was offended someone had trespassed our hallowed halls. Corrinne was troubled by the apparent ease with which the break-in had occurred. Viv tracked my every move as though concerned someone would appear from thin air to harm me. Adrian's head swiveled around as though afraid to miss a moment of this unexpected drama. Had I mentioned I was concerned about him?

The librarians closed ranks around me as we faced Jed and Errol. Viv rested her hand on my shoulder. Her touch was comforting and bracing. I was grateful for both.

"Are y'all sure you locked up last night?" Jed stroked his upper lip as he scrutinized each of us in turn.

Corrinne clasped her hands in front of her and repeated her earlier answer in an even tone. "I was the last to leave yesterday. I assure you, Deputy Whatley, I checked all the doors and offices on my way out."

I nodded my confirmation. "And I was the first one in this morning. The entrance was locked when I arrived. So was my office."

"Are any of y'all missing keys?" Errol looked up from his notepad. We shook our heads. He continued. "Ms. Marvey, did you notice if the lock'd been tampered with?"

I spread my arms. "No, but I wasn't paying close attention."

Jed's grim gray eyes surveyed the surroundings again. "Are you sure nothing's missing?"

I roamed the close confines of my office, weaving round the librarians and the deputies as I studied my desk and scanned my file cabinets, shelves, and bookcase.

"I'm certain. Everything appears to be here, although I don't keep anything of value in my office." Besides photos of my family and my emergency bag of chocolate-covered peanuts. "And I believe the only reason the killer came to my office was to deliver that threat in the most invasive and threatening manner they could." And they'd succeeded. I couldn't suppress a shiver.

Errol gestured toward the door with his pen. "Did y'all happen to notice if anything in the main area had been disturbed or's missing?"

My four colleagues exchanged looks while shaking their heads.

Corrinne wrapped her arms around her waist. "It doesn't appear to be, but we'll do a thorough search and let you know whether we discover anything."

Errol gave her a comforting smile. "That would be real helpful, Ms. Corrinne. Thank you."

Corrinne's offer triggered a thought. I waved a hand toward my desk. "I don't think this is significant, but papers from one of the project folders on my desk were disturbed."

"Which project?" Errol asked.

"The Summer Solicitation Drive." I shrugged. "I don't know why the killer would be interested in our list of donors."

"Like you said, it's probably not significant." Jed held the evidence bag with the note aloft. "I warned you not to get involved in this investigation."

I unclenched my teeth. "Is 'I told you so' the most constructive response you can offer right now?"

"We don't have the resources to protect Spencer Holt, Brittany Wilson, *and* you." Jed lowered the bag. "I don't suppose this note has made you come to your senses and convinced you to leave the investigation to us."

Gripping my hands together, I struggled to keep the anger from my voice. "Deputy Whatley, tomorrow will be two weeks since Nelle's murder. Hank had been murdered two weeks before her. If the serial killer sticks to a pattern, either Spence or Brittany will be harmed tomorrow. So no, that note has not convinced me to mind my business. Spence's safety *is* my business."

I didn't want to stand here talking about the killer's timetable. I wanted to *do* something.

But what?

The darkness in Jed's gray eyes eased and appeared to be replaced by grudging respect. I could have been hallucinating, though. I hadn't yet had my third cup of coffee.

"Don't you worry about Mr. Spence and Ms. Brittany, Ms. Marvey." Errol sounded so earnest. "I'll do extra patrols of their houses myself."

"Y'all just about done there?" Jed snapped over his shoulder at the two younger deputies. They'd stopped packing their evidence kits and were gaping at us with identical expressions of wide-eyed interest.

At Jed's order, masquerading as an inquiry, the deputies collected their kits and hurried from the room. They each gave me a lingering look as though I was one of the specimens they were gathering from the crime scene.

Errol closed his notepad. "If there's nothing else, ma'am—"

I held up my right index finger. "There's one thing. Based on the message, I think we can take June Bishop permanently off of our suspect list."

Jed interrupted. "What makes you think Ms. Bishop was on our list?"

I arched an eyebrow at the contrarian. "I like June too. But either way, I'm now convinced she's not the killer."

"Why's that?" Adrian asked.

I turned my attention to him. "In the message, the killer references seeing Spence and me at the kickoff. They called it the cocktail party. June wasn't at the event, remember? She'd RSVP'd but then one of her employees was ill, so she'd had to deliver the flowers to the wedding he was going to work. If she'd written the note, she wouldn't have made a reference like that."

Floyd nodded. "Good point."

"It's as though the killer wanted you to know they'd

been watching you that night." Viv squeezed my shoulder before dropping her arm.

I saw the flash of fear in her eyes. I'm certain she saw mine. "Exactly. They wanted to emphasize the threat in their message."

June and Delores were cleared, but Lucas, Philomena, and Reba were still on the list. I wasn't even close to identifying the killer—or killers—and there was only twenty-four hours to go.

"You have to stop investigating." Spence's response had been expected. This was a replay of the argument we'd had yesterday afternoon when I'd told him I'd followed Lucas.

It's the reason I'd dreaded sharing this latest update with him. We were having lunch with Jo and Nolan at the conference table in his office Friday afternoon. The room smelled like fried chicken and gumbo, but the mouthwatering aromas didn't affect me because the other three people in the room were angry with me. My tension made everything taste like wood.

I could disregard Jed when he ordered me to leave crime solving to the professionals because there was too much at stake. But it was harder to ignore friends, especially when one of those friends was the reason for my investigation.

"We've already been through this." I strove for a reasonable tone when all I wanted to do was pull my hair out. Everything in my life seemed to be moving in circles: our disagreement, this investigation, and re-placement options for the lead library donor.

"That was before you received a direct threat to your life." Spence's voice was tense as though he also was striving to sound reasonable. "Obviously, we need to discuss it again."

"All right. Consider it discussed." I returned to my Italian sub. This might be what woodchips on a toasted whole grain bun taste like.

"Marvey, it's not safe." He gestured toward my cell phone on which was the photo of the anonymous note.

"Spence has a point." Jo was hesitant. She seemed torn between protecting one friend over another. "You've brought all of your information to the deputies. Let them do the physical investigation. We'll focus on keep-ing Spence safe."

"That's a good idea." Nolan looked at Spence. "You can stay with me until the deputies find the killer."

Spence appeared caught off guard. "Thank you, No-lan, but I don't want to impose on you."

I added my support of Nolan's solution. "Thanks, Nolan. I'd feel better knowing Spence wasn't alone."

Jo interrupted. "And Marvey, you and Phoenix should stay with me. Someone broke into the *locked* library, then into your *locked* office to leave a threat on your desk. It's not safe for you to be on your own, either."

Her offer warmed my heart. Jo was more than a friend. She was my sister from another mother. "I ap-preciate that but unlike the library, I have an alarm system. I'll be safe at home."

"All right. If you're sure." She didn't seem happy with my decision, though.

I turned to Spence. "You should consider getting an alarm system. In the meantime, I'm certain your mother will be relieved to know you're staying with Nolan until the serial killer is captured."

Jo packed up the remnants of her lunch. "I wish we knew how long that'll take. Considering how stubborn Jed's being about the information you've brought him, it could take weeks. Or months."

I groaned. "We don't have that kind of time."

Spence gave me a pointed look. "If we continue this investigation, it has to be a group effort."

"I agree." I swept my gaze over Spence's conference table. "We're dealing with a remorseless killer. No one should confront any of the suspects on their own."

Nolan turned to me. "What's our next move?"

I was reluctant to admit the truth. "I don't know, but we have to stay alert. If the killer sticks to their apparent routine, someone's going to be in harm's way tomorrow."

CHAPTER 23

"**M**ARVEY? IS THAT YOU?" PHILOMENA'S voice stopped me.

I turned to face her on the walkway leading to the library's front door. I'd been deep in thought after lunch with Spence, Jo, and Nolan. It took me a moment to adjust to addressing one of the suspects of the investigation we'd just been talking about.

"Hi, Philomena. Are you coming in?" I noticed the two books she carried in the crook of her right arm.

She smiled. "Yes. I like to stock up on library books for the weekend."

"I'm happy to hear that." Pulling the door open, I allowed her to proceed me.

"I'm so glad I saw you." She led me to a relatively deserted section of the book stacks. "I wanted to apologize for causing a scene during the library's fundraiser kickoff."

A perfect opening! Hold on. Hadn't I just promised Spence, Jo, and Nolan not to confront suspects on my own? But Philomena had approached me. What was

I supposed to do, walk away? I was safe here in the library.

That was my story, and I was sticking to it when I gave them my update later today. "That was a pretty heated argument. And it was over a business loan?"

She pressed a hand to her chest over her pink and blue patterned blouse. Her laugh was forced. "Obviously, Nelle and I have never been friends. I'm just sorry the last memory I have of her alive is of our exchanging cross words. I hope it didn't give you the wrong impression."

"What do you mean?" I gave her a questioning look.

She glanced around the stacks as though reassuring herself we couldn't be overheard. "I mean, I hope you don't think I had anything to do with Nelle's *murder*. But then, I read in the *Crier* that the deputies think Nelle's and Hank's deaths are connected. What do *you* think?"

I think you have more explaining to do.

"If the deputies believe the cases are connected, they're probably connected. Philomena, I'm sorry about Hank. I heard the two of you dated for a while. How are you?"

Philomena waved away the question. "Hank and I were over months ago. He was never the settling-down type. But you know a woman has to find that out on her own."

"I have a feeling he and Nelle could've made a go of it. They'd dated in high school, didn't they? He must've been carrying a torch for her all these years." I searched Philomena's features for even the slightest reaction to my comments. Had she really moved on after her breakup with Hank as she wanted me to believe? Or did she feel like a woman scorned? She didn't respond to my comments. Perhaps she was telling the truth about her and Hank.

"Hmmm." She gave me a speculative look. "The deputies questioned me a couple of days after your event. I couldn't give them much, though. You didn't tell them about our tiff, did you? I mean, not that it would've mattered." She shrugged a shoulder, shifting her feet. "I just don't want the deputies getting the wrong impression."

Or was it the right one?

"What made you think Nelle blocked your loan application? She was in charge of corporate giving. She didn't have anything to do with loans."

Perhaps the argument was motive enough for Philomena to poison Nelle. And perhaps a woman scorned would poison Hank. But why kill Spence? Even if she was working with Lucas, why would either of them want to kill Spence?

Her lips tightened. Anger rolled off of her like waves from the ocean. "Nelle had always been jealous of me. She can't stand the idea of my success. She probably lost her mind, thinking of me expanding my shop. That's why she smeared me to the loan officers who turned down my application. I wasn't her only victim. She had a reputation for doing that type of thing."

I adjusted the strap of my handbag across my chest. "You and Nelle had been rivals since high school? It must've upset you when Hank asked her out after breaking up with you."

Philomena stepped back as though I'd threatened her. "If you're going to point the finger at anyone for murder, you should take a look at Reba McRaney. Hank dated her *before* me. And she has a temper. Yeah, I'd look at her for Hank's and Nelle's murders and anyone else's."

With that, Philomena flounced to the book return counter before pivoting on her heels and disappearing deeper into the stacks. I tracked her progress. Ice sped down my spine.

I'd look at her for Hank's and Nelle's murders and anyone else's.

How had she known other people were being targeted—unless she was the killer?

"We're moving Lucas off of the main suspect list." I was meeting with the librarians in my office at the end of the day Friday to review the investigation.

"Why? His wanting to keep his NCAA violations secret was the strongest motive for killing Hank and Nelle." Floyd looked frustrated.

I shared his pain. "Spencer spoke with a friend on the school board who confirmed Lucas had told them about the violations. They were impressed by his candor—and his qualifications—so they hired him, but with a longer probationary period, just as he'd said."

"And poison's typically a woman's method of murder," Adrian reminded us.

Floyd inclined his head. "There's that."

"We've removed Ms. Delores, Ms. June, and Mr. Lucas from our main list." Adrian counted off our suspects with his fingers. "That just leaves us with Ms. Philomena and Ms. Reba."

"I think we should remove Reba from the main list

too." Viv looked at us seated around the small conference table. Her dark eyes were clouded with concern.
"She'd been close friends with Nelle for years. I don't
think she'd get involved in a scheme that would hurt
her."

We crossed Reba off our lists.

"That leaves us with only Philomena." I tapped my
pen against the sheet of paper.

Adrian's expression was hopeful. "I ran into Ms.
Philomena the other day at the pharmacy. She said
she's had dry-eye syndrome ever since she had the cor-
rective vision surgery."

"That's an important tip." I made a note of that on
my suspect list. "She was also very concerned about
whether I'd told the deputies of her argument with
Nelle."

Viv tapped her copy of the list. "But what connects
her to Spence and Brittany?"

I stared at the dwindling list. It lay in my manila case
folder on top of other lists, notes, copies of important records, and printouts of Internet searches. We'd started
with five names and motives we'd considered viable.
After additional research, follow-ups, and consultations,
we were down to one suspect and her reasons for committing murder seemed shaky at best.

"We've already lost two good people." Viv's voice was
soft and unsteady. "I don't want to lose even one more."

"Neither do I." Floyd offered grim agreement.

A short silence followed. Then Adrian cleared his
throat. "How do we find more suspects?

That question had driven us since the beginning of
our investigation. "Have you found anything notable in
the high school papers?"

Between Brittany's 2006 and Spence's 2008 editions, we had thirty-four high school newspapers to review, averaging sixteen pages per issue. At the time, the papers had been distributed electronically to students, faculty, administration, and staff. Fortunately, Brittany and Spence had saved the editions for which they'd been editor onto jump drives and stored them in their versions of keepsake boxes. I'd printed every file and given four issues each to Floyd, Viv, Adrian, Spence, Jo, Nolan, and Brittany. I'd taken the remaining six.

My editions were a mix of 2006 and 2008. I'd reviewed seven of the issues. So far, the most controversial story I'd come across was one Brittany had written about the growing discontent among teachers who believed coaches were placing athletics above academics. But why would that article be a motive for murder fifteen years later, and how did it connect to Hank, Nelle, and Spence?

"There's an ambitious series exploring the interests of different groups of students, Athletes, Scholars, and Recluses." Viv flipped through her folder for the copy. She offered it to me. "The reporter is Hank Figg and he's pretty tough on the Recluses. Maybe it's worth looking into?"

"Maybe." I skimmed the article before passing it to Adrian. It didn't seem promising. "I also want to research Trudie Truman. She's very concerned about Hank's and Nellie's murders, but she didn't tell the deputies about the conversation she'd overheard between Nellie and Lucas. Something about that bothers me."

Adrian frowned. "She's only been back a coupla months. Taking over her family's business has kept her busier than a one-legged woman in a butt-kicking contest. She's in Anna May's café every Saturday with piles of papers everywhere."

Floyd spread his hands. "She didn't graduate from Mother Mathilda."

"You both make good points, and Trudie seems very nice." I held onto my book pendant. The image was the original cover of Terry McMillan's *Waiting to Exhale*. Ms. McMillan's name appeared in bold blue letters against a black background, and the four women were illustrated in vibrant orange, yellow, green, and blue. "But I'd feel better if we checked into her. There's too much at stake not to."

"I called Brittany this afternoon to check on her." I slipped into the blue University of Florida sweater Jo offered as I followed her into her office at To Be Read Friday evening.

"Did you tell her about your concern an attack might be planned for tomorrow?" Jo took her seat behind her faux wood desk surrounded by University of Florida Gator paraphernalia.

"I wish I had." I massaged the back of my neck, trying to ease the knotted muscles. What more could I do to protect Spence—and Brittany? "I did stress the need for her to remain vigilant. But I called the deputies to remind them. Who knows if Jed will take me any more seriously this time?"

"I bet he will." Jo threw herself back against her chair. "You've been right about everything so far: the list; the connection to the high school. I'm working Saturday, but call me if you need help with surveillance or something. I'm sure Nolan would be available to help, too."

"Perfect!" I'd originally planned to stick to Spence like his shadow. New plan. "Nolan can stay with Spence while you and I continue the investigation. Fortunately, the killer doesn't know we've identified the poison, but we don't know how they plan to get the poison to Spence."

"You know, Marvey, part of the reason Spence's so upset about this case is he really cares about you." Jo's intense stare seemed to reach into my mind. "That threat against you rattled him. I've known him for years and I've never seen him like that. I'm scared for you, too."

My throat grew tight. I didn't want my friends to be afraid for me, and I didn't want to be afraid. Every day, Spence was becoming more important to me. The threat of something happening to him was by far my greatest fear.

"Please don't think I'm not taking that message seriously. I'm being careful and taking precautions." Including working at home instead of staying late at the library. I'd packed my fundraiser project binder into my tote bag. I was going to work on my donor consortium pitch within the safety of my home security system.

Some of my neighbors looked askance at the security company's sign in my yard. I wanted to shrug and say, "Overprotective parents." Instead, I smiled. That added security already had proven useful. *Thanks, Mom and Dad.*

"Good." Jo grabbed one of her blue Gator stress balls and squeezed it between her palms. Her fingernails were neatly shaped. She hadn't bitten them in quite some time. Was that Nolan's influence? "If anything happened to you, Spence would never forgive himself."

I blew an impatient breath. "If anything happened to him, I'd never forgive myself if I hadn't done everything I could to stop this serial killer."

Jo raised her eyebrows and gave me a side look. "But the two of you are still in the friend zone."

"What about you and Nolan?" I gathered the blue Gator sweater more tightly around me. Jo was wearing the orange one. Neither sweater would be necessary if she'd just turn down the fan in her office. "Watching the two of you circling each other is painful."

"He does like me, doesn't he?" Jo's cheeks flushed.

"Yes, he does. So...?" I struggled to hold back a smile.

"We're getting there." Her brown eyes sparkled with anticipation. "It's a work in progress."

"Urgh." I pressed my fists into my eyes. "Painful."

"Stop it!" Jo laughed. "I want you to admit your relationship with Spence has romantic elements. Go on."

"All right. I'm still breathing so, yes, I've had romantic thoughts about Spence and me. Who wouldn't? He checks all the boxes: smart, funny, kind, ambitious—"

"*Fine,*" Jo sang.

"Very." I chuckled. "But you know I'm a private person. And Spence is the Prince of Peach Coast. If we started dating, I think all the attention and speculation would put a strain on our relationship. I'm not made for a royal romance."

Jo's eyebrows strained up her forehead. Her grunt was very Floyd-esque. "If you ask me and three-quarters of the women in this town, Spencer Holt's worth the aggravation of love in the limelight."

"Good one." I smiled at her alliteration. "More and more, I'm feeling that way too. But we got some news yesterday about the library." I drew a deep breath. "If this year's fundraiser isn't successful, I could be out of a job next year."

"What?" Jo's jaw dropped. She straightened in her chair. Her eyes searched mine for evidence I was lying. She didn't find any. "Marvey, I'm so sorry."

"So am I." I tried to curve my lips into a smile. When they trembled, I gave up. "I don't think I should start a romantic relationship with someone if I'm not certain I'll be here in a year."

"I understand, but maybe Spence would be willing to move with you."

I shook my head in disbelief. "I can't see that. He loves this town."

Spence had lived in other cities, including New York, but I couldn't imagine him anywhere else. He was so important to the town and the town meant so much to him.

"We know he cares about the town, but we're concerned he might not want to stay. People have noticed that he gets restless."

"His mother's here. His roots are here, and he's running a successful newspaper and several profitable businesses here."

Jo spread her arms. "He didn't come home because of those companies. He was successful in Chicago. He came home because his father got sick. After his father passed, he seemed restless again."

My heart broke all over again for Spence and Cecelia's loss. "It's understandable he'd be withdrawn after his father's death. They were very close. I'm sure if Spence didn't want to be here, he would've left by now."

"You're right." Jo nodded. "People in town just want Spence to be happy, and since you've moved here, he's the happiest we've ever seen him."

I loved this town and my feelings for Spence were growing. But could I commit to a future here without knowing whether my career was secure?

CHAPTER 24

"A S MUCH AS LITTLE CLAY has enjoyed daycare, he's excited to start preschool next year." My mother laughed as she concluded the latest anecdote in her Adventures of My Grandson Chronicles. Something told me my four-year-old nephew, Clayton, was going to be "Little Clay" until he had children of his own—or perhaps the rest of his life.

I loved these Friday evening chats with my parents as much as I enjoyed catching up with them Saturday mornings and Sunday afternoons. Still, I couldn't wait to visit with them.

After dinner, Phoenix spread out on the sofa, and I settled into my navy blue recliner. The cloud-soft cushions welcomed me. Considering a serial killer was still running loose in Peach Coast, I felt guilty being so relaxed—and keeping the threats against me from my parents.

I hurried to break the silence before Mom and Dad noticed it. "It sounds like Clay enjoyed his surprise visit from his grandma."

"I don't know about Clay, but it was definitely

the highlight of your mother's day." Dad's tone was indulgent.

Mom laughed. I imagined her squeezing Dad's hand as it rested beside her on the sofa. "Now tell us about your day. Have you found a donor to replace that thoughtless banker?"

Stress rushed back, tightening every muscle in my torso. I went down the mental checklists of companies I'd contacted versus those I still needed to approach. I had a long list of *no* and only a handful of businesses left to try. My parents didn't know what was at stake if I couldn't find a new lead donor. I hoped that conversation wouldn't be necessary.

When I'd first told my parents about Malcovich Savings and Loan dropping out of the fundraiser, Mom had gone on a tirade over what she'd labeled the bank's "unprofessional" and "untrustworthy" actions. I was tempted to have her call them. That fantasy conversation restored my good humor.

"I haven't found a replacement yet." I pushed back on the recliner, activating its footrest. "I need to think outside the box."

There was a pause as though my parents were considering my words. From outside came the sounds of evening traffic and neighbors socializing on their front stoops.

Dad finally spoke. "Which is more important to you, having a big-name donor like the bank or investment company, or reaching your fundraising goal?"

Mom hummed. "That's a good question."

Yes, it was. "Without a doubt, it's much more important I achieve my fundraising target."

"Then redesign your strategy based on meeting that goal," Dad advised.

Frustration started to creep in again. "That's the problem. My strategies aren't working. I'm appealing to their civic duty, their commitment to education, their position as community leaders. Nothing's working."

"You've said yourself you need to think outside of the box." If Mom's response was meant to encourage, it wasn't quite working.

I pushed my way out of the recliner and stood to pace. Phoenix stirred himself to acknowledge me before returning to his nap. "I just need one big donor, but several of these companies have already donated as much as they can—" I froze. "But what if I replaced that one big donor with a group—a consortium—of smaller donors?"

Excitement pushed me away from the bookcase and into my dining room. "Like you said, Dad, meeting my goal is what's most important. Not whether the donor is a high-profile company."

"I didn't actually say that, honey. You—"

"You guys, that's a great idea." I hadn't meant to interrupt. My enthusiasm carried me away. "If I could convince even one of the smaller companies to back this idea, I could then leverage their commitment to appeal to other companies to join the consortium."

My mother spoke slowly as though baffled. "This wasn't our idea, Marvey. It was yours."

Her words confused me. "I would never have come up with it without you. I'm going to start a list of companies to approach. I have a feeling Corrinne's going to love it. Thanks so much. You two are the best. Love you!"

After disconnecting the call, I spread my project papers and memos across my dining room table and got to work strategizing this Hail Mary for the library.

"How do you want to handle this?" Jo had parked her orange compact sedan in the Shoreline Souvenirs' parking lot near the pier Saturday afternoon. Her owning an orange car showed how much she loved her Florida Gators. My sitting in her orange car showed how much I loved her.

The store had opened at 10 a.m., a little more than three hours ago. From the passenger seat beside Jo, I'd spent the past almost thirteen minutes monitoring the thin but steady stream of customers who strolled through its wooden double doors. The clientele was young and old, male and female, residents I recognized and those who appeared to be tourists.

The one-story, cottage-style structure had a fairytale charm. Asphalt shingles crowned its white oak façade. Three flint stone steps led to its wraparound porch. Large pane picture windows flanked the entry doors. Its lush landscaping included sugar maple trees, big bluestem, black-eyed Susans, and white sage. I scanned the area for battalions of tinker fairies and seven industrious dwarves whistling while they worked.

Dragging my attention from the shop, I considered Jo's question. "The one thing we know Hank, Nelle, Brittany, and Spence have in common is that they worked on the high school paper."

"Spence wasn't on the paper with them, though."

"Philomena was." I stared through the windshield again as I played with my book pendant. I was wearing the one with the image of Dr. W.E.B. DuBois's *The Souls of Black Folk*. I used the cover of the version on my bookcase. It was black with an image of the author in the upper-right corner. His surname appeared in white text in prominent cursive letters on the left.

Jo frowned. "I didn't find anything in those four issues you gave me that would incite someone to commit murder fifteen years later. Did anyone else?"

"No." I sighed. "But let's start with the papers and see where it takes us."

Jo and I crossed the threshold, blending in with a handful of other shoppers. The store was bigger on the inside than I'd expected. It took us a few minutes to locate Philomena as we wound our way around displays of Peach Coast-themed T-shirts, crafts by local artisans, and tourist guides and postcards.

She noticed our approach. "Marvey. Jo. This is a surprise. Can I help you find anything in particular?"

I glanced at Jo. "I was hoping to find more information on Mother Mathilda Taylor Beasley. Jo and I haven't found any titles widely distributed. There's nothing at the library or at her store. Do you have any books about her?"

Philomena gave us a smile of satisfaction. "I might have something. Follow me."

She led us toward the back of the store. Along the way, we passed glass casings of sculptures replicating local landmarks, foliage, and fauna. Had Lucas created them? If so, he really was talented.

A collection of framed needlepoints hung on a wall beside us, highlighting quotes by famous Georgia natives past and present. Philomena brought us to a stop in front of three floor-to-ceiling, refinished, antique bookcases. Each shelf contained a decent display of titles on local attractions and history.

"These bookcases are beautiful." I ran my hand over the smooth mahogany wood.

Philomena glowed with pleasure. "They're by a local artisan." She reached for one of the titles on the shelf. "I've been saving to expand my store to allow room for more books and crafts. But as I told you, the bank rejected my loan application. I'll have to use my expansion money for repairs instead."

As a possible motive, killing Nelle in an effort to have the bank reconsider her loan application had been a stretch. Knowing Philomena had alternate resources to pay for her repairs removed the money motive altogether. I was torn between sighing with relief to have cleared her and clenching my fist in frustration that we'd removed our last suspect from the main list.

Could she have another motive? "I'm sorry about the delay in your plans. It looks like you could use the room."

Philomena scanned the center bookshelves. "That's all right. It'll all work out in the end, unless Brittany Wilson's dang lawsuit takes me to the cleaners." She stretched to reach a high shelf. "Here's a book on Mother Mathilda. It's an independently published title by a local author."

"Wonderful." Excitement shot through me, almost making me forget the reason we were here. "Did you say Brittany's suing you? Why?"

She waved a dismissive hand. "Oh, some nonsense about a local artisan who claims I've been cheating him.

Bull pucky. Don't even know why I brought it up except I have a lot on my mind."

"Good luck with the lawsuit." I passed the book to Jo, nudging her to remind her to stay focused on our investigation. "It would be a shame if you aren't able to expand your store."

Tearing her attention from the book, she gave me an apologetic grimace. "There aren't many available titles about Mother Mathilda. I'm envious you found this one. You probably know a lot about her, though, having attended the school."

"Actually, no." Philomena faced us. "She wasn't part of the curriculum, but I wrote an article about her for the paper."

"That's right." Jo returned the book to me. "You worked on the paper with Hank, Nelle, and Brittany, didn't you? That must've been fun."

Philomena arched an eyebrow. Her expression soured as though she'd gulped some bad milk. "Not really. I'm sure you know how high school cliques are. Brittany was Ms. Popularity, and Hank and Nelle were her pet reporters."

"I'd like to get this, please." I held the book aloft. "Could you ring it up for me?"

Philomena's expression brightened with news of the sale. "Well, absolutely."

We followed her back across the store. I nudged my partner in criminal investigation past the display of Southeastern Conference memorabilia displays. She already had enough University of Florida fan gear to open a store. "I know it's not easy being a Gator alumna in Bulldog country, but could you stay focused, please?"

"Sorry." Her gaze lingered on the conference display a moment more before she caught up with Philomena.

At the checkout counter, I hoped my shrug and light tone made my question seem more casual than it was. "Those are tough memories. I could understand your still being upset, especially since Brittany's representing that vendor against you."

Philomena scanned the book, then announced my total. "I'd gotten past Hank's and Nelle's snobbery years ago. That lawsuit with Brittany, well, she has bills too."

I paid for the purchase. "You dated Hank for a while, didn't you?"

She gave me a half smile and a guarded look. "Hank dated half the women in this town."

I collected the sales receipt and my book. "Good luck with that lawsuit."

"Thanks." Philomena's tone was dry. "Enjoy your book."

Through silent but mutual agreement, Jo and I waited until we got back to her car to discuss the informal interview.

Jo put the key in the ignition. Her shoulders rolled forward as she slouched behind the steering wheel. "We need to take her off the list. Unless she's an accomplished actress, she's not carrying a torch for Hank, and the bank rejecting her loan application hasn't really hurt her."

I scowled through the windshield. "And why did she volunteer that information about the lawsuit? If she was the killer, she's basically telling us Brittany's her next victim."

"She doesn't even blame Brittany for representing the vendor who's suing her. 'Brittany has bills too.'" Jo's voice was strained as though she was trying to control her aggravation.

"And what's her connection to Spence? What is *anyone's* connection to Spence?" I scrubbed both hands over my face.

"What should we do now?"

I don't know.

I sat up and buckled myself in. "I need to go back to Spence's yearbooks. We'll have to start from the beginning to try to solve this case, but with less time to do it.

CHAPTER 25

THE SERIES OF MEOWS WAS Phoenix's version of throat clearing. They would become increasingly aggressive the longer I ignored them, which was incentive enough to respond.

I glanced at my cell phone on the dining room table beside my binder Saturday evening. "Oh, wow. It's after five. I'm sorry Phoenix. I lost track of time."

I sprang from the dining room chair and strode into the kitchen to prepare his dinner. But when faced with the various choices for his meal, I was stumped: grilled seafood, classic seafood, chicken, chicken and beef ...

"What are you in the mood for?" I asked over my shoulder.

The wide-eyed look he gave me was a mixture of amazement and disdain. I interpreted his expression as, *Just pick something.*

"Classic seafood it is." I opened the can. As I poured its contents into his bowl, my phone demanded my attention from the dining room.

Phoenix crowded me away from his dish.

"I see you've got everything under control." I straightened and crossed into the dining room to take the call. The phone screen identified Jo's number.

"Hey, Jo. What's—"

"Someone broke into my house and knocked me out."

My body went cold. I grabbed my car keys and raced to the door that led to my attached garage. "Are you all right?"

"Yes." Jo sounded dazed, as though she couldn't quite comprehend what had happened.

"Are you sure?" My voice was sharper than I'd intended. I pressed my garage door opener, gritting my teeth as it slowly lifted. I could've opened it faster manually.

"My head hurts." Her words were muffled by the sound of the door rising, but I could hear her growing anger and outrage. "As I came through my front door, the person hit me on the back of the head, knocking me unconscious."

Another splash of fear washed through me. It was so cold, it made my muscles hurt. "Are you certain the intruder's gone?"

"I think so." The trace of fear in her voice squeezed my heart. "But could you come over? I've called the deputies, but I really don't want to be alone."

"I'm on my way."

I had to remind myself to breathe as I sped toward Jo's house.

Someone broke into Jo's house.

Someone hurt her.

Breathe. Breathe. Breathe.

I pulled into a spot in front of her cottage as the deputies arrived. As Jed and Errol parked their cruiser,

I yanked my key from the ignition and launched myself from my sedan.

Jo was waiting on her porch. She had her arms wrapped around her waist, and she was shivering as though she were freezing in Peach Coast's seventy-degree evening temperatures. "I started thinking about what you said. That the person might still be in the house. I thought I'd better wait out here. Just in case."

I wanted to hug her with relief, but first things first. I searched her eyes. Her pupils were fine. She had a bump on the back of her head, but the blow hadn't broken skin. "Do you hurt anywhere other than your head?"

"No. I'm just cold." Her teeth chattered.

"Sounds like you're in shock." Jed's assessment made sense. He also checked her pupils with a flashlight, examined her scalp, then checked her pulse. "You seem okay, ma'am. Do you want us to call the EMTs?"

"No, I'm all right." Jo's voice was weak and wobbly. I'd wait until the deputies completed their interview before asking her to reconsider seeing a doctor.

Jed nodded once. "All right, then, ma'am. Let's get you inside."

I gave her arms a brisk rub to help her get warm before putting my arm around her waist to steady her as I guided her up her front steps. I could feel her shaking and it broke my heart. As we crossed the threshold, I almost collided with the deputies who'd planted themselves just inside her house. Their hands were on their holstered weapons as though preparing to defend the home and everyone in it.

"What's wr—" My puzzled gaze landed on the television monitor across the room.

Stop protecting him!

Someone had scrawled those angry words in what appeared to be coral lipstick across Jo's forty-eight-inch, black, high-definition television screen. In addition to the exclamation point, the intruder had underlined each word twice.

I tightened my hold on Jo's shoulders. "You didn't tell—"

"I hadn't seen it." Jo sounded as dazed as I felt. "I called you as soon as I came to, then left the house to wait for you and the deputies."

Jed stepped forward with careful strides. Echoes of his tension seemed to reach out to my muscles. "Come on, Errol. Ms. Harris, Ms. Gomez, y'all wait right here."

While we waited for the deputies to finish their reconnaissance, I made tea for Jo and took several photos of the message on her TV.

"Who do you think they're referring to?" Jo sipped her tea. Her teeth had stopped chattering.

"I'd guess Spence." I studied the message on the television. The penmanship didn't appear rushed. The intruder had pressed the lipstick into the monitor, leaving behind thick coral strokes. I sensed the anger in the act. "But if the killer left this message, why wasn't it more specific, like the one they left in my office?"

"Good point." Jo frowned. "They left you a typewritten note. I got three words, written in lipstick."

I nodded. "It's strange. Your message feels more personal."

Jed returned, leading Errol into the living room. "We've searched your whole house and your yard. Whoever broke in is gone."

Errol scanned the room as though prepared for

someone to leap out from behind a bookcase at any moment. He crossed to her TV and opened a kit similar to the one used by the deputies who'd fingerprinted my office after the break-in. I didn't think they'd found prints after my event. I didn't think they'd get any here.

"You're sure?" Jo held her mug in a death grip. I empathized with her anxiety. If someone had broken into my home and rendered me unconscious, it would be weeks before I felt safe in my house again.

Errol gave her an encouraging smile. "We sure are, Ms. Jo. We even checked the attic. All's clear."

Jo managed a smile in return. "Thank you, deputies."

I nudged her elbow to stop her from biting her nails.

Jo's home was similar to mine. We both had separate living rooms, dining rooms, kitchens and foyers. Long, curving staircases carried us to the second floor where we each had three bedrooms and a full bath.

Our interior decorating styles were different, though. Jo preferred modern, sleek furnishings in earth tones. I gravitated toward comfortable, cushiony pieces in pastels. I often wondered if our design choices were a reflection of our reading preferences. Jo liked action-packed novels where the conflict started on the first page. I enjoyed stories that took a bit more time with the worldbuilding.

Jed gave Jo a considering look. "Take us through your day."

When she hesitated, I started the recap. "Jo and I went to Shoreline Souvenirs at two o'clock this afternoon."

He narrowed his eyes. "What'd you go there for?"

"I bought a book on Mother Mathilda Taylor Beasley." I tried to appear and sound as innocent as someone keeping secrets could be. "Neither the library nor Jo's bookstore have much on her. Although the library has access to *The Savannah Biographies Volume fifteen*, which does have a few pages—"

Errol interrupted me. "Ms. Marvey, can we talk about that later, ma'am? For now, it'd be real helpful if you could just help catch us up on the events leading to Ms. Jo's attack."

"Of course." I closed my eyes briefly, frustrated with myself. "Jo and I lingered at the shop, then she drove me home. That was about 2:52 p.m."

"Are you sure about the time?" Jed's tone was dry.

Although suspicious of his demeanor, I took Jed's question seriously. "Yes, I checked my cell phone as Jo pulled up to my house."

Jo picked up the narrative, frowning at the Berber area rug beneath her glass and metal coffee table. "I went into my store to check on my team and to see if there were any issues they needed me to address."

"And how long did that take?" Jed asked. "Fifty-two minutes?"

I gave him a sharp look, but he avoided my eyes.

Jo hesitated, seeming to search her memory. "I stayed a little longer than I'd intended. I think I left around five."

I nodded my confirmation. "That makes sense. I got her call at almost five-thirty." Just before her fingernails could connect with her teeth, I caught her wrist and returned her arm to her side.

"When I got home from my store, everything seemed fine." She jerked a finger over her shoulder toward the front door. "Nothing looked out of place or unusual. My front door was locked as it should've been. I let myself in. The attacker must have been waiting for me behind the door. As soon as I walked in, she hit me from behind."

I tilted my head, looking at Jo. "You referred to your attacker as she. What made you think it was a woman?"

Jo pointed toward her TV. "She wrote the message with lipstick."

I looked from Jed to Errol. "Deputies, I'm sure you recognize the similarities between this break-in and the one at the library. In both cases, the intruder got through locked doors without leaving any signs of tampering. How had they accomplished that?"

"Well, now, I don't think the doors were locked, at least not properly." Jed glowered at me. "And I warned y'all *not* to investigate these killings, didn't I? I told you to stay out of law enforcement business. This isn't some TV show. This is real life and you could've gotten your friend killed."

Jo interrupted his lecture. "I recognize that lipstick. It's the same shade Philomena Fossey wears. She was in the salon the evening Reba did my hair. She asked for that shade by name, Wet Kisses."

Errol scribbled it down. "That's a great tip, Ms. Jo. Thanks."

That was the same night Philomena had met Lucas for dinner. "Who else was at the salon that night?"

Jo pursed her lips and stared across the room. "It was pretty crowded. There were two or three people I didn't recognize. Philomena was just there for the lipstick. I remember seeing Delores Polly, Trudie Trueman, and Zelda Taylor."

"Why are you asking, ma'am?" Errol paused with his pen above his notepad.

I met Errol's eyes. "I don't think Philomena is the serial killer. She doesn't have motive to kill Hank, Nelle, Brittany, or Spence. Someone's framing her."

Jed's features settled into his familiar scowl. "Y'all got all that from some lipstick?"

"And research." I shrugged.

He grunted, then pinned Jo with a no-nonsense look. "Just make sure you lock your doors and windows."

Jo gave a frustrated sigh. "I *am* locking my doors and windows. Someone broke in."

Errol looked from Jed to Jo. "Do you keep a spare key outdoors?"

Jo's ponytail swept her shoulders as she shook her head. "No, Marvey talked me out of that."

Jed led Errol to the front door. "Well, we'll look into this, but it may take us a few days to get to the bottom of things. Until then, just make sure everything's locked up securely."

Behind me, I sensed Jo shaking with annoyance at the unnecessary reminder. I patted her shoulder, then went to see the deputies out.

"Let's get you to the medical center." I returned to Jo's side. "I'd feel better if a doctor examined you to make sure you're okay."

We locked up her house before getting into my car. She turned to me once her seat belt was secured. "You're not going to get us lost, are you?"

I turned the key in the ignition. "I can't make any promises."

The Coastal Care Medical Center staff checked Jo in, commiserated with her misfortune, and escorted her back to the examination room in twelve minutes. Impressive. I especially liked the way they balanced ruthless efficiency with tender care.

I took a pinch of credit for the center's efficacy. By participating in the Peach Coast Cobbler Crawl last month, Spence and I had helped raise money for the clinic. Nearly half the town—including Jo, her team, and the librarians—had sponsored the Harris-Holt team. I was certain Spence was the reason for our overwhelming support. It was a good feeling to know our efforts had benefited such a worthy cause.

The facility's white paneled walls and pink and white tiled flooring made the waiting area seem spacious. Vases of flowers and roses on the blond faux wood tables picked up the room's floral theme. Bowls of apple cinnamon potpourri battled the scent of disinfectant.

Grabbing a magazine, I sank onto one of the lounge's poofy floral armchairs to wait for Jo. I opened the publication, but couldn't concentrate on a single word. My mind was restless. Who'd broken into Jo's home and why? How had they known Jo would be out? Were they surveilling her? If so, how long had this been going on—and why? I checked my phone: half an hour had crawled by. How much longer would Jo's exam take?

I gripped my book pendant with my right hand and cradled my forehead in my left palm. Had someone attacked her because I'd involved her in the investigation? I breathed deeply, hoping I wouldn't be sick.

"Marvey? Are you okay?"

I stood at the sound of Jo's voice. "I should be asking you." I forced a smile as I gestured toward the chocolate chip cookie and disposable cup of what appeared to be apple juice in her hands. "Where'd you get the treats?"

"The nurse gave them to me. They're to take the edge off of the visit." Her eyes were still dark with concern as she returned my gaze. "The doctor gave me a clean bill of health. She checked for external as well as internal injuries, and I'm fine."

"Great." My relief was bone-deep. "I'd feel better if you stayed with me at least for a couple of nights."

Jo started to bite her nails, caught my look, then lowered her hand. "I don't know, Marvey. I don't want to put you in danger."

"If you stay with me, we can protect each other. Besides, I have an alarm system. The killer won't be able to break into my house without setting it off."

"That makes sense." She turned to leave the center.

Keeping pace with her, I pulled my cell phone from the front pocket of my shorts. I hadn't checked on Spence or Brittany since late this afternoon.

I stumbled to a stop in the parking lot.

Jo steadied me. "What is it?"

Wide-eyed, I looked at her. "Was that the killer's point? Did they attack you to distract us from their actual targets?"

Jo shook her head. "Nolan was with Spence and Brittany was staying with her parents. If the killer wanted to get to them, they'd failed."

This time.

CHAPTER 26

S PENCE AND NOLAN WERE WAITING for us on my porch when Jo and I pulled into my garage Saturday evening. I opened the front door and Nolan rushed in.

"Are you all right?" He caught Jo's shoulders. His eyes, wide with concern, scanned her face and head before sweeping over her body.

Phoenix sidled up to my leg and issued a feline throat clearing. Translation: *We need to talk.*

Jo filled in the details of the disturbing events for Spence and Nolan while Phoenix and I carried her suitcase up to the guest room.

"It's just for a few days." I lowered my voice as I carried Phoenix in my left arm and dragged Jo's suitcase up the stairs with my right. "And you like Jo, although not as much as Spence. It must be the whole male-bonding thing."

Phoenix gave me a cat eye roll, which I took as his grudging approval of our temporary houseguest. After depositing Jo's luggage, I made quick work of putting fresh sheets on the guest bed before returning to the living room.

"Would anyone else like dinner?"

My unexpected guests accepted my invitation. I was a little intimidated by the thought of cooking for Mr. Spencer Holt, Peach Coast's most lauded chef, but what could go wrong with spaghetti and meat sauce?

Nolan pinned me with wide, worried eyes. His blunt features were tight. "This is the killer's second warning. We need to either find another way to identify them or leave the investigation to the deputies."

While I made the pasta, Spence made the salad, and Jo drew Nolan aside to help set the table.

"I'm puzzled by the differences between the two messages." I scrolled through the photos on my cell phone to bring up the image of the message left on Jo's TV. I handed the device to Spence. "The first message was a letter written by the killer. It was very specific. They admitted to planning to kill Spence and threatened to kill me."

"'Mind your business or you'll be added to the list.'" Spence gave my phone to Nolan. "But this one's an order, 'Stop protecting him!' I assume they're referring to me."

It was chilling to think of Spence as the subject of the message, delivered by an intruder who'd assaulted Jo. They'd put one friend on their hit list, assaulted another, and threatened me. We needed to stop this person. "Could those messages be from different people?"

"That would support our theory that two people are behind these killings." Jo laid out the placemats and folded dinner napkins at each setting.

"We should take this information to the deputies."

Nolan followed Jo around the table, adding glasses and silverware to the placemats.

Jo shook her head with enough force to propel her ponytail. "The deputies think the intruder got into my house because I'd left my doors unlocked. I *didn't.*"

Nolan leaned back, apparently caught off guard by her vehemence. "You need to be kept safe."

Jo spun to face him. "And this threat needs to be taken seriously. The only person doing that is Marvey."

I rushed to correct her. "And I couldn't do this without all of you and the librarians."

A heavy silence settled over the kitchen and dining room. Tensions were reaching a boiling point. We were starting to snap at each other when the real villain was someone out there. A few minutes of peace would help us to refresh and regroup. Spence made quick work of the salad and I served the spaghetti and meat sauce. We gathered around the dining table, accompanied by the scents of oregano, tomato sauce, and parmesan cheese.

"I'm sorry I snapped at you, Nolan. I didn't mean to." Jo's smile was a warm olive branch.

Nolan squeezed her hand. "I know. You've been through a terrible experience." He shifted his eyes to me. "Thank you for being there for her and keeping her safe."

"Of course." A sip of iced tea eased my dry throat. Jo's was one of the worst calls I'd ever received. "And thank you for keeping Spence safe."

Nolan's eyes twinkled as he considered Spence from across the table. "You learn a lot about someone when you live together even for a short time."

"Nolan's a slob." Spence nudged aside his empty salad bowl.

"And Spence likes to sneak up on people." Nolan spun his spaghetti around his fork.

I shook my head, smiling as Jo rolled her eyes. "We have to find out how the intruder got into your house, our library, and my office. If we could figure out their trick, we may be able to identify them."

"We have to be careful." Nolan looked to Jo. "Just because you're not on the list doesn't mean you're safe."

A sobering but necessary message. "The good thing is Spence and Brittany are safe tonight. Our investigation may have disrupted the killer's schedule."

"But now we don't know what to expect from them or when." Nolan looked around the table before returning his troubled gaze to me. "They're going off script."

"That's fine. I didn't like the original one." The one that marked four people for death.

"Marvey Harris. May I help you?" I was working through lunch late Tuesday afternoon when my desk phone rang.

I'd hesitated before swallowing a bite of my chicken parmesan on whole grain sandwich to answer the call. I hadn't found an eatery that sold chicken parm sandwiches. It wasn't popular in the South. I'd had to make my own. It wasn't bad for my first effort.

"Good afternoon, Marvey. It's Trudie Trueman. How're you?"

The New Yorker in me wanted to speed the conversation along and get back to work. But when in Rome..."I'm fine. Thank you, Trudie. How are you?"

"I've been busier than a moth in a mitten." She sounded exhausted. Even if I hadn't heard the saying before, I'd have understood her meaning. "There's a lot of work to do and things to learn as I take control of my family's business. That's the reason I haven't been able to return your messages. I'm so sorry."

"I understand. Taking control of the company's a huge responsibility. It's been in your family for nineteen years, hasn't it?"

"That's right." Trudie's tone was surprised as though she hadn't expected me to know that. "My parents started it my first year of high school. But I didn't call to bend your ear with my life's story. You probably didn't expect to hear from me about your fundraiser, did you now? Mama and Daddy weren't known for their charitable gift giving. They were richer than Croesus, but they'd still squeeze a quarter so tight the eagle would scream."

I smiled at that Southernism, too. "I appreciate your returning my call."

"Of course. But I'm not contacting you to make a standard contribution. Rumor has it you're looking for a replacement donor since Malcovich backed out of its commitment to the library."

Awkward. I searched my mind for a diplomatic response. "Malcovich Savings and Loan has been a valued library supporter."

"Well done." Trudie laughed softly. "It was shabby of them to pull out of the fundraiser, especially at such a late date. I'm sure if Nelle was still alive, she would've pitched a hissy fit with a tail on it."

Probably. "Peach Coast has a lot of charitable causes and the bank wants to contribute to as many as possible. We're just grateful it's willing and able to continue to support us."

"Well, I'm calling because I'm willing to take the bank's place as your lead donor, or rather my company is."

For a moment, I lost my breath. Was I dreaming? I struggled to breathe again. "Trudie, that's very generous of you. Thank you."

"Please, no thanks are necessary. It's my pleasure. I consider this part of making Peach Coast my home again."

My relief was incredible. I felt as though a fifty-pound backpack had been removed from my shoulders. Seriously, was I dreaming? "Thank you so very much, Trudie. I'm beyond grateful and I know the other librarians will be too." Now no one would have to worry about being out of a job next summer.

"You're all very welcome. I'll just fill out the paperwork that you sent me and we'll be good to go."

I couldn't wait to tell Corrinne and the other librarians. Maybe our summer goals were achievable after all. At least Trudie had given us another chance.

"We're still a bit short of my fundraising goal." I shared the disappointing news about the library's Summer Solicitation Drive campaign with Jo, Spence, and Nolan over lunch at To Be Read Wednesday afternoon. After spending the rest of the weekend at my home, Jo had returned to her place Monday. Thankfully, she hadn't had any trouble since her scare Saturday.

We'd chosen a table toward the front of the café, surrounded by the scents of seasoned meats, fresh rolls, savory soups, and strong coffee.

"How short?" Nolan asked. He sat across the table from Jo with Spence beside him.

Spence had started referring to Nolan as his bodyguard since his friend was doing his best to stick to Spence like gum until we found the killer. I suspected he was only partially joking. Spence had remarked more than once that he found the situation frustrating.

On the other hand, acting as Spence's shadow was giving Nolan a lot of extra opportunities to spend time with Jo. I watched his gaze once again drift toward my friend as though pulled by a magnetic force. Jo smiled at him before dropping her gaze. Knuckleheads.

I named the estimated fundraising shortfall in response to Nolan's question. "It's discouraging because we would've exceeded our goal if the bank hadn't withdrawn its support."

"I'm sorry, Marvey." Jo's expression crumbled with disappointment as though it was her campaign and ultimately her job on the line. "I know how hard you worked on this project."

Spence jumped in. "Let's not admit defeat yet. There are ten days left to the campaign. More contributions will come in and some of the companies that haven't responded to your solicitation yet might come through."

"You're right." I gave him a grateful smile. "I'd given up hope of hearing from Trudie Truman, but she called me yesterday afternoon and offered to take the bank's place as our lead donor."

Jo applauded. "Congratulations!"

Spence lowered his sweet tea. "That's terrific."

"Trudie Trueman?" Nolan asked. "She's your new lead donor?"

I regarded Nolan from a warm bubble of joy. "Yes, I was so relieved to get her call. She didn't offer as large a gift as the bank, but if it wasn't for her donation, we'd have an even greater deficit to overcome to reach our goal."

Nolan didn't appear as relieved as the rest of us. If anything, he seemed even more troubled. "Is Trudie making a personal contribution or is this coming from her family's company?"

"The gift's in her company's name." This couldn't be heading in a good direction. "Nolan, what's on your mind? You're making me very uncomfortable."

"I'm sorry." His sandwich forgotten, Nolan slid a look toward Jo and Spence before returning his attention to me. He lowered his voice. "Trudie's company's no longer a client, but I'm still not comfortable betraying her confidentiality."

"And I wouldn't ask you to." I sensed his turmoil from across the table. It was like a sound wave pushing against me.

"At the same time, I don't want to put you or the library in a bind." Nolan lowered his voice again. "Let's just say, if Trudie's made a generous donation on behalf of her family's company, well, that dog won't hunt."

My eyes dropped to my ham and cheese sandwich. Having lost my appetite, I nudged the plate aside. "When you suggest I shouldn't rely on a *generous* gift from Camden County Construction Contractors, how generous do you mean?"

Nolan shook his head. "If I were you, I wouldn't depend on *any* gift from Trudie's company."

Jo gaped at him. "Are you saying her company doesn't have any money? But Camden County Construction Contractors is one of the biggest employers in town."

Nolan raised his hands. "I'm not comfortable saying anything more."

Spence's eyes were dark with regret. "I'm so sorry, Marvey." He frowned at Nolan. "I hadn't realized Trudie's company was in such a dire situation. They submitted a bid for expanding my family's bed and breakfast. It was the lowest one, but we turned them down. One of the higher bids included better quality materials."

I took a deep drink of my soda to ease my dry throat. That bubble of joy hadn't lasted long. "Thanks for the warning, Nolan. Our volunteers and I are still working the phones and making other contacts. At least we're on track to do better than break even, which will help persuade the board to support it again next year."

Nolan sat back against his chair. "I'm sorry to be the bearer of bad news, and sorry that I can't give you any more details."

I exhaled a heavy, frustrated breath. "This isn't your fault at all. Why would Trudie do this? Surely, she knows she doesn't have this kind of money. Then why would she make a promise she can't possibly keep?" I pressed my lips together, cutting off the rest of my rant. I could hear the stress and temper in my voice.

Nolan spread his hands. "I've gotten to know Trudie. There are a number of reasons she would have made this offer. She probably thought the donation would help her to appear successful. Appearances have always been important to her family."

Jo shook her head. "Maybe she thought replacing Malcovich and being listed as the fundraiser's lead donor would be a good advertising opportunity for her company?"

"That's possible." Spence nodded as he considered Jo's theory. "The fundraiser's supported by several prominent companies. You can't underestimate that kind of positive exposure. It could help boost her company's profile."

"Those are all good theories." I looked from Spence to Jo and Nolan. "There's just one problem."

Nolan frowned. "What's that?"

I held his gaze. "What was she planning to say when we asked for her check?"

Nolan dragged his hand over his close-cropped hair. "That would've been bad. I could see her writing the check. And I have no doubt it would've bounced."

Urgh! "Now I have to tell Corrinne, Viv, Floyd, and Adrian that Trudie's donor pledge is bogus." I blinked back tears. The thought of delivering that crushing news to my friends broke my heart. It made our fear of future layoffs seem more real.

"We've got enough on our plate, Phoenix." I'd settled at my dining table to enjoy an after-dinner cup of lemon herbal tea Wednesday evening. "The bank backed out of its donor commitment. The replacement donor isn't as flush as she'd led me to believe, and I'm running out of time to stop a serial killer. I don't think I can take on anything else."

Phoenix didn't stir from his napping position, curled up like a ball beside my chair.

"Thanks for caring, pal."

I shifted my attention to the index cards on which I'd taken notes on the investigation: impressions on the high school newspaper articles and yearbooks, summaries of the targets' social media accounts, and interview synopses.

I'd been shuffling and reshuffling them for almost an hour, spreading them across the table, hoping reviewing them out of order would trigger a fresh perspective on the case. So far, nothing.

When my doorbell rang, I leaped from my chair. Hopefully, it would be Spence or Jo—or both. Three heads were better than one. Maybe they could look at the random cards and find a clue or link I'd missed.

I checked my security peephole. My porch lights weren't on. The sun was still strong at six o'clock on a June evening. But my eyes must have been playing tricks on me.

"What in the world?" Cautiously, I opened the door.

CHAPTER 27

"MOM? DAD? WHAT ARE YOU doing here?"
Was I dreaming?

"Right now, we're waiting for you to invite us in." Dad's deep voice rumbled with humor.

Laughing, I stepped back, pulling the door wider to welcome them. "I'm so happy to see you!"

I hadn't realized how much I needed to see them, feel them—and yes, smell them. I locked my front door. They dropped their suitcases, then I launched myself into their embrace.

Ah! This is what I'd been missing the past five months: A parental embrace that wrapped me in safety, acceptance, and love. All those things rolled up together said, *Everything will be okay. You'll be fine.*

A soft, warm brush against my ankles meant Phoenix had joined the family reunion. Stepping back, I scooped him up for a proper greeting. Mom and Dad exclaimed their joy at being reunited with their grandcat.

Mom took Phoenix from my arms. "We brought a present for you. You knew we would, didn't you? Didn't you? Oh, we missed you so much, kitty cat."

She and Dad nuzzled and petted Phoenix while they spoke nonsense words to him for several minutes. He ate it up.

My parents were both tall and fit, like Dre. As a child, I'd thought they'd taken all the height and there hadn't been any left for me. For the trip, Mom had worn olive wide-legged pants with a cream shell blouse. Dad was in tan lightweight khakis and a brick polo shirt.

"What are you doing here?" I asked again. "I'm glad to see you." *Understatement.* "But what happened to our plans for you to visit next month?"

As ecstatic as I was to have them here with me, their surprise visit further complicated my projects, both personal and professional.

And why hadn't Dre warned me Mom and Dad were on their way? He was slipping in his sibling responsibilities.

"We couldn't wait, Marvey. Next month is just too far away." Mom returned Phoenix to the floor, then looked around the living room.

Dad shoved his hands into the front pockets of his pants. Phoenix did a figure eight around his ankles before moving on. "We're concerned about those murders. We needed to see for ourselves that you're safe."

Mom wandered the room. "This is even prettier in person. The tour you gave us with your phone's camera was nice, but it didn't do justice to this space." Her expression softened as she paused to study the framed photos lined up along the fireplace mantle.

"Thanks, Mom."

"Our daughter's a homeowner." Dad grinned as he joined Mom in front of the fireplace.

"I understand you're both worried, and I really am

glad to see you. But I can't take time off right now. I'm in the middle of a big project." *And a murder investigation I don't want you to know about.* "Remember?"

"We remember." Mom turned from the fireplace with a nonchalant wave. "But don't worry about us. We can entertain ourselves."

Dad nodded his agreement. "While you're at work, we'll tour the town on our own."

My phone chimed, indicating a text had arrived. It was from Dre. *911 mom dad otw*

"Is that your brother?" Dad asked.

"Yes." I was distracted. *OTW?* My frown cleared. *On Their Way.* I rolled my eyes. No punctuation and now unclear initialisms. Again I wondered, what were those students teaching him?

"Tell him we said hi." Mom strolled past the fireplace, leading Dad into the dining room.

I sent Dre a reply: *They're here. They said, "Hi."*

I returned my phone to the front pocket of my shorts—then froze. The index cards with notes on the investigation were scattered across the dining table, inches from my parents. They didn't seem to have noticed them. Yet. But I had to move fast.

"Mom! Dad! Let me show you to your room." I advanced on my parents, crowding them away from the table and ushering them back to the living room.

"All right. All right. We're coming." Mom protested around a chuckle.

"We're not tired." Dad picked up his suitcase. "It's only six o'clock. We were hoping to stay up and chat with you for a while."

"And we will. But first let me get you settled." I grabbed Mom's suitcase, then led them upstairs.

My parents followed me into the guest room. The bright, cozy space was clean. Jo had been a very tidy guest. I only needed to make the bed and place towels in the guest bathroom. We left their suitcases at the foot of the queen-sized bed. Area rugs in vivid patterns broke up the dark hardwood flooring.

I stepped back to do a final visual check. A row of hangers hung in the closet ready for use. Empty draws in the dark wood laminate dressing table waited to be filled.

Mom stood in the center of the room, taking in the decor. "This is lovely."

Dad crossed the room, moving aside the venetian blinds to look out the windows. "You should see the view."

I hadn't realized how anxious I was for their approval until I exhaled. "Why don't you get cleaned up? Are you hungry? I've already eaten, but I can make you dinner."

Mom shook her head. "We're fine, honey."

Dad spoke over his shoulder. "We ate before the flight."

I linked my fingers together in front of my hips. They were really here. Suddenly, I couldn't stop smiling. "All right. I'll make us some tea."

Dad faced me, his hands in his pockets. "That'll be great."

"Yes." Mom crossed her arms over her chest. "And while we drink it, you can fill us in on your investigation and the index cards on your dining table."

My smile disappeared.

"Let's have it." The next morning at work, I called Dre. That's right. This time, we were having a phone conversation. No more grammatically challenged, headache-inducing texts. A real, honest-to-goodness talk.

"Hey!" Dre's voice strained with diffidence. "Mom and Dad didn't text me until they'd already landed in the Jacksonville airport. What was I supposed to do?"

Yes, the closest airport to Peach Coast, Georgia, was Jacksonville International Airport in—you guessed it —Jacksonville, Florida. Ironic, isn't it? The airport that served this Bulldog safe haven was in Gator country.

Dre's defensiveness was understandable. He'd broken the cardinal sibling rule requiring plenty of advance warning of parental surprise visits.

"You didn't have any idea they were planning this trip?"

"Of course not." He sounded irritable, a sure sign he was telling the truth. "I don't live with them anymore, Marvey. Unless they tell me, how would I know? And if they did tell me, I'd've called you right away."

"Fair enough. All's forgiven." I considered his picture, one of several framed family photos arranged beside my computer monitor.

"Thank you?"

I could've done without his sarcasm. "I'm glad Mom and Dad are here. They loved Anna May's peach cobbler." I smiled at the memory of their confusion every time a Southernism popped up during their conversation with Anna May, Dabney, and Etta.

"Anna May, she's the café owner, right?" Beneath Dre's words, I heard low, rumbling conversations.

Students must have been wandering the hallways of John Jay College of Criminal Justice where my older brother taught forensic accounting. Their voices carried through the open door into his office.

"Good memory. I also introduced them to my colleagues and gave them a tour of the library." Adrian's enthusiasm at meeting members of my family had the Southernisms flying. Fortunately, I'd been able to translate most of them. We'd also gone jogging together this morning. They loved the trail.

"It sounds like everything's going well, so why are you making such a big deal about my not warning you?"

I rolled my eyes. *Was I the only one listening to me?* "Now's not a great time for a visit. Remember?"

"Marvey." His tone was low with warning. "Are Mom and Dad right? Are you investigating these murders?"

Sigh. "Yes, they are, and yes, I am. And before you ask, Mom and Dad know. I came clean with them last night after they saw my notes and demanded to know everything."

"Not for nothing, Marvey, but you brought this on yourself. You promised you wouldn't do this again." Dre abruptly went silent, probably cleaning up his language.

"I'm sorry." I squirmed on the inside, the way only a sibling could make you squirm. "In fairness, when I made that promise, I'd no idea it would *happen* again."

"You know what? I'm glad Mom and Dad are there, too. Maybe they can talk some sense into you."

I took a moment to collect my thoughts. "Dre, the same person who killed the first two victims also is threatening Spence." *And me*—but there wasn't any need to worry my family with that right now.

"What?" A wealth of emotions filled that word: shock, concern, fear. "How do you know that?"

I brought him up to date with our investigation. "I

feel as though the librarians, Spence, Jo, Nolan, and I are going in circles."

"What about the deputies? Murder investigations are their job. What're they doing?" There was an edge to Dre's voice. His inner overprotective older brother was on display.

"They're at a loss as well. But with all of us working together, I'm hopeful we'll get on the right track. Soon."

"I don't like this."

"I understand."

"You need to stay away from him."

"From Spence?" I gritted my teeth. "Is that what you'd do if someone you cared about was in danger?"

His silence was longer this time. "No, I wouldn't."

I didn't think so.

He added, "Be careful."

"I will be."

"And keep Mom and Dad safe."

"Count on it." That promise I'd keep no matter the cost.

CHAPTER 28

"HELLO, MARVEY? IT'S ADRIAN. I'M here at the circulation desk. Ms. Nancy and Ms. Natalie Kenton would like to speak with you, please." Curiosity threaded through the library assistant's voice and down the phone line.

"Thanks. I'm on my way."

Adrian's curiosity was contagious. Why were Nelle's sisters here? Cradling my phone, I stood from my desk. The text notification chimed on my phone. My parents had sent another photo from their adventures in Peach Coast sightseeing. They'd made it to the beach, which was practically deserted on a late Thursday morning.

Wish we'd brought our swimsuits.

I chuckled. *LOL! Next time.*

Pocketing my phone, I went to meet the Kenton sisters. It was a short trek from my office to the circulation area. I located Nelle's sisters right away. They stood within an arm's reach of the intricate weathered oak desk. Even if Nelle hadn't shown me photos of them, I would've known they were her younger sisters. They could've been triplets, which would've been strange considering they were each about three years apart.

"Good morning. I'm Marvey Harris." I waited for the two women to return to the counter. "My sincere condolences on your sister's death. I miss Nelle. I considered her a friend."

"Thank you." The one on the right was Nancy, the middle sister at twenty-nine. I was pretty certain. She had dark brown hair that hung in straight tresses to her shoulders. Her big cornflower blue eyes were full of shadows and grief.

Natalie was silent beside her. At twenty-six, she was the youngest Kenton sister. She'd dragged her dark brown hair into a hurried knot at the nape of her neck. Her turquoise blue eyes were a balanced mixture of anguish and anger. Nancy wore a simple brown dress that hung to her knees. Natalie was clothed in baggy gray shorts and an oversized black T-shirt.

I shared a look between the women. "Would you like to speak in my office?" I sensed Adrian and Viv straining to hear our conversation even as they assisted customers.

Nancy nodded. "Yes, please."

I held open the oak, half-waist swinging door that separated our guests from the library's employees-only section. "May I get you a coffee or some tea?"

Natalie broke her silence. "No. Thanks."

"No, thank you," Nancy responded at the same time.

After gesturing them to the two guest chairs in front of my desk, I closed the door to ensure our privacy.

"I wish we'd met sooner." I circled my desk and settled onto my chair. "Nelle spoke about you a lot."

Nancy took the seat to my right, leaving Natalie with

the chair closest to my conference table. "She's...She'd mentioned you as well. She said you were really nice for someone from New York City."

I blinked. How should I take that? "Please let me know if there's anything I can do to help."

"Thank you." Natalie was speaking again. "And thank you for the cards you sent. They were beautiful."

"She was a special person." The words felt so inadequate. I wish I could say more, do more.

Nancy cleared her throat. "The deputies finally released Nelle's body to the funeral home. We're making arrangements for her wake now. We hope you can attend."

"Of course." That went without saying. My heart hurt for them. I couldn't imagine the pain and sorrow I'd feel if someone killed my brother. I blinked away tears just thinking about it. "I'm certain a lot of people will want to pay their respects."

"And there are a lot of people I'm fixin' not to invite." Natalie's voice trembled with anger.

"Nat, don't be ugly." Nancy's voice was quiet, sympathetic, but firm.

Nelle's younger sisters' sorrow was like a being that had entered my office with them. I sensed Nancy's battle with depression and it tore me apart inside. Natalie was entrenched in the second stage of grief, anger. How much of that was caused by her sister's as-yet unsolved homicide?

I took a breath to settle my nerves. "I'm sorry to ask, but do you have any idea why anyone would want to harm Nelle?"

"No." Nancy shook her head.

"Yes." Natalie sat straighter on her chair.

I gave Nancy an apologetic grimace, then turned to Natalie. "Who?"

Agitation added volume and texture to Natalie's voice. "A lot of people were jealous of my big sister all of her life. She was sharp as a knife, successful, admired, and beautiful."

I offered both women a tissue from the box on my desk before taking one myself. Natalie's assessment of Nelle's qualities were true. "But who would be jealous enough to kill her?"

Natalie gave me a pointed look. "Who benefited from my sister's death?"

Chet Little was promoted to Nelle's job, but would he have killed for it? And what motive would he have to kill the other people on the list—a list I couldn't discuss with Nancy and Natalie? This may not be the right time to pursue the investigation with Nelle's sisters.

Nancy changed the subject. "We're here because we heard Malcovich Savings and Loan has declined to keep the gift commitment it had made to our sister and the library."

Natalie scowled. "Our sister secured that commitment and gave her word to the library. The bank didn't have the right to withdraw it."

Tread gently. "Chet Little explained there were other charitable programs the bank wanted to support at this time. We were disappointed but don't begrudge another nonprofit the opportunity to receive donations."

"Chet Little." Natalie spoke the name of her sister's interim replacement like she was spitting out rotten meat. "Isn't he precious."

I blinked. To my understanding, *aren't you precious* was a close relation to *bless your heart.* Both were ambiguous as to whether the speaker was being empathetic or insulting. In this instance, it was obvious Natalie wasn't paying a compliment to her sister's former coworker.

I continued. "Nelle understood the library's value to the community. In fact, she came to us to offer support. I'm hopeful with a little time and effort, I can persuade Chet to be a champion of the library also."

"You'd be better off talking to a fence post." Natalie shifted on her chair, crossing her legs and folding her arms. She was tall but slight, and her anger seemed to swallow her, just like her shorts and T-shirt.

Nancy gave her younger sister a worried look before returning her attention to me. "We realize the bank's decision has put the library's fundraiser in a bad spot. That's why, as Nelle's sole beneficiaries, we want to make a donation to the library in her memory."

I pressed a hand to my heart. "Thank you so much. That means a lot to me personally, and I know the library team will be very moved by your gift."

For the first time, a trace of humor eased the strain and sorrow that shadowed Natalie's thin features. "You don't even know how much we're giving you yet."

I spread my hands. "We're grateful for every donation, especially one made in your sister's name."

Nancy revealed the size of the gift. My eyes stretched wide. Shock knocked the breath from me. I opened my mouth, then closed it.

"It's not as much as what the bank had originally promised." Nancy shrugged. "But it's what Nelle would've wanted. She's always loved libraries."

I swallowed the emotion that fought to settle in my throat. "I don't know what to say. 'Thank you' doesn't feel like enough. It's a very generous gift. On behalf of the library, thank you so very much."

Natalie stood. Nancy and I followed suit.

The youngest sister adjusted her tan purse on her left shoulder. "We've heard that you're trying to find the person who killed our sister. That's more than enough thanks. But please be careful. Nelle wouldn't want anything to happen to you."

My thoughts went to Spence. I didn't want anything to happen to him or anyone else.

"Why can your parents read a map but you can't?" Jo was lending a hand clearing the dining table after my impromptu dinner party Thursday evening.

"Don't be judgey." I packed the dishwasher as my guests carried plates, glasses, silverware, and serving trays in from the dining room.

Unlike Spence, I wasn't opposed to my guests helping with the cleanup. Did that make me a horrible host? Probably.

"I'm not judging." Jo started to wash the pots and pans I'd left soaking in the sink. "I'm just curious as to why the first day your parents arrive in Peach Coast you can set them loose with your car and a map, yet after five months you still can't find your way around town even using your phone's GPS."

"It would help if she'd listen to it." Spence's voice was dry as dust. He set the entrée plates on the counter above the dishwasher.

"She's always been too impatient to read instructions. I think the same thing applies to directions." Humor thickened my father's words. He added the silverware and serving spoon to the counter. "Cooking instructions, assembly instructions—not even with a bribe."

Lifting my head, I gave my father a taunting look. "Perhaps you had the wrong bribe. Should've tried chocolate."

"The dinner was wonderful, Marvey." Nolan returned the pitcher of lemonade to the refrigerator. "Thank you again for including me."

"Of course." I smiled. "Thank you for coming."

Mom set the leftover rigatoni on the counter beside the refrigerator while she hunted through cabinets for the aluminum foil.

The whole house smelled of spicy pasta sauce, savory meats, garlic and sharp cheeses. I hadn't intended to make that dish for my parents' welcome dinner. I'd planned on something a bit more regional as a special, surprise treat. But they'd arrived in between trips to the grocery, and my cupboards were almost bare. Rigatoni ingredients were all I had that would stretch for my parents and the friends I wanted them to meet: Spence, Jo, Cecelia, and Nolan. In addition to the meal, my dining table also had strained to accommodate the seven of us. My father and I had lugged the extra leaf from my basement.

Plucking the aluminum foil from a top cupboard shelf, Mom wrapped the leftover rigatoni in preparation for storing it in the fridge.

"After a while, one would think you'd get tired of always getting lost." There was a definite teasing tone in my mother's voice.

Cecelia carried in the salad bowls. "If impatience is her worst fault, I'd say you should be thankful. You've done a wonderful job raising your daughter. She's quickly become a valuable member of the community. In less than a year, she's already left her mark on this town."

I looked toward Spence's mother in surprise. "Thank you for saying that."

My parents exchanged a proud look.

"That's always nice to hear." Mom led the group into the living room. "But we wish those marks didn't include homicide investigations."

She and my father sat together on the sofa. Phoenix curled up on her lap. Spence, Nolan, Jo, and I carried blond wood dining chairs into the living room.

My stomach muscles knotted in dread. I loved my family and didn't want to give them any reason to worry about me. But I also loved my friends and didn't want to desert them when they needed me most. I was torn between two loyalties that shouldn't have to be in conflict.

"Mom, Dad, you taught me the importance of helping people in need, especially family and friends." I set my hands on my hips. "That's all I'm trying to do."

"We understand." Mom looked at Dad beside her. "And we're proud of you, Marvey. We're not opposed to you helping your friends, but you can't expect us not to worry, especially when you don't tell us what's going on."

Fair enough. I gave my parents an apologetic smile. "I'm sorry."

"I can imagine how unsettling that's been for you." Cecelia gracefully lowered herself onto the armchair. She smoothed the skirt of her linen dress over her knees and crossed her feet at her ankles. "You're hundreds of miles away and unfamiliar with the town and its residents." She met my gaze from across the room where I'd set my chair beside my parents. "But if it hadn't been for your daughter making the connection between the list she found and Hank's and Nelle's suspicious deaths, we wouldn't have realized Spence's life was in danger."

Dad shifted on the sofa to face me. "You believe the connection between the people on the list is the local high school?"

"That's our strongest theory." My eyes dropped to the sofa cushion. Dad had wrapped his right hand around Mom's left hand as they lay on the sofa between them.

Mom frowned at Spence. "But you're class of 2008. The other people on the list are class of 2006. Besides your alma mater, what did you have in common during your high school career?"

Spence was seated across the room near his mother. "Ma'am, the one thing we all had in common was the school newspaper. Brittany Wilson was its editor in 2005 and 2006. Coach Hank Figg and Nelle Kenton were her top reporters. And I was editor in 2008."

Dad's eyes circled the room. "One thing's certain. Everyone on the list is very successful in their careers."

I stood to pace. "I've wondered if that's significant as well. But there are other lawyers, business owners, and executives who've graduated from the local high school and still live here."

Dad turned to Spence. "Your times on the newspaper are two years apart. Did you cover any of the same stories?"

Spence spread his hands. "Sir, Brittany and I kept

computer files of the newspapers we edited. We all went through them, but nothing jumped out at us."

I gestured toward Cecelia. "Ms. Holt brought me the 2006, '07, and '08 yearbooks. There weren't any commonalities across those years."

Mom shifted Phoenix from her lap and rose to wander the room. "What happens when we set aside their graduation dates and focus on the school paper? Hank, Nelle, and Brittany worked on the paper in 2006."

"And only Spence worked on the paper in 2008." I paced toward the fireplace.

Mom faced me from the other side of the mantel. "What happened while Hank, Nelle, and Brittany were on the paper in 2006 that affected the paper in 2007? That's what connects Spence to the other three."

"We've been looking at the wrong year." My eyes grew wide with realization. I turned to Spence. "It's not 2006 *or* 2008. We need to look at 2007."

Dad looked around the room. "So, who had a really bad 2007?"

CHAPTER 29

"WHEN YOU TOLD US YOU were leaving New York and moving to Georgia to work for a library in some obscure town with barely a thousand people, your mother and I were... concerned." Dad looked amused as he sat on the sofa across from me.

"'Concerned,' Dad?" I arched an eyebrow. "Admit it. You thought I'd lost my mind."

"Don't put words in our mouths." But Mom didn't deny it.

Minutes before, we'd bid our dinner-guests-slash-sleuthing-team farewell. The evening had been fun and productive, even better than I'd hoped. It felt good to have the investigation out in the open instead of hiding it from my parents. As a bonus, they'd spent part of the evening trying to help us solve the murder mystery.

I'd curled up on the armchair Cecelia had vacated, hoping to get Mom's and Dad's first impressions of the town and its residents.

Mom studied the view from one of my two front windows. I had the sense she was committing it to memory. What would she tell Dre, Kaylee, and Clay about it?

"We knew the move would be a good professional opportunity for you." She turned from the window. "But we were worried about how it might affect you personally. Could you flourish in a small town? Would you be accepted, or would it be too much of a culture shock?"

I smiled at this. The first couple of months *had* been a challenge. I'd wondered whether I'd made the right decision for myself and for Phoenix, and if we'd ever be happy here. The realization my parents had had the same conversation with each other that I'd had with myself as I'd considered relocating was both disconcerting and reassuring.

Dad continued. "But it was important to support your decision, whatever you chose to do. We understood that. If you believed this was a good opportunity, we had to trust your judgement."

"That's right." Mom moved away from the window to peruse the novels on my blond wood bookcase. "We knew you didn't have to be in New York to be close to us, especially with modern technology. We also knew if Peach Coast didn't work out, you could always come home."

Dad's chuckle was self-deprecating. "Although to be honest, the idea of going from seeing you several times a week to maybe twice a year wasn't sitting well with me. Your mother and I worried about the effect that would have on our relationship with you."

I hadn't liked that adjustment, either. "But we're talking several times a week."

"True." Dad pet Phoenix as my tabby kneaded his lap. "And this town has impressed us. Everyone we met today has been nice—strangers as well as your friends. It's like you've been telling us, the people in this town are genuine and welcoming. We just needed to experience it for ourselves."

Mom returned to the sofa, sitting so close to Dad I doubted even a molecule could squeeze between them. "Mmm. Now we can reassure your brother that you're fine."

Oh, *Dre* needed reassuring? I shook my head and smiled. Somehow I didn't think he was the only one, but I let Mom's comment slide.

Dad gave Mom an indulgent look, before turning back to me. "I like your friends. They're smart, funny, and kind. They'll look out for you. Dre will be happy to know that."

I exchanged a teasing smile with Mom. "I'm sure he will."

"I like your friends, too. All of them." Mom wrapped her arms around one of Dad's. "What we're trying to say, dear, is that you shouldn't have any reservations about settling here in Peach Coast. If you're happy here, then so are we. That's all that matters."

I gave her a wobbly smile. "Thanks, Mom, Dad. That means the world to me."

As I crossed the room to embrace them, they stood to greet me with open arms. Phoenix seemed a little peeved at being set aside, but he waited patiently for the group hug to end. I returned to the armchair and my parents settled back onto the matching sofa.

Mom shifted to face me. "Now, tell us about Spence."

Homeownership had its challenges, such as selecting a replacement door knob for one's main floor bathroom. So many choices and they were all so nice: knobs and levers; brass and nickel; turn locks and buttons. I stared wide-eyed, at the display on the wall in the hardware store's doors & hardware aisle Friday afternoon.

"This is going to take my entire lunch hour," I complained to myself. "I need a second opinion."

"Afternoon, Ms. Marvey." Bobby Hayes's slow Southern drawl preceded him down the aisle. It was an answer to my prayer.

I turned to greet him—and my smile froze. Running into Bobby was awkward enough. But he wasn't alone. His helicopter mother, Betty Rodgers-Hayes, was with him. Her face was as stiff as the door models around us. Betty couldn't stand me.

Swallowing a sigh, I braced myself for the encounter. "Hello, Bobby. Betty. How are you?"

Bobby's guarded expression relaxed. Beneath the brim of his red University of Georgia ball cap, his hazel brown eyes warmed. "Fit as a fiddle, thank you, ma'am. I've used the money Fiona left me to make some changes to my daddy's business."

The twenty-something-year-old was the late Fiona Lyle-Hayes's stepson. He and his mother had been vocal in their opposition to my investigating Fiona's murder. With time, Bobby had accepted my interference. It seemed more than a month later, Betty's resentment still had a grip on her.

"What changes did you make?" Bobby's news intrigued me. That and the fact he seemed different from when I first met him: happier, relaxed, confident.

He flashed a grin and crossed his arms over his

faded black short-sleeved shirt. The circular logo on the right chest pocket read Hayes Home Remodeling. "I've converted it from real estate to home renovation. It's what I've always wanted to do."

His joy was infectious. It blew away the twin fogs generated by my stumbling investigation and faltering fundraiser. "That's wonderful, Bobby. I wish you every success."

"Thank you, Ms. Marvey." He took off his cap and dragged his long fingers through his dark hair before settling it back into place. "I didn't think I'd be able to pull it off, but like my daddy always said—God rest his soul—can't never could."

"No, I'm sure it...couldn't." It would take me a while to unravel that. Taking another breath, I turned to his mother. "You must be proud, Betty."

Her milky features relaxed and a proud smile curved her thin lips. "Bobby always makes me proud." She seemed content. I thought I heard angels singing. Then she looked at me. Her expression soured and the music stopped. It had been nice while it lasted.

"I'm sure he does." I started to turn away, but her hand on my arm surprised me.

She released me immediately. "I've given this a lot of thought." Her brown eyes gleamed with defiance. "I suppose there's something I need to say to you."

I straightened my spine. "What is it?" *Take your best shot.*

"Thank you." Her milky complexion was flushed. Was the cause anger or embarrassment?

I looked to Bobby, then back to his mother. They seemed stiff with nerves. The air between us was heavy with discomfort. That added to my confusion. "Why are you thanking me?"

Betty sighed and shifted on her feet as though explaining the reason for her gratitude was torture. "It's because of you that Bobby and I were able to have an honest conversation about the past and how my behavior toward Fiona had hurt him."

After Betty's husband and Bobby's father, the late Buddy Hayes, had divorced Betty to marry Fiona Lyle-Hayes, she began a smear campaign against Buddy's new wife. Bobby had liked Fiona and had been happy for his father, but his loyalty to his mother had prevented him from defending Fiona against Betty's lies. His silence had caused him a lot of guilt and distress.

I shook my head. "You're giving me too much credit. I asked a couple of questions. You did the rest yourselves."

"Getting everything out in the open helped us to grow closer." Bobby glanced at his mother before giving me a crooked smile. "Although I did move out of Mama's house. I'm living out in Fiona's cabin now."

My eyebrows flew to the top of my forehead. "That's a big change."

Betty gave him a dry look. "I'm still coming to terms with it."

As uncomfortable as she was expressing her gratitude, I was just as uncomfortable receiving it. "I'm glad you and Bobby have a better relationship, but I didn't have anything to do with it."

"We'll have to agree to disagree." Bobby stepped aside to select an item from the wall beside me.

I'd noticed the display earlier. The tools' name had stirred my curiosity. In bold red letters, the packaging read *Lock Key Bump Pick Gun Repair Tool Kit*. The mechanism inside reminded me of a smaller, thinner version of the tag guns grocer's use to affix price labels to their inventory.

I nodded toward the packet in Bobby's calloused hand. "What does that do?"

His eyes jerked to mine as though my interest surprised him. I was a librarian. Everything interested me. "It's a lock-pick gun. You use it to pick a tumbler lock without damaging it. I've locked myself outta the home I'm renovating a coupla times." His smile was self-deprecating.

I stilled. My eyebrows knitted and my eyes narrowed as I looked from the tool to Bobby and back. "So, if I didn't have my key but I needed to get into my house, I could use this lock-pick gun to get in and it wouldn't damage the lock?"

Bobby nodded. "That's right, ma'am. Provided you had a tumbler lock. It wouldn't leave a mark at all."

The library.

My office.

Jo's home.

Had someone used this device to enter those places without leaving a trace?

"Who'd know about lock-pick guns?" I certainly hadn't.

"Well, anybody can own a lock-pick gun." Furrowing his brow, Bobby gestured toward the wall display. "They're legal in Georgia, as long as you don't use them to commit a crime. Locksmiths use 'em. So do repo agents and contractors."

I swallowed hard. "Like construction workers?"

He shrugged. "Sure. They could use 'em."

An image of Trudie came to mind. But what was her connection to Hank, Nelle, Brittany, and Spence?

Coastal Cycles was crazy busy Friday evening. Tourists and even residents were lined up to rent bicycles and kickoff their weekend by exploring the shoreline. Brittany and her small staff kept the customer line moving with courteous efficiency.

Spence and I watched the activity as we waited for Brittany to finish helping a customer. I stole a few glances at his spare, sienna profile. He seemed off today. He'd been quiet as he'd driven us here. When I'd asked if there was something troubling him, he'd responded, "Nary a thing." I was certain he was using that Southernism incorrectly, though, since it was obvious something was wrong. And although he seemed strained, I didn't think it was because of the wait.

"My parents enjoyed meeting you and your mother yesterday evening."

He gave me an absent smile. "We enjoyed meeting them, too."

I waited a beat, then tried another approach. "Having a hard day?"

Spence rubbed the back of his neck. "Yeah, you could call it that."

I nodded as though satisfied. I wasn't, but I decided to let it go for now.

Brittany approached us with an apologetic smile. "Thanks for coming on such short notice. I'm sorry to keep you waiting."

"It's not a problem." Spence shrugged under his tan linen suit.

I was more direct. "When you called this afternoon, you said you had some information for us. What is it?"

Brittany looked surprised. Perhaps I should've eased in by asking about her mama.

She glanced around her showroom. "Let's go to my office. We'll have more privacy there."

Brittany and I had a very different definition of privacy. The room she took us to was behind the customer counter. It was like a fishbowl for humans, with two glass walls that allowed an unobstructed view of the showroom and customer counter. Conversely, visitors to the bike shop had an unhindered view of us. The space even smelled like window cleaner.

Looking at the bare walls and empty desk, I wondered if this was an open office available to everyone who worked for the shop or whether Brittany just didn't spend much time in it.

"Please have a seat." She gestured toward the chairs in front of the desk and took a seat behind it.

I moved toward the chair on the right. Spence's hand was on it. "Are you holding it for me?"

He nodded. "That's right."

"Thank you." I struggled with my patience as he and Brittany took a few minutes to go through the normal Peach Coast greetings.

She turned to me. "My family and I appreciate your calling on me every day. That's very considerate of you."

Spence gave me a surprised look. I hadn't told him I'd also been checking in with Brittany. He might've thought I was being histrionic, which I wasn't.

I shifted on my chair. "We want to make sure you're safe. About this information you mentioned ...?"

"Yes, well, I haven't been completely honest with

you." Brittany's opening words didn't bode well for the rest of our meeting. "When you first asked if I could think of anyone who'd want to harm me, I said no, but that's not completely true."

I pressed back against my seat, eyes wide and lips parted. *I knew it!*

I exchanged a look with Spence before responding to Brittany. "Tell us everything."

With a big sigh, Brittany collapsed back against her chair. "Do y'all know Gertrude Trueman? She goes by Trudie."

"Her daddy died recently." Spence propped his right ankle on his left leg. He was a master of disguise. His body language was a study in relaxation, but I sensed his tension. "She's been back now a couple of months. He left her the family construction business."

Unease caused the hair on the back of my neck to stir. "Why are you asking?"

Brittany glanced at me, then looked at Spence. "I crossed paths with Trudie when she got back to town in March. I was coming out of Big Boy's Sporting Goods Store. You know the one? It's on Elm. The owner, Peaches, runs these specials on cold winter gear when the weather's turning warm."

Oh, my goodness. Seriously? "What did Trudie say?"

Spence and Brittany looked at me as though I'd slapped them across the face without provocation. My cheeks burned with embarrassment.

Before I could apologize, Spence turned to Brittany. "She's from New York."

I scowled at him. He arched an eyebrow as though daring me to dispute the claim.

Brittany nodded as if Spence's statement explained

everything. "Well, as I was saying, I was coming out of Big Boy's Sporting Goods Store, I think it was a Tuesday, when I saw Trudie on the street. Well, first I heard her voice. She said, 'Brittany Wilson.' Just like that. 'Brittany Wilson.' Without any emotion. So I looked up and there was this woman standing right in front of me, blocking my path. At first, I didn't recognize her."

Spence spread his hands. "It's been fifteen years."

"Exactly. And she's changed a lot. She's much prettier now. Her acne's cleared up and she's pulled her hair back from her face." Brittany leaned forward. "But she got this smug look on her face and she said, 'Don't you recognize me, Brittany?' in a real creepy way. I was about to tell her to kiss my..." Her eyes widened and a blush filled her cheeks. She must have just remembered she was speaking with Peach Coast royalty.

I nodded in an effort to get her train back on track. "You were annoyed. Then what happened?"

Brittany drew a breath before continuing in a more moderate tone. "Anyway, I did recognize her after she did her Ghost of Christmas Past impersonation. And I said, 'It's been a while, but of course, I recognize you, Trudie. How you doin'?' I was trying to show some manners, unlike her."

Is there a point in my near future? I briefly closed my eyes.

Brittany didn't stop. "And that's when she said the strangest thing. 'How d'y'all think I feel?' That's weird, right?"

Spence frowned. "What did she mean by that?"

Brittany swept her hand aside. "I just thought she meant she was still grieving her daddy, but when I told her I was sorry for her loss, she just stepped around me and walked on by. That's weird, right?"

Maybe not weird, but her anger seemed out of proportion to the exchange. "Have you been able to figure out why she'd reacted that way?"

Brittany sighed, throwing up her hands. "To tell the truth, at the time, I put her out of my mind. I just thought, *That's Trudie.* She's always been a little different. And we didn't move with the same crowd. I was with the athletes and she was with the recluses."

"*Recluses.*" The memory hit me like a shove to my back. "That's what Hank had called one of the student groups in the series he'd written for the paper."

Spence shook his head. "I don't remember much about Trudie from high school."

"Neither had I. But then I started wondering if she could be behind this." Brittany covered her face with both hands before straightening in her seat. "It took me a while to remember. Trudie was a year behind me, Hank, and Nelle."

My mother's words came back to me. "Then she was in the class of 2007." I could tell Spence also remembered what my mother had said.

"That's right." Brittany continued. "Hank and Nelle found out Trudie and her friends were selling answers to the school's standardized tests. They did an investigation. It was a whole thing with Nelle going undercover. I asked the administration for approval to run it. They approved our running the story, provided we leave out the students' names. But *they* kept the names and those students were brought up for disciplinary review by the school board."

"What happened to them after the disciplinary hearing?" I asked.

Brittany shrugged. "I graduated that May. The hearing was scheduled for the summer. The last thing I heard, Trudie was the only one who didn't return in the fall."

Spence glanced at me before turning back to Brittany. "That explains why she didn't graduate with her class."

I tightened my hand on the chair's cool metal arm. "Could she really be angry enough to kill you for something that happened fifteen years ago? What about Spence? He didn't have anything to do with that article."

Spence held up a hand, palm out. "In 2006, my father was the president of the school board that apparently voted to expel Trudie."

Surprise eased the furrows on my brow. "You think she's threatening *you* as a way to get back at your father?"

I sat back on my chair and considered Spence and Brittany. We had a suspect with a reason to want revenge against all four victims, but I needed to be certain she was the right suspect. "This happened fifteen years ago. Why would she wait that long for revenge? And is being expelled a strong enough motive to kill four people?"

There was a shift in Brittany's expression that warned me she was withholding more information. "Well, there was a more recent incident. It was March, right before Trudie's daddy died. Hank asked me to represent him in a lawsuit against Camden County Construction Company. Mr. Trueman was threatening to put a lien on his house if he didn't pay for the repairs

they'd done. But he wanted them to fix a bunch of problems with the work first."

Eyes wide, I turned to Spence. "You rejected the
company's bid on the expansion for your bed and
breakfast. And Nolan said Malcovich Savings and Loan
had rejected its loan application."

Spence rubbed the back of his neck again. Tension
seemed to be building there. "Her resentment may have
started in high school, but these recent events have
contributed to bankrupting her family's company."

I looked from Spence to Brittany and back. "I think
Trudie's the one who broke into my office at the library
and Jo's house, using a lock-pick gun."

Brittany frowned. "And what's that?"

I summarized my conversation with Bobby Hayes
about the lock-pick gun.

Spence's expression was grim. "We need to share
this information with the deputies right away."

"I agree, but this is all still speculation." I pushed
away my shock and dread, forcing myself to focus on
next steps.

Spence reached into his right front pants pocket.
"We can also tell them about this."

He pulled out what looked like blue felt cloth. My
breath caught in my throat. My body went ice cold. *Was
that ...?* He unfolded it to reveal the Mother Mathilda
Taylor Beasley High School pennant circa 2006. Or was
it 2007?

My mind went blank.

CHAPTER 30

"WHEN WERE YOU GOING TO tell me about the pennant?" I strapped myself into the passenger seat of Spence's black SUV. My hands were shaking. My pulse was racing. And I wasn't certain, but I might be blinking back tears.

A serial killer had left their calling card with Spence. I was definitely blinking back tears. I was that scared for him.

"I found it as I was leaving my office to meet you." Spence backed out of the parking space and maneuvered the car toward the lot's exit. "I didn't want to bring it up before we spoke with Brittany. It would've been a distraction."

It was a reasonable explanation, but I was still irritated with him. Or maybe I was irritated with myself. I'd felt something had been troubling him on the drive over here. I should have pressed him harder to tell me.

Glancing out the rear window, I spotted Brittany's silver compact sedan, following a safe distance behind. We were driving separately so Spence wouldn't have to chauffeur both of us after our meeting with the deputies.

On route to the sheriff's office, I called Nolan. He answered on the first ring. "There's been a development in our investigation. Can you meet us at the sheriff's office like now?" He agreed immediately without asking any questions. He was a good friend.

Spence pulled into the sheriff's office's parking lot. "Why did you ask Nolan to meet us here?"

I hopped out of the SUV before Spence could open my door. When we'd left the bike shop, he'd capitalized on my distraction to hold the car door open for me. "First, Nolan's your friend and he needs to know the threat against you has escalated. Second, he's going to play a major role in our sting operation, provided the deputies approve the plan."

Brittany pulled into the parking lot behind us. Nolan arrived minutes later. It didn't take much to convince Jed to meet with us. Perhaps it was the tension on Spence's and Brittany's faces, the two surviving members of the hit list. Jed led the four of us plus Errol to the department's break room.

Spence pulled out the pennant. "I found it on the floor beside my desk as I was leaving my office. It must've fallen there shortly after the killer delivered it."

Brittany, Nolan, Errol, and Jed looked at Spence with increased concern.

Jed stroked his upper lip. "Did you notice anyone near or around your office this morning? Has there been anyone new coming into the newspaper building?"

Spence narrowed his eyes as though scanning his memory. "No, I haven't noticed anyone new or anyone acting suspiciously lately."

"I didn't think so, but I had to ask." Jed sighed. "We'll stop by later to dust for prints and have a look around. Doubt we'll find anything, either, but we need to process the scene just the same."

I lifted my right index finger. "Could you hold off on that for just a few hours?"

Jed pinned me with an irritated stare. "Now, why would I want to do that?"

I lowered my arm to the table. "So we can set a trap for the killer. But the plan depends on the killer believing Spence doesn't understand the significance of the pennant."

Jed and Errol exchanged a look before the senior deputy returned his flat-eyed stare to me. "What's your plan?"

I gathered my thoughts. I had to be persuasive. More importantly, the plan had to work. Too much was at stake for it to fail. "Hank received the first pennant. We don't know when, but shortly afterward, on a Saturday, he was poisoned. Then Nelle received a pennant. Again, we don't know when, but we do know she had it the night of the fundraiser kickoff because she'd asked Lucas about it."

"That Saturday, two weeks to the day after Hank was found dead, Nelle was killed." Spence's voice was somber. Was he thinking of Nelle or the fact that he'd received a pennant? I suspected it was both.

"With the same poison." I picked up the narration. "That was the pattern until the deputies announced the deaths were homicides and likely connected."

"That made it harder for Trudie to sneak around." Nolan frowned. "I can't believe one of my clients could be a serial killer."

Brittany leaned forward to catch my attention. "That's why you thought I was in danger last weekend. It's because I received a pennant and you noticed the pattern in the timing."

I nodded. "But you were staying with your parents so Trudie, *if* she's the killer, couldn't get you alone." My gaze drifted to Spence and a chill swept through me. "Now you have a pennant and tomorrow's Saturday. I think Trudie's getting impatient. I think she's going to go after you tomorrow. We have to be ready."

He held my gaze. "What do you propose?"

I turned to Jed and Errol. "We've explained why we think Trudie's the killer, but we don't have evidence to support our theory."

Jed's gray eyes glittered with impatience. "That could be a problem."

I lifted my index finger again. "Not if we get a confession."

Brittany frowned. "How do you plan to do that?"

"Yes, please share." There was laughter in Jed's voice. "How're you going to make Trudie Trueman confess to serial murders? Do you have Wonder Woman's Lasso of Truth in your purse?"

I blinked. Was Jed a comic book fan? If so, he and I may have found common ground. "No, not Wonder Woman's lasso. Something better." I leaned into the table and looked to Nolan, drawing everyone's attention to him. "We have the suspect's crush."

Showtime!

My arms were shaking so badly, I was afraid I'd drop my cell phone. I braced my right forearm with my left hand, pressing the phone hard against my ear.

"Hello?" Trudie's voice was relaxed and carefree as it traveled through my phone late Saturday afternoon. It was sickening.

"Trudie! Thank goodness! It's Marvey Harris." Sitting in Coastal Care Medical Center's floral-themed waiting area, I dug deep for any crumbs of acting ability I may have developed over the years.

My performance would've been easier if half the town wasn't watching me. Spence stood beside me. Mom, Dad, and Cecelia had insisted on coming in case Trudie became violent. Corrinne, Viv, Adrian, Floyd, and Brittany wanted to be present to close the case.

Jed and Errol were in the treatment room with Nolan, Jo, and the doctor who'd treated Jo during her last visit here. Once Trudie was on her way, I was to alert Jed so everyone could take their places.

"Marvey? Has something happened?" Her question was delivered with pitch-perfect solicitousness.

Did she have any idea how it would have destroyed me, Spence's mother, and so many other people if anything had happened to Spence? Did she even care?

I clenched my fist and struggled to keep anger from my voice. "Trudie, it's about Nolan." I managed to make the words wobble with emotion. Or perhaps it was my nerves.

There was a pause. "Nolan? Do you mean Spence?"

Do tell. Why would I mean Spence, Trudie?

I checked my phone to make sure it was recording this conversation. Like most states, Georgia had a "one-party consent" wiretapping law. It was a crime to secretly record phone conversations unless one party to the call consented to the recording. I'd looked it up. So this recording would be admissible in court because trust and believe, I was consenting.

"No, no. It's Nolan." I concentrated on sounding agitated and concerned. "I know how much you care for him. That's why I'm calling."

This morning, Spence had put our sting in motion by going to On A Roll. Trudie had been there, just as she'd been every Saturday morning since returning to Peach Coast. She'd engaged Spence in conversation, and he'd given her an opportunity alone with his coffee. If she was the serial killer, she'd only need seconds to tamper with it. Spence had then gone straight to the newspaper where Nolan had been waiting for him.

"What's happened?" Trudie barked down the line. Her air of gracious solicitation had vanished.

"He was with Spence this morning. Spence said Nolan collapsed after drinking coffee. The EMTs said he's having a heart attack. They're treating him now at the medical center."

"No!" Trudie screamed. I jerked the phone from my head. Her response still reverberated against my eardrum. "It's not a heart attack! Tell them it's not a heart attack! I'm on my way!"

The line went dead. I stopped the recording. "She's on her way. I've got to let Jed know."

I surveyed my audience. Their eyes were wide with amazement. I felt their tension bouncing around the room.

"Oh, my gosh! You were great."

"I knew you had it in you."

"You sold it."

I clapped my hands. "Focus, people. Focus. Trudie'll be here any minute. Hide your faces in a magazine. Turn your backs to the door. Do something to make sure she doesn't recognize you." I pointed to Brittany. "Take off the sunglasses. She may become suspicious if she sees someone wearing sunglasses indoors. Just pull the scarf further over your face if you're worried about being noticed."

Brittany adjusted her scarf, wrapping more of it over her shoulder. "How's this?"

"Perfect." I tugged on Spence's shirtsleeve. "Come on. We've got to warn the others."

Spence and I alerted Nolan, Jed, and Errol. Then we returned with Jo to the front desk so we could to escort Trudie to Nolan's room when she arrived.

In the first treatment room down the hall, the doctor had helped us arrange pillows and a mannequin head to create the illusion that Nolan was in the bed. An oxygen mask further distorted the fake head. Dimmed lights kept the windowless room in heavy shadow. The scene called for him to be asleep. Meanwhile, Jed, Errol, and the real Nolan were waiting in the connecting bathroom for Trudie's confession.

It sounded easy, didn't it? Why didn't anything ever go according to plan?

CHAPTER 31

"WHAT'S TAKING HER SO LONG?" I checked my watch for the fourth time in as many minutes.

Jo, Spence, and I kept passing each other as we paced the hallway. The scent of disinfectant was almost imperceptible beneath the fragrance of roses and apple cinnamon potpourri.

"She should be here by now." Spence's somber tone added fuel to my unease.

We looked up and down the hallway, craning our necks to see as far as we could. There was no way we would've miss her. Unless she saw us first and somehow knew she was being set up.

"We've been made." I tugged on Spence's sleeve and motioned for Jo to follow.

With my heart in my throat, I hustled back to the treatment room. As I turned the corner, I saw Trudie enter Nolan's room. My breath caught in my throat.

Go time.

I ran on my toes to minimize the sound of my footsteps. I raised my arm, silently warning Spence and Jo that our target had arrived. I rushed toward the room. Her voice was muffled. I strained to hear it.

"Nolan?"

I inched closer to the room. Slowly. Quietly. Peaking in, I located her standing just inside the doorway. I crouched low so Jo and Spence could see over my head. Hopefully, the shadows in the room were deep enough that the mannequin head and pillows we'd arranged could pass for Nolan, or at least buy us some time.

"That poison wasn't for you." Trudie's words were speeding up as she crept toward the bed. "Can you forgive —?" She reached out to touch him— or rather his mannequin-and-pillow stand-in. "What—?"

The bathroom door slammed open with the speed and bang of a gunshot.

"Freeze!" Jed's command whipped across the room. His gun was trained on Trudie.

Errol stood beside his veteran partner. He also aimed his gun at Trudie. Nolan stood behind them, thankfully safe.

"Get the lights." Jed barked the order.

"Got it." I flipped the wall switch, flooding the room with fluorescent lighting.

Trudie spun to face the door. Instinctively, I hopped in front of Jo and Spence, using my back to push them into the hallway. My eyes remained on Trudie. Hands pulled at me from behind as though trying to drag me from harm's way. I didn't move.

"Freeze!" Errol repeated the order in a voice almost as ferocious as Jed's.

Trudie gaped at us in horror. "You. And you." Her line of sight was above my head. She must have been referring to Spence and Jo. Her face crumbled and she collapsed onto the floor, sobbing and wailing. "It wasn't supposed to end like this. It wasn't supposed to end like this."

With Errol backing him up, Jed holstered his gun, switching it for handcuffs. As he read her Miranda rights, Jed took the sobbing serial killer into custody. Once she was secure, Jo dashed from behind me, racing into the room to embrace a safe and healthy Nolan.

Spence pulled me into the hallway, giving Jed and Errol plenty of space to escort Trudie from the room. Her face was a mask of hatred as she stared at us.

I turned to Spence. "Thank God you're safe."

"And thank you." His dark eyes were warm with relief and gratitude.

I wrapped my arms around him and held on tight.

"Coming back to Peach Coast reawakened Trudie's resentment against Hank, Nelle, and Brittany for exposing her role in the exam cheating ring. That resentment turned into homicidal rage when she blamed them for her family's business failing." I leaned against the far right wall in the library's second floor activity room early Saturday evening. The refreshment table under which I'd found the hit list had been set up against that wall the evening of the library's cocktail kickoff.

My parents had joined the librarians at the table in front of me to my right. Spence had joined his mother, Nolan, Jo, and Brittany at the table next to them.

Corrinne had suggested we gather for a debriefing. The sting had been emotionally and mentally draining.

She'd claimed talking it over would give us closure and help put it behind us.

"What made her think it was their fault?" Corrinne's puzzled gaze shifted from Brittany to Spence.

The lawyer explained. "Hank hired me to represent him in a lawsuit against the company. Apparently, Trudie thought Nelle had cautioned the bank against approving her father's business loan application." She glanced at Spence. "Your role in Trudie's vengeance rampage is more complicated."

Spence made the attempt to explain it. "My father had been school board president at the time Trudie had been expelled. Since he's passed, she transferred her resentment to me. She also learned that I'd rejected her father's bid for an expansion project for the hotel. Trudie believes the strain of his financial problems triggered her father's fatal heart attack."

"So she blamed Hank, Nelle, Brittany, and Spence not only for her father's death but also for her family's company going bankrupt," I concluded the recount.

Jo, Spence, Nolan, and I had spent about half an hour after Trudie's arrest at the sheriff's department, giving our witness statements. Then Jed and Errol told us as much as they could about the events that had triggered Trudie's murderous plans.

"But the board didn't expel her solely because of the cheating ring." Jo looked between the two tables. "Trudie had been involved in other questionable activities as Marvey discovered last night."

Everyone looked to me. I shifted my shoulders, trying to unknot the tension that had collected there. "Trudie was the only member of the ring who'd been expelled. I thought that was harsh, so I checked with the board yesterday. They couldn't give me details, of course, but a very nice man in the archives department said Trudie had been a repeat offender. She and her parents had been warned if she committed even one more infraction, she'd be expelled." I addressed Spence and Cecelia. "The board hadn't voted. They'd adhered to the terms they'd previously presented, which Trudie and her parents had agreed to."

I pictured the activities room as it had been the night of the kickoff: long tables with hot and cold hors d'oeuvres, pastries, and punches; mismatched decorations; classical music; and pub tables surrounded by revelers. I could almost smell the pralines Adrian had scarfed down as though someone had announced a pending shortage.

That had been only three weeks and two days ago. It felt like six months to a year. In that time, Trudie had killed a second person, had attacked someone, and had almost killed two others. I wrapped my arms around myself to ward off a chill.

"Trudie had hated the private boarding school her parents had sent her to." Nolan shook his head with a sigh. "The school had been very strict. There were curfews with mandatory lights out, and punishments for everything. Strip searches, random drug tests, and room inspections. On top of that, she'd been bullied as an outsider. Those memories added to the grief of her father's death caused her to snap."

"Well, I for one don't feel sorry for her." Cecelia threw up her hands. "She murdered two people in cold blood, tried to kill my son and his best friend, and for what? Because she refused to accept responsibility for her actions and her father's mismanagement of their company."

Conversations broke out around the room. People were talking with and over each other.

Mom left her seat at the table with Dad to join me. She wrapped her right arm around me as though trying to help me get warm.

"What's on your mind, darling?" She asked under cover of the cacophony of conversations around us.

Spence sent me a questioning look. I responded to him with a smile and answered my mother. "Cecelia's right. Trudie was lashing out at everyone except the person most responsible for her actions: herself."

"True. *She* was solely responsible for everything she did. The policies she violated in high school that led to her expulsion and the lives she ended." Mom rubbed her right hand briskly up and down my arm.

My blood started to flow again. I leaned into her. She knew what I was thinking without my having to say it. I whispered it anyway. "I almost got two people killed today. Suppose Spence had drunk that coffee?"

"He didn't."

"Supposed Nolan had been in that bed?"

"He wasn't." She hugged me harder. "You saved four lives today: Spence's, Brittany's, Nolan's and yours."

"You could be right." I shivered with alarm.

Mom rubbed my arm again. "Your father and I are very proud of you. What you did to protect your friend took a lot of courage—and a lot of smarts."

"Thanks, Mom. I really do hope this is the last one, though. This investigation was even more stressful than the last."

Mom chuckled. "We hope so too." She guided me to

the table she shared with Dad and the librarians. "Between reading and making your book pendants, you have enough activities to occupy your mind during your free time."

I laughed as I imagined my mother had intended. "I'd much rather solve a murder mystery in the pages of a good book than in real life."

CHAPTER 32

"IT'S SO NICE OF THE librarians to host a luncheon send-off for your father and me." Mom wrapped her arms around Dad's as I escorted them across the library's parking lot early Sunday afternoon.

Withholding comment, I gave my parents the side eye. Dad was the portrait of serenity while Mom was a little too exuberant—almost giddy—for the occasion. Meanwhile every step that brought me closer to the Peach Coast Library's entrance was weighted with reluctance and dread. I know. I know. First, I didn't want my parents to visit because the timing wasn't convenient for me. Now, I didn't want them to leave. Ever.

Make up your mind, Marvey!

"I'm so glad you came." Was this the hundredth time I'd said those words? "Your being here for me this week was such a gift. Thank you. I'm not looking forward to driving you to the airport this evening."

"Oh, darling." Mom hugged my shoulders. "We've really enjoyed our visit—despite the murder investigation."

Dad reached across Mom. I took his hand and he squeezed mine. "We'll be back in July."

I forced my lips into a smile for him. Maybe focusing on that will cheer me up tomorrow. Right now, not so much.

"Our upstairs activities room probably hasn't seen this much action in a decade." I shook off my gloom and held the library's front door for them.

As we reached the staircase, I heard laughter and music floating down from the activities room.

I frowned over my shoulder at my parents. "I thought we were early, but it sounds like we may be late." I hurried up the stairs.

"We can't be late to our own party," Dad said cheerfully.

Why did they sound so happy? In less than five hours, a plane was going to fly them away from me.

I entered the room—and froze. Why were all these people here?

Betty Rodgers-Hayes and her son, Bobby Hayes. Deputy Errol Cole and...*Wait*. Was that Deputy Jed Whatley? Was I in the wrong place?

"There you are, Marvey." Corrinne greeted me with an embrace. Mayor Byron Flowers was with her. What was he doing here?

My head was swimming. "I'm sorry, Corrinne. I thought you said noon." I gestured to my parents beside me. "We got here a little early to help with the preparations, but it looks like we're late..." My voice faded away. I was totally confused.

Corrinne flashed a warm smile. Her green A-line dress complemented her green eyes. "You're not supposed to help set up your own party."

"Mr. Harris and Ms. Bennett-Harris?" The mayor switched his attention to my parents. He was dapper in linen pants and purple polo shirt. "I'm Mayor Byron Flowers. It's so nice to meet you. I hope you've enjoyed your visit to Peach Coast."

"Yes, we did." Dad inclined his head. "We're looking forward to our next visit."

Mom's smile beamed. "You have a beautiful town. We had a lovely time."

Byron rocked on his heels. "Glad to hear it. And when you come back, please stop by my office. I'd love to give you a tour of town hall and some of our historic sites."

Dad nodded. "We'll take you up on that."

"Corrinne, thank you again for arranging this event for my parents, and on such short notice. It was very generous of you." I surveyed the room, amazed at how many people had attended as well as who'd come. I supposed Dabney McCoy would make the extra effort for free refreshments.

"Marvey, how are you?" Viv gave me a searching look before pulling me in for a hug. Her amethyst romper was casual elegance. "I hope you were able to get some rest."

"I'm fine, Viv. Thank you for asking." I stepped back, switching my attention to Floyd and Adrian. "Adrian, I see you've found a way to keep your hair out of your face."

He'd pulled his hair into a ponytail that rested on his thin shoulders. The style was a little reminiscent of the 1980s, but the look was coming back.

Adrian gave me a half smile as he smoothed his hand over his tightly gathered tresses. "It's starting to become a hassle, but Ms. Reba asked me to keep growing it. She said it should be long enough to work with in a little while."

"You're growing it for the salon?" Floyd looked as confused as I felt. He and Adrian wore almost identical dark baggy shorts and T-shirts. They looked like they were wearing uniforms.

Adrian dropped his arm. His brow creased as though he didn't understand Floyd's question. "Well, sure. They make the free wigs for cancer patients. What did you think I was growing it for?"

Floyd shrugged. "I don't know. You didn't say."

Adrian nodded. "My nana died of cancer my second year of college. The treatments made her hair fall out. But she loved those wigs. Said they made her feel pretty as a peach."

I pressed my hand to my heart. "It's wonderful that you're going to donate your hair to such a worthy cause in memory of your grandmother."

"I'm sure she would be proud of your gesture," Mom said.

Floyd grunted. "I'm proud of it and I'm not even related to you."

I smiled, remembering the concerned looks Floyd had given Adrian as the younger man's hair kept growing and growing and growing.

Adrian nodded again. "She was a homicide detective before she got sick. She used to read true crime books to me as a child." He laughed. "My mama would get madder than a wet hen. She thought for sure I'd have nightmares. I didn't."

Never again would I worry about Adrian's fascination with true crime stories. He came by it honestly.

I looked around, realizing my parents and I were still standing at the entrance to the room. "Would you like me to get you some refreshments?"

Dad linked his fingers with Mom's. "Why don't we go with you?"

I turned to my colleagues. "Excuse us."

Spence, Cecelia, Jo, and Nolan intercepted us on our way to the refreshment table in the center of the room. Spence offered my parents and me disposable glasses of iced tea.

"I'm so glad we were able to spend some quality time together on your trip." Cecelia stood beside her son.

"So are we." Dad looked at each of my friends in turn. "Marvey has told us so much about each of you. It was nice to finally meet you."

"On your next visit, I'll host a dinner party and serve a regional dish." Spence gave me a wicked smile. "Perhaps Georgia Peaches and Chicken with Southern Green Beans."

"Peaches with chicken." Mom's smile looked stiff.

"Stop taunting my parents." I laughed. "It's delicious, Mom. Promise."

"Meeting you has solved some of the mystery that is Marvey." Jo's dark eyes sparkled with good-natured teasing. "I still have a few questions, though."

I raised my right hand, palm out. "And I'm sure my parents would love to humor you—next time."

Spence stepped closer to me. "May I speak with you in private?"

"Sure." I searched his spare features for an idea of what he wanted to talk about. "Have you moved back into your house?"

He took my elbow. His touch was warm and firm,

reminding me he was someone I could depend on. "Last night."

Surprised laughter tumbled from my lips. "You didn't waste any time, did you?"

Spence escorted me into the hallway. "Nolan is a good friend. I'd like to keep it that way." He faced me, linking his hands in front of him. Whatever he wanted to say didn't seem to come easily. "I haven't properly thanked you for saving my life."

"Yes, you—"

He lifted a finger, halting my interruption. "The thing of it is, Marvey, I don't know how to thank you."

I shook my head. "Your being alive is thanks enough."

"No, it's not." He laughed without humor. Lifting his hand, he massaged the muscles at the nape of his neck. "When no one believed you, not even me, you kept pushing. You involved yourself in the investigation, which could've gotten you arrested. You risked your life for me without hesitation, which could've gotten you killed. I was scared to death something would happen to you."

"*I* was scared to death something would happen to *you.*"

Spence took my hands and kissed the backs of them. "Thank you from the bottom of my heart, Marvey." His voice was rough.

I cupped the side of his face. "You're so very welcome, Spence."

A surprised look shifted across his features. I'd never touched him so intimately before. I read a question in his dark eyes. My breath caught in my throat. Even if I could speak, I didn't know whether I had an answer for him. He was still the Prince of Peach Coast. Was I made for a royal romance?

I took his hand and led him back into the activities room. I released him once we rejoined our family and friends. With just hours to go before their departure, I was determined to stick close to my parents.

"Good afternoon, everyone and thank you for coming." Corrinne spoke at a podium microphone we used for library events and presentations. It seemed a bit much for my parents' farewell luncheon, but I brushed the thought aside. "Many of you already have had the pleasure of meeting Isaac Harris and Ciara Bennett-Harris, the wonderful parents of our wonderful Marvey Harris." Corrinne gestured toward Mom and Dad, who stood on either side of me. "They're returning to New York this evening. The librarians and our board of directors wanted to host this luncheon today to thank them for coming to Peach Coast, and wish them a safe and uneventful journey. We also wanted them to be part of our Summer Solstice Donor unveiling."

I straightened, caught off guard. *We wanted to do what now? Why?*

I looked around the room. Viv, Floyd, and Adrian stood near the front, seemingly unruffled, as they listened to Corrinne.

My eyes met Cecelia's gaze from over her shoulder. "What're we doing?" I whispered.

Shrugging, she turned back around.

Corrinne continued. "We still have three days left for our donor drive, but I checked our summer fundraiser total this morning."

And I'd checked it Friday evening. We'd past the break-even point, but our gift level wasn't nearly impressive enough for a public announcement. *What was going on?*

"Are you all right, honey?" Dad's voice was low. "You seem tense."

I forced my muscles to relax. "I'm fine, Dad. Thank you."

"As of today, three days before wrapping up the campaign, our gifts total... Do you want to know what it is?" Corrinne paused for the applause and cheers. She smiled, then revealed the amount.

"What?" I slapped my hands over my mouth. But it was too late. The room had heard my exclamation and burst out laughing, including Corrinne.

It must've been a very substantial donation that came in between Friday evening and this morning. The value Corrinne announced put us where we would've been if Malcovich Savings and Loan hadn't withdrawn its donation. I wanted to jump up and down and scream with joy.

Thank you, generous donor, whoever and wherever you are!

She gestured toward me. "It's not surprising that our director of community outreach would be unaware of the gift that came in this morning. It's from a consortium of donors that she's unaware of. But I'll let our consortium administrator and the president of the Peach Coast Library Board of Directors discuss the details. Ladies and gentlemen, Cecelia Holt."

Cecelia laughed at the thunderous applause, cheers, and whistles. "Stop it, now. You make me feel like Yolanda Adams, standing up in here." Her audience laughed when she compared their reaction to those of the award-winning gospel singer's fans. With her attention on me, she continued. "As Corrinne explained, I'm the administrator of the Friends of Marvella Harris Donor Consortium."

I caught my breath. My pulse pounded in my throat. Blood was rushing in my head. I looked to my parents, Mom on my left and Dad on my right. They looked proud, pleased, and...giddy. "Did you know?"

Mom's smile was big and bright. "Yes, we're so glad we were here for the announcement."

Dad hugged me. "We're thrilled for you, honey."

Cecelia continued. "Since moving to our town five months ago, Marvey Harris has been a tireless advocate for our community. She's proven herself to be a fiercely loyal and fearless friend." Spence winked at me. Jo gave me a sweet smile. "And her caring and empathy for others have helped build bridges and heal wounds." On the far side of the room, Betty and Bobby smiled at each other. I was happy for them.

"I can't believe this." Shaking my head, I wiped tears from my eyes.

Cecelia addressed me. "Marvey, everyone in this room is a Friend of Marvella Harris."

There must have been more than two dozen people in the room. I was too overwhelmed to count: My parents, library colleagues, On A Roll regulars, book club members, June Bishop, Lonnie Norman, Brittany Wilson, and so many others.

"Everyone?" I called back, around.

Cecelia chuckled. "Yes, every last one."

I pointed across the room at Jed. "You like me. You really like me."

Bubbles of laughter circled the room. Jed waved both hands at me, but I noticed his reluctant smile.

"Speech! Speech! Speech!" The chants built in enthusiasm.

Mom and Dad pushed me toward the podium. I looked at the sea of friendly faces and warm smiles. My mind went blank. All I could think was that my job was secure and I could remain in this beautiful, friendly, quirky town that had stolen a piece of my heart.

"I don't have the words to describe how grateful I am for your incredible gift. Thank you so much." I spread my arms to encompass them all. "And I hope to see everyone at the library."

THE END

Anna May's Southern Style Pralines

A Hallmark Original Recipe

Prep Time: 20 minutes
Cook Time: 20 minutes
Serves: 12

Ingredients

- 2 cups light brown sugar, packed
- 2 cups sugar
- 1 cup half and half
- 3 cups pecan halves
- 4 tablespoons butter

Preparation

1. Combine brown sugar, white sugar and half and half in a heavy 2 quart saucepan and bring mixture to a boil over medium heat, stirring occasionally with a wooden spoon, until mixture reaches 227 degrees or soft ball stage on the candy thermometer.

2. Add pecans and butter. Cook over medium heat, stirring frequently.

3. Remove saucepan from heat and let cool for 2 minutes.

4. Using a tablespoon, spoon rounded balls of warm praline mixture onto a sheet of wax paper leaving about 3 inches between each ball (this will allow them to spread). Let cool.

ABOUT THE AUTHOR

Patricia Sargeant, a bestselling, award-winning author, writes mysteries as Olivia Matthews and romance under her own name. Her work has been featured in national publications such as *Publishers Weekly, USA Today, Kirkus Reviews, Suspense Magazine, Mystery Scene Magazine*, and *Library Journal*. Her mysteries put ordinary people in extraordinary situations to have them find the Hero Inside.

For more information about Patricia and her work, visit **PatriciaSargeant.com**.

Thanks so much for reading
Murder Out Of Character. We hope you enjoyed it!

You might like these other books
from Hallmark Publishing:

Murder By Page One: A Peach Coast Library Mystery
Dead-End Detective: A Piper and Porter Mystery
Out of the Picture: A Shepherd Sisters Mystery
Behind the Frame: A Shepherd Sisters Mystery
Still Life and Death: A Shepherd Sisters Mystery

For information about our new releases and
exclusive offers, sign up for our free newsletter at
hallmarkchannel.com/hallmark-publishing-newsletter

You can also connect with us here:

Facebook.com/HallmarkPublishing

Twitter.com/HallmarkPublish

Turn the page for a sneak peek of

Murder by Page One

A PEACH COAST LIBRARY MYSTERY
FROM HALLMARK PUBLISHING

OLIVIA MATTHEWS

CHAPTER 1

"I WAS PROMISED CHOCOLATE."
I directed the reminder toward my new best friend, Jolene Gomez, after entering the bookstore. I threw my gaze into every visible nook and cranny of To Be Read in search of chocolate-covered pecan clusters.

Jo owned To Be Read, an independent bookstore on the southeast side of Peach Coast, Georgia. It wasn't that I needed the food bribe to come to her bookstore—or any bookstore—especially when a bunch of authors were signing their books. It was just that, well...promises had been made.

"Marvey." The tattooed businesswoman's tan features warmed with a welcoming smile. Her coffee-colored eyes shifted to my right. "Spence. I'm glad you both made it."

Jo seemed relieved, as though she'd worried we wouldn't come. Why would she have thought that? I kept my promises, especially those made to another book fanatic. Jo and I had bonded over our love of books, our newcomer status—she was from Florida and

I was from New York—and chocolates, which reminded me today's stash was still conspicuously absent.

"Of course we came. We're readers. On top of that, we're here supporting our friend." I nudged Jo's shoulder with my own.

"The others are on their way," Spence said, referring to the members of the Peach Coast Library Book Club.

Spence and I had walked over from the library after our Saturday afternoon meeting. It was about a fifteen-minute walk, and the weather on this May Day had been comfortably warm. As geographically challenged as I was, I'd been glad to have Spence with me. On my own, I probably would've still been circling the library's parking lot.

Spencer Holt was a local celebrity, although he'd deny it. The Holts were the richest family in Peach Coast and one of the wealthiest in Camden County. They owned a bed and breakfast, a hotel, a local bank, and the town's daily newspaper, *The Peach Coast Crier*. It was considered required reading among the residents, and Spence was the publisher and editor-in-chief.

The family was also philanthropic: Peach Coast's answer to Gotham City's Wayne Foundation. Spence's mother, for example, served on the board of directors for the Peach Coast Library—which technically made her my boss.

For all his money, prestige, power, and good looks—think Bruce Wayne with a slow Southern drawl—Spence was very humble. He was more interested in listening than talking about himself, and he seemed to prefer comfort over fashion. I once again noted his brown loafers, faded blue jeans, and the ruby-red polo shirt that showed off his biceps and complimented his warm sienna skin.

Spence shifted his midnight gaze to mine. "If you want pecan clusters, we can get some at the coffee shop after the signing."

After the signing? "It wouldn't be the same." Translation: that would be too late. Far too late. I continued scanning the store, my mind rejecting the truth my eyes had confirmed.

"I haven't put the chocolates out yet, but I'll get you some in a minute." Jo waved a hand as though the treats weren't important. The right sleeve of her citrus-orange knit sweater, which she'd coupled with leaf-green jeans, slipped to reveal the University of Florida Gators logo inked onto the inside of her small wrist. Jo was a proud alumna. "First, let me introduce you to Zelda Taylor. She's the president of Coastal Fiction Writers. The authors who're signing today are members of her group. Zelda, you know Spence."

"Ms. Zelda, it's nice to see you again." Spence's greeting rumbled in his Barry White voice.

"Mr. Spence, it's always such a pleasure," the redhead gushed. Her porcelain cheeks glowed pink. "How is your mama?"

"She's very well, ma'am. I'll tell her you asked after her." Spence's smile went up a watt. The poor woman seemed dazed.

I tossed Spence a laughing look. "Is there anyone in this town you don't know?"

Spence's smooth forehead creased as he pretended to consider my question. "Well, nearly one thousand people reside in Peach Coast. I'm sure I've yet to meet one or two of them."

Jo gestured toward me. "Zelda, this is Marvella Harris. She moved here from New York—the city—four months ago. She's the library's new director of community engagement."

Zelda tugged her attention from Spence. Her appearance was flawless: well-manicured nails, perfect makeup, and salon-styled hair. She was camera-ready for a photo spread in a Southern homes magazine.

"Oh, yes. I read the article about you in the *Crier* a couple of months back." Her voice was now imposing, as though she were reading a town proclamation. "Welcome to Camden County. What brings you all this way, Ms. Marvella?"

Referring to the county of residence instead of the town was taking some getting used to. I supposed it was like New Yorkers saying we were from Brooklyn, The Bronx, Queens, or Staten Island. Only people from Manhattan said they were from "the city."

"Just Marvey, please." The Southern custom of adding a title to a person's name was charming, but it was a lot to say before getting to the point. "I want to help the library increase its outreach and services. Do you have a library card?"

Zelda's eyes widened. "Why, yes." Her commanding tone had faded. "Yes, I do."

Although suspicious of her response, I gave her the benefit of the doubt. "Excellent. I look forward to seeing you at the library. You should join our book club. We meet the first Saturday of each month."

"Oh. That sounds nice." Zelda smoothed her silver cotton dress in a nervous gesture. I sensed her casting about for a believable excuse to get out of the meetings.

Spence offered an incentive. "Marvey serves Georgia Bourbon Pecan Pie and sweet tea after every meeting—

but you have to stay till the end of the meeting for the refreshments."

Panic receded from Zelda's eyes to be replaced by interest. "Oh, well, now. That would be nice indeed."

I turned my attention from Zelda to survey To Be Read. I loved the store. It was like a giant welcoming foyer, flooded with natural light. Closing my eyes briefly, I drew in the scent of crisp new paper from thousands of books and magazines. Fluffy furnishings in pale earth tones popped up at the end of aisles and in quiet nooks. A multitude of blond wood bookcases stuffed with stories offered the promise of adventures and the thrill of knowledge.

A couple of Jo's employees were setting up for the book signing. They'd already arranged the wooden chairs and matching tables. The twenty-somethings transferred books from wheeled metal carts to each author's assigned table. Jo's third employee processed purchases at a checkout counter while engaging each customer in conversation as though they were lifelong friends. Every now and then, a burst of warm laughter rolled across the store.

But there still wasn't a single chocolate-covered pecan cluster in sight.

"I'm sorry I missed the meeting." Jo's gaze swung between Spence and me, twinkling with curiosity. "How was it?"

"It was great," Spence said. Slipping his hands into the front pockets of his jeans, he turned to me. "I'm impressed you were able to get the club up and running so quickly, within a month of your arrival."

"We librarians are known for our efficiency." It was a struggle to keep the smugness from my tone.

Spence's compliment filled me with a massive sense of achievement—and relief. Even though it was only our third meeting, I'd known the book club would be a success. We'd already attracted twenty-five book lovers, all from diverse backgrounds and each strengthening our argument for a bigger budget. *That* continued to be my motivation.

Leaving my parents and older brother in Brooklyn to relocate to Peach Coast with my cat had been hard. My roots were in Brooklyn. I'd lived my entire twenty-eight years in the New York borough, but I'd grown increasingly frustrated by my lack of opportunities to shine in my public library system. There, I was just one of many small fishes in a very big pond. I couldn't generate any waves. Not even a ripple. But I'd been confident that, if given a chance, my ideas for growing the community's interest in and support of the library could make a big splash. Here, in this small town, I'd finally be able to try. The library's success would make at least some of my homesickness worth it.

Jo grinned. "So who came in costume, and what did they wear?"

Spence ran a hand over his close-cropped hair. His voice was devoid of inflection. "Mortimer painted himself blue and called himself Aquarius."

This month's member-selected read was the latest paranormal fiction release by Bernadine Cecile. I loved paranormal stories. This one featured a world in which meta-humans used the power of their zodiac signs to defeat villains—hence Mortimer's costume. He wasn't the only one who'd gotten carried away. Most of the members hadn't wanted to read *Born Sign*, but the first rule of book club was to keep an open mind. To my relief, the novel had been a hit.

Zelda spoke over Jo's laughter. "Marvey, if you don't mind my saying, that's a lovely pendant." Her gaze had dropped to my sapphire cotton T-shirt, which I wore with cream khakis and matching canvas shoes.

"Thank you." I touched the glass pendant. I'd suspended it from a long antique silver chain. It held a silver-and-black illustration of the cover of Lorraine Hansberry's *A Raisin in the Sun*, the version depicting the Younger family's dream home.

Jo inclined her head toward me. Her long raven ponytail bounced behind her narrow shoulders. "Marvey makes those herself. And the matching hair barrette. She draws the pictures and puts them in the pendants and barrettes."

Zelda glanced at my shoulder-length, dark brown hair, but she couldn't have seen my barrette, which gathered my hair behind my head.

"You're very talented." Her eyes glinted with admiration—and longing. "Do you sell them?"

This question came up a lot. Each time, I stood firm. "No, it's just a hobby. I'd like to keep it that way."

I'd been making those pendants and barrettes since high school. The craft fed my love of art and jewelry making, and allowed me to pay homage to great works of literature. It was the kind of activity I could do while listening to an audiobook. Although I often gifted sets to family and friends for birthdays and holidays, the hobby was something I did for enjoyment, not for money. If I mass-produced them, it wouldn't be fun anymore.

Jo's dark eyes twinkled with mischief. "With all the

interest people have shown in your pendants, you may have to break that rule."

Spence flashed his silver-screen smile. His perfect white teeth were a dentist's dream. "Maybe you should give a class. That way, you can teach people how to make their own pendants."

"That's a great idea. The course could be a fundraiser for the library." New books. Updated software. Additional periodical subscriptions. Every little bit would help. I shelved the idea to consider in depth later.

"Ready for another great idea?" Spence's lips twitched with humor. "Run the Cobbler Crawl with me."

The man was relentless. I responded to his winning smile with a chiding look. "For the fourth time, no, I will not."

The Peach Coast Cobbler Crawl was an annual three-and-a-half-mile race to raise money for the local hospital. Each two-member team had to stop and eat a large, heaping spoonful of peach cobbler at the one-, two-, and three-mile points. The first team to cross the finish line together won.

"I can't enter the Cobbler Crawl without a running partner." Spence had been trying to convince me to form a team with him almost since the day we'd met.

I was running out of ways to say no. "Why don't we both just give a donation and watch the event from the sidelines?"

Jo laughed. "You should do it, Marvey. You run six miles every day. Three and a half miles will feel like nothing."

Now they were ganging up on me. "If we only had to run, I wouldn't hesitate. But I don't think I can run *and* keep down the cobbler." I shuddered to think of the consequences.

Zelda came out of her spell, dragging her attention from my pendant. "I'm the exact opposite. I could eat the cobbler, no problem. But I couldn't run a mile in a month of Sundays."

Determined to change the subject, I turned to Zelda. "How many members of the Coastal Fiction Writers are published?"

"We're a small group, but we're growing. At the moment, there are twelve of us. Four of our members are published."

"Five." Jo lifted the requisite number of fingers. "I ordered books for five members. I think you're missing Fiona." She addressed Spence and me. "Fiona Lyle-Hayes just released her first book, *In Death Do We Part*. It's a mystery, and it's gotten great advance reviews."

Spence sent me a look before switching his attention to our companions. I could tell he wasn't giving up on the Cobbler Crawl. "We ran a piece about her book in the *Crier*."

"Oh, yes. How could I have forgotten Fiona?" Zelda clutched her pearl necklace. Her smile seemed fake. That was curious.

"Fiona helped coordinate the signing." Jo glanced at her employees who were setting out the books before returning her attention to Spence and me. "She's also the writing group's treasurer."

"Yes, Fiona manages our money. She's good at that." Zelda flashed another tight smile, then looked away. Tension was rolling off her in waves. I really hoped it didn't bubble over and ruin Jo's event.

I glanced toward the entrance again to see more of

our book club members arriving, as well as quite a few strangers—each one a potential new library cardholder. Four of the newcomers made a beeline for Jo, who identified them as the local authors who were signing today. I concentrated on the introductions, but keeping names and connections straight strained my brain. Of course, Spence knew all of them. I resolved to stick to him like gum on his shoe.

The authors dressed up their displays with promotional postcards and trinkets. Jo's employees put the finishing touches on the arrangements, which included the bowls of the long-promised-but-seemingly-forgotten chocolate-covered pecan clusters. Jo and I had only been friends for four months, but I'd known she wouldn't let me down. I began drifting toward the signing area—and the chocolates—when Jo's voice stopped me.

"I wonder what's taking Fiona so long?" Jo checked her silver-and-orange wristwatch. A frown cast a shadow over her round face. "The signing starts in ten minutes. I thought she'd have her books out long before now."

Zelda scanned the store. "Fiona left our writers' meeting early, saying she needed to get ready. Where is she?"

Jo jerked her head toward the back of the store, sending her ponytail swinging. "She's been in the storage room. She wanted to examine her books and bring them out herself."

Weird. "Why?"

Jo shrugged nonchalantly, but I saw the aggravation in her eyes. "She didn't say, but I suspect it's because she thought my staff and I would damage her books."

Zelda's smile didn't reach her eyes. "Fiona can be a pain in the tush. Bless her heart."

Bless her heart. That was a Southern phrase I'd heard before. It didn't mean anything good.

Read the rest!
Murder By Page One is available now!